She surprised him

He didn't know what to say when she took his hand and led him into her bedroom.

He watched as Cassie slowly unwrapped the tie to her robe and let the robe slip from her shoulders. The rain drummed on the roof, or was it his heartbeat pounding in his ears? His mouth went suddenly dry.

I know her and yet I don't know her. How well do we know each other? How well does anyone kn... another person? Cassie had denied hi... e to her tortured mind and though... s preparing to allow him e... ody was brown and gl... uld not refuse. No... because hers c... he could reach her. ... doon would be the utmost in ...

ABOUT THE AUTHOR

Pamela Browning has been a reporter, columnist and feature writer for local, regional and national publications. She began writing fiction when her children were small and is also well-known for her young-adult romances, written under the names of Pam Ketter and Melanie Rowe. Pam makes her home in South Carolina with her husband, son and daughter.

Books by Pamela Browning

HARLEQUIN AMERICAN ROMANCE

101—CHERISHED BEGINNINGS
116—HANDYMAN SPECIAL
123—THROUGH EYES OF LOVE

HARLEQUIN ROMANCE

2659-TOUCH OF GOLD

These books may be available at your local bookstore.

Through Eyes of Love

PAMELA BROWNING

Harlequin Books

TORONTO • NEW YORK • LONDON
AMSTERDAM • PARIS • SYDNEY • HAMBURG
STOCKHOLM • ATHENS • TOKYO • MILAN

With special thanks to my friend,
singer and songwriter Sandy New,
who made the right choice all those years ago.

Published October 1985

First printing August 1985

ISBN 0-373-16123-9

Printed in Canada

Prologue

Somewhere South of San Francisco
February 1982

Cassie stared in horror at her husband, who was unconscious and slumped forward over the yoke of the small airplane, and she choked back a scream.

"Kevin? Kev?" Frantically she shook his arm, but he didn't respond. The plane's single engine droned monotonously, as though nothing untoward had happened. Outside, beyond the plane's propeller, she saw only darkness overlaid with stars—no earth, no horizon, nothing.

Calm. It was important to remain calm, but she couldn't believe this was happening. The three of them had been cruising along through a night full of stars, comfortable at sixty-five hundred feet, and her husband had suddenly gasped and fallen forward, straining against his shoulder strap.

"What's wrong with Daddy?" asked her son Rory, peering wide-eyed and frightened through the space between the two front seats.

"I don't know," Cassie said tremulously, panic rising with the bile in the back of her throat. "God help me, I don't know."

She swiveled in her seat, facing front again, and clenched her fingers around the yoke in front of her. Kevin had shown her how to fly the plane a few times, and once she had practiced landing on their runway at home with him beside her at the plane's dual controls. He'd always been safety-conscious, and he knew that sometimes things happened in the air to incapacitate a pilot. But she'd never thought anything like this would happen. Not to Kevin. He was the picture of good health and only thirty-three.

"Mommy, Mommy," cried Rory from the backseat. "I'm scared." He began to whimper.

He was barely five years old, a sweet blond cherub of a boy, and Cassie's instinct was to gather him in her arms and comfort him. She was scared, too. But she couldn't worry about the boy now. She was going to have to fly the plane somehow. And land it.

She summoned every ounce of concentration she possessed. The radio. First, the radio. She slipped the control to the emergency frequency. Then she grabbed the microphone.

And she was thinking, *oh, Kevin, what is wrong?* His face, what she could see of it, with his head sagging against his chest, looked pasty in the luminescent glow from the dials of the control panel. Was he breathing? Was he? She couldn't tell, couldn't spare the time to take care of him any more than she could take care of their son, not with their lives in peril as they hurtled through the sky in their pilotless plane.

"Mayday, Mayday," she gasped into the mike, and then too late she realized that she hadn't pressed the transmission button down. She fumbled with the button and repeated the distress call. The radio speaker crackled, but there was no response. She clutched the mike in her hand as she slid her eyes across the complicated control panel in front of her. Which gauge was the altimeter? Which was the directional gyro? She was so petrified that she couldn't think straight.

No one answered on the radio. Cassie saw no other aircraft in the wide black sky. Where were they, anyway? If she managed to reach somebody on the radio, she'd have to give their location. They'd been traveling north toward home, but they hadn't reached San Francisco yet. Cassie would have noticed the lights below as they passed the city on their way to Wildflower, their estate near Occidental; she always noticed the lights. But were they flying over land or over the ocean?

She hadn't realized it until now, but tears were streaming down her face. She was so damned *scared.* She tried to think of something that would help her. She swiped at the tears rolling down her cheeks, and her arm inadvertently struck the yoke so that the plane dived sharply. By instinct, she yanked the yoke upward. The plane stabilized and she fell back into her seat and sobbed out loud in relief, drawing great gulps of air into her lungs. Hearing her distress, her son flung himself across the width of the backseat and wailed.

It was Rory's fright that lent her strength. She didn't care about herself anymore, but she cared about her husband and son. She had to save them.

Cassie jammed the microphone to her lips. "Somebody please help me," she sobbed. "Please, somebody. I'm all alone and I don't know how to fly this plane. Please help me."

The microphone fell to her lap as she buried her face in her trembling hands. She was losing control, fighting to hold her balance on the thin sharp edge of panic. They'd all die, all three of them, and it would be her fault because she couldn't fly the plane.

The radio speaker crackled, and then, like a miracle, she heard a garbled transmission.

"Where...you?" rasped a male voice.

He was asking where she was. She grappled at the mike and depressed the button. "I don't know. I don't know," she said brokenly. "My husband is unconscious. I can't fly the plane."

"Don't..." and there was too much static to understand the transmission.

But then, after what seemed like an eternity, more than an eternity, the voice transmitted clearly. "I'll help you," he said.

Cassie hardened herself to ignore her child's screams of terror and sent up a silent prayer of desperation.

"Tell me what to do," she said into the microphone.

And they sailed through the sky, the three of them, halfway home.

Chapter One

Near The Town of Scot's Cove, North Carolina
June 1984

Cassie measured her breathing. In, out. In, out. Above her, the leaves of a giant black oak rippled in the wind. The muscles of her face slid into repose, and she rested her hands with palms upturned on her knees. Cassie found the lotus position comfortable for meditation; now she concentrated on the quiet place inside her and didn't detect the stranger's approach.

She focused her mind on the steady rhythm of her breathing, rising upward on each exhaled breath, allowing her mind to float free of her body, free as a leaf, free as air wafting upward from Flat Top Mountain.

The stranger approached quietly, wondering how to present himself. He had traveled too far, had tried too hard to find her. He would not back off now.

She was not what he had expected, this woman whose stillness contrasted so sharply with the riotous magenta blooms of the rhododendrons behind her. Of course, John had known very little about her when he had started out. But this earthy creature, nut-brown and clothed in a shapeless garment of hyacinth blue, did not look like the woman he had sought at the secluded estate in northern California, nor did she appear to be the type who would feel at home in the glitzy apartment complex in Century City, near Los Angeles.

John studied her intently. Her hair was buoyant and curly and long, springing from its roots with a life of its own. The color of it was pale brown, and it looked like a crackling extension of her nut-brown skin. Fascinating hair, he decided. But her face was the most interesting thing.

It was a face of great individuality. If he were to draw a line down the center of it, dividing her face neatly in two, each side would be different. The same eyes, nose, mouth, except that the left eye was ever so slightly more elongated than the right one. The left nostril flared ever so slightly more than the right one. The left side of her mouth tilted ever so slightly upward, and the right side did not. Each side was beautiful, but each side was different, like a sketch blurred on one side by a careless finger.

Cassie's scalp tingled with the sensation of someone watching and, startled, she opened her eyes. The man's expression was so concentrated, so intense, that she gasped from the impact of its energy.

She scrambled to her feet, frightened. "Who are you?" she said, and her voice was pleasantly soprano and had a breathless little-girl quality that made it sound as though her syllables were filtered through a whisper. To him, her voice sounded familiar. But of course it wasn't. He'd never met her before.

"I'm your neighbor," John said easily, letting her get a feel for him. He hadn't meant to frighten her.

"My neighbor?"

"Yes, I've rented the cabin." He gestured over his shoulder toward the path through the woods.

"No...no one rents the cabin," she stammered. "No one has, not for years."

"Well, I have. I talked Ned Church into renting it to me for the season. I needed a place, and..." He shrugged.

"Why didn't you rent a place near Linville? That's where the tourists go." There was no doubt in Cassie's mind that this man was a tourist, and tourists seldom came to Scot's Cove. With that streaky blond hair and his sun-bronzed skin, he looked like the lost denizen of a land where aquamarine swimming pools were standard equipment in every backyard. She could almost smell it on him—a scent of Someplace Else, a place where the sun shone year round and the air was flavored with chlorine and the smoke of barbecue grills. She was sure he wasn't a native of the North Carolina mountains.

John laughed. "Linville's not for me. I'm not a tourist." His laughter rang rich and wholesome, booming out over the clearing. The candor of such a laugh was, above all, reassuring.

By this time, Cassie couldn't contain her curiosity, and she was no longer afraid. How could she be? She had already pegged him as a good person, a decent person. She could always tell. Something in the eyes. Goodness and decency were the characteristics Cassie divined in this man even before she took note of his high cheekbones, the cleft in his chin, his broad shoulders straight as the crossing of a T.

"Well, what are you doing here, then? Flat Top Mountain is definitely off the beaten path."

He'd come prepared for this. "I'm a nature photographer," he told her. It was a line that he'd carefully rehearsed. Actually, he'd never held a camera more complicated than an Instamatic in his hands until two weeks ago, when he'd bought the Nikon.

"And you're going to photograph the mountains?"

"I'm going to photograph the plants native to the area," he said. God, he'd schemed so elaborately. Would she buy it?

But apparently she didn't sense anything odd about a nature photographer being on Flat Top Mountain.

Generations of inbred Southern hospitality surfaced, and she smiled and stretched out her hand. "Welcome," she said. "Neighbor."

Her hand in his was not soft and small, nor was it rough. There was a hardness to it, a competence. He looked down at it before she withdrew it too quickly from his.

But at that point all hell broke loose.

A ramshackle car, a real bomb, tick-ticked up the winding unpaved road, belching clouds of exhaust before lurching to a stop in front of her house. Out of the car piled several people in assorted shapes and sizes, as well as a dog or two.

"Grampa's got the colic again," called one of them, but he couldn't tell which one. At least he was sure that it wasn't one of the dogs, which were snapping and yapping and chasing each other through the underbrush.

"Excuse me," Cassie said, not at all discomfited by the commotion, and then she headed for the house. She walked with a slight limp, which drew his attention to her legs. Looking at them was anything but an unpleasant task, although the left one appeared to be shorter than the other, causing the limp. But her body within the short, shapeless garment she wore was supple and lithe and exquisitely graceful.

Not knowing what else to do, and not willing to let her so soon out of his sight, John reluctantly followed her. By the time he reached her porch, she had stepped briefly inside the house and reappeared in the doorway. She carried a small brown medicine bottle.

"Tell your grandfather to drink this," she said into the milling group. "It's the same thing I sent last time."

"Sure do thank you," said the man to whom she handed the remedy. He grinned, revealing gaps in his teeth.

At that point one of the dogs, a big brown coon dog with spots the exact shade of liver mush, leaped out of the shrubbery and all but bowled John over. With the dog's paws planted in the middle of his chest, John did his best to fend him off, but before the animal galloped away, his claws had left two angry red welts on John's right arm.

Without bothering to apologize for their pet's misbehavior, two raggedly dressed boys rounded up the dogs and shoved them into the backseat of the automobile. Then the people piled in after them and, amid a cloud of oil fumes, the car jolted off down the mountain.

This left Cassie and John staring at each other.

"I—" he said.

"You—" she said at the same time, looking down at the scratches on his arm.

They stopped and laughed self-consciously.

"You'd better let me take a look at those," she said.

"You're a nurse? A doctor?"

"Not exactly. But you should wash the scratches off so they won't get infected."

"I didn't bring any antibiotic ointments or Band-Aids to the mountain with me," he said with chagrin. "I didn't even think about it."

She stepped aside. "Come in," she said. So he did. "Let me get my things." She had disappeared into the kitchen, leaving him holding his hurting arm.

This was a small, sturdy house, no more than a cottage. The house was built partly of stone and partly of wood, and there were many windows. The windows afforded a breathtaking view of Magnus Mountain to the right and Pride's Peak on the left, plus a host of lesser mountains in between.

"I'm Cassie Muldoon," she said over her shoulder, busying herself in the long rectangular kitchen adjoining the front room. She stood at an oaken counter, pouring a clear liquid out of a bottle onto a cloth.

"I'm John Howard," he replied, glad that she couldn't see his eyes when he said it. Somehow he knew she'd detect this bit of falseness in him. But was it false? Not quite. It wasn't the complete truth, either. Not that he had any choice. He had no doubt whatsoever that if he told her his complete name, she'd send him packing immediately.

This place where she lived was a comfortable house. He stood in a combination living and dining area beside a table hewn from a square slab of wood and covered with a woven cloth laid diagonally across it so that the curly-maple corners showed. Rag rugs allowed the polished oak floor to peek out here and there, and the walls were painted a pleasant cream color.

Wide, dark hand-hewn beams supported the ceiling, and from them bunches of flowers and leaves hung drying, their fragrances commingling to lend the room a pungent, aromatic scent that he found quite inviting. A magnificent fieldstone fireplace took up one whole wall. A handmade quilt, very old, decorated another. The quilt's time-mellowed colors glowed in the sunlight that streamed through the many windows.

Cassie limped over to the table. She gestured with her hand for him to sit down; it was a graceful gesture. Her breasts bobbed round as plump apples beneath her shapeless dress. John pulled his eyes away from that part of her anatomy. His interest in her wasn't sexual.

When he was seated, she announced, "I'm going to wash those scratches with tincture of marigold in water."

"What?" he said, recoiling slightly. He'd expected plain soap and water.

"I use tincture of marigold all the time for bleeding wounds. It's an old herbal remedy of my grandmother's."

Nonplussed, John watched her as she dabbed at the scratches with the liquid. Her touch was soft but sure. She knew what she was about.

Cassie concentrated on what she was doing. Nevertheless, it didn't escape her notice that John Howard was an undeniably handsome man, a terribly attractive man. She felt no response to him at all. She hoped that he would not mistake her attempt at neighborliness for something else, something sexual. She was celibate, a decision she had not arrived at lightly; nevertheless, she had made celibacy her way of life, and she intended to stay that way.

She shot him a surreptitious look as she poured more of the marigold tincture on the cloth. His tall, blond good looks were stunning, and those laser-beam eyes, an intense blue, revealed an active intelligence. The cleft defined his chin and rendered it bolder than it would have been uncleft. His chin was bold, but not aggressive. Or maybe it was aggressive but softened by the warm blue of his eyes. At any rate, the man definitely did not blend in with the rest of the scenery here on Flat Top Mountain.

John had noticed the profusion of wildflowers growing along the edges of the path to Cassie's house and the more tame varieties massed in beds in her garden in the back. "Do you make this tincture stuff from your own marigolds?" he asked.

"Yes. I make other remedies, too, from herbs I grow here. For some reason Flat Top Mountain has always been especially fertile, and the rich soil ensures a good harvest."

"What do you do with your herbs? Sell them to dealers?"

"No, they're for my own use in my herbal remedies. You know the family that was just here? I gave them a garlic potion for their grandfather's stomach spasms."

His eyebrows flew up skeptically. "Does it work?"

"Of course it works." She smiled gently. "Herbal medicine isn't new, you know. It's been around since the cavemen."

He looked at the red welts on his arm. The bleeding had stopped, and they didn't look as angry.

"Aren't you worried that you'll hurt someone? Give someone the wrong remedy? Keep people from going to a doctor if they're really sick?"

"My herbal remedies are meant to work in conjunction with medical care, not against it. You have to realize that I'm using old recipes, ones that my grandmother used for fifty years. You won't find many doctors in this part of the country. There's a place here for herbal remedies."

"But how did you learn everything you needed to know? And how do you remember what remedy to use for what problem?"

She set aside the cloth and went to a nearby bookshelf. She pulled down a thick volume and returned to the table, opening the book in front of him. As she bent over it, he became aware of the sun-warmed scent of her skin. He tried to concentrate on her words and not on her physical presence.

"This is Gran's recipe book. She wrote everything down, from how to identify the plants, to how to make a tonic, to how to put together an effective insect repellent. See, it's all here—what to do with marigolds, elm bark, cucumber. Gran learned from her mother, and her mother learned from her mother before her." Cassie flipped through the pages. They were covered with an elegant slanting script, faded to brown with the passing of the years.

"Amazing," he said, shaking his head. He'd noticed that the family earlier hadn't paid her for the stomach remedy. "And you do this free?"

"That's right," she said. She shoved the book back into its place on the shelf.

"But—"

"I don't want to talk about it," she said firmly, and her silvery eyes—why hadn't he noticed them before—darkened. He stared at her for a moment, puzzling about this. But before he could think about it too much, her eyes lightened again, became bright. They were remarkable eyes, prominent and very round, arresting in their beauty, and he was pulled into their depths, so that he had to struggle his way out again.

By that time she was gathering up the cloth and the tincture of marigold, a signal for him to go. He stood up.

"Here," she said, thrusting the bottle toward him. "Take this with you and bathe those scratches in it from time to time. If by any chance they get infected, let me know."

He took the bottle, but he didn't want to go. What he would have liked was to sit with her as he absorbed the atmosphere of this house, which seemed ideally suited to her, with its hanging plants, its small clay pots of herbs in a sunny window, its woven baskets holding magazines and firewood and balls of brightly colored yarn.

At that moment, a skunk rambled through the room, waddled under the table, sniffed briefly at his shoes, and hopped into a cardboard box in the corner. John stared in disbelief as it burrowed under a few handfuls of wood shavings until all he could see was a patch of black-and-white fur.

A skunk?

"That looks like a skunk," he said, stating the obvious in a tone of disbelief.

Cassie, in the kitchen, was drying her hands on a length of huck toweling. She came and stood at the kitchen door.

"It is," she said, grinning. "That's Bertrand."

"He's descented, of course," John said, more of a question than a statement in his voice. Bertrand twitched beneath the wood shavings.

"No, he's not. He's a fully equipped, almost grown skunk." She almost laughed at John in her amusement.

"Your choice of house pets is a little, um, strange, don't you think?" She was enjoying this, and as startled as he was, he liked to see that playful expression on her face, her face that was so pleasingly different. He had the idea that she probably didn't laugh much.

"Oh, well," she said. "Bertrand won't be here long. He'll be going back to the woods soon."

"He looks pretty comfortable," John observed, getting up and pushing his chair back under the table. Suddenly he wanted to get out of there. Fast.

"I know, but he's a wild thing. I haven't tried to domesticate him because I know he has to go back where he came from. He couldn't if I'd had him descented. And don't worry. He's never gassed me yet."

"There's always a first time," he said, keeping a wary eye on Bertrand and edging around the table toward the door.

"Somebody brought him to me a couple of months ago. He'd been hurt. He's almost recovered now." Cassie knelt at the side of the box and absently stroked the skunk's fur.

John shook his head as if to clear it. Yoga, skunks and herbs. So this was the long-sought Cassie Muldoon! She was hardly what he had expected.

"Thank you for taking care of my scratches," he told her, barely remembering his manners in time.

Cassie smiled up at him from her place beside Bertrand's box. "You're welcome," she said. Her hips looked solid beneath her dress, her legs limber. She was barefoot, and in those few seconds, he admitted to himself that she was very beautiful.

As though he found John's unvoiced thoughts unacceptable, Bertrand wiggled out from beneath Cassie's quiescent hand and scrambled out of his box, scurrying to John and sniffing his shoes again. Then Bertrand backed off a few feet and whipped his backside around, shifting from side to side in a funny little dance with his front feet. When the fluffy black-and-white tail shot up in warning, John knew enough not to prolong his good-bye.

"He only does that with men," Cassie explained as she snapped her arm out to scoop an unprotesting Bertrand up and replace him in his box. "Maybe because he feels threatened. Maybe a man hurt him."

John backed out the door, mumbling a hurried farewell. Once out of skunkshot he wheeled and walked swiftly away down the clean-swept earthen path, so neatly edged with its swoop-stemmed wildflower border. He inhaled the sweetly scented mountain air.

For almost two years Cassie Muldoon had declined to answer his letters, finally returning them unread. She had written him a cool note refusing to meet him at any time, under any circumstances or for any reason. And now that he'd found her, she was protected by a fully functioning skunk named Bertrand who didn't like men.

John smiled jubilantly to himself. It didn't matter. It didn't matter at all.

There was nothing, absolutely nothing, that John enjoyed more than a challenge.

Chapter Two

In June in the Great Smoky Mountains of North Carolina, the promise of spring is fulfilled by the bounty of summer.

Great fragrant roses in radiant shades of red and pink droop their sleepy heads over split-rail fences, yellow roses no bigger than a thumbnail flare like candle flames in the sun, and tiny pale pink rosebuds sprinkle their confetti petals in celebration of the season. The fruity scent of creamy elderberry blossoms mingles with air deepened by the scent of the roses, and tart wild strawberries nuzzle out from beneath heart-shaped green leaves. Melons burgeon, sweet-smelling grass throbs with the tuneless song of insects, and banks of rhododendron deck the mountainsides with color.

For Cassie the new growth of summer pulsed inside her body with unexpected energy. It was her second summer in Gran's house; she was unprepared for this new strength and the tentative happiness. No, it was not happiness. She could never know happiness again. Perhaps contentment was a better word. The contentment gave her courage to go on, a feeling that she was making progress within herself. Once, she would have thought that progress was impossible.

For the next several days after his arrival, John saw Cassie grubbing regularly in her garden, wearing a faded old sunbonnet that must have belonged to her grandmother. On the first day he called from his car, "My scratches are fine. You should market that marigold stuff commercially." She only smiled.

After that, as often as not she'd turn her back in a way that told him she'd rather not be friendly. Maybe she was embarrassed about the way she looked; most women, he supposed, would prefer to be approached when their fingernails weren't underscored by a line of dirt.

Yet at other times—say, in the evening after dinner, when he would have enjoyed a congenial conversation—he'd ramble through the woods toward her house and wait at the edge of the clearing for some sign that he was welcome. But by the time it was dark, her lights were out. He never hung around. The last thing he wanted was for her to think he had inclinations toward being a Peeping Tom.

He finally hit upon an excuse to approach her. When he was out jogging one morning, he realized that her rural mailbox, almost hidden behind a tangle of weeds three feet tall, was located around the curve in the road not far from her house. One day soon after that, he met the letter carrier driving his U.S. Mail jeep on his route up the mountain.

After tipping his hat and introducing himself as Joe Clutter, the mailman asked curiously, "Do you know this Cassie Muldoon?"

"I've met her," acknowledged John, who had engaged a post office box in Scot's Cove and had no need of rural delivery.

"Well, I've got mail for her. A lot. She hardly ever empties her mailbox."

John leaned down and rested his elbows against the open window of the jeep. He emitted a long low whistle when he saw the stack of mail Clutter indicated. "You mean all that mail is for Cassie?"

"Sure is. I drive up to the top of Flat Top and honk my horn, but she never comes out to the jeep and gets it like she's supposed to, and if I knock on the door, she doesn't answer. Guess I'll have to send it all back where it came from."

"Want me to give her her mail? I see her outside sometimes."

The mailman brightened. Then his face fell. "It's against postal regulations. I'm supposed to put it in her mailbox. There's too durned much of it to fit in her mailbox, you can see that."

John switched on his most engaging smile. "I'll give it to her. Promise." He made an absurd little gesture, a child's cross-my-heart-and-hope-to-die.

The mailman studied John's face, finally deciding that John could be trusted. "Here," he said, handing the armful of packages and envelopes out the open window. "I sure appreciate this. Don't know why she doesn't want her mail." He shook his head.

"Tell you what," said John, thinking fast before Clutter could drive away. "You deliver the mail to Cassie's mailbox and I'll check it every day and see that she gets it. I jog past here every morning."

"You'd do that for me? You really would?"

"Sure I would."

"You know, my boss is beginning to think there's something wrong with me, bringing all this Cassie Muldoon mail back to the post office all the time. 'Refused,' she writes on it sometimes. I been working for the post office for thirty-three years and I do a good job. Ain't my fault if somebody doesn't want their mail.'' He looked indignant.

''I'll see that she gets it,'' repeated John soothingly.

''Sure would appreciate it. Sure would.'' Clutter threw the jeep into gear. John waved cheerfully as the red-white-and-blue vehicle bounced down the rough road.

He stared down at the armload of letters and packages. Then he grinned and began to climb the steep road toward Cassie's place.

''Male call,'' he said out loud to a redbird sitting on a fence rail, and then he chuckled.

CASSIE SAT AT THE TABLE, nibbling on the eraser at the end of her pencil. She'd long ago given up trying to write music; she simply didn't have the heart for it. But writing her thoughts and feelings on paper helped her to understand herself, and understanding herself was somehow the key that would open the lock to—what? To what? That was what she didn't know.

The knock on her door startled her; she had been lost so deep in herself that she hadn't heard anyone walk up the steps.

''I brought your mail,'' John said when she threw the door open.

The disorientation and then the dismay on her face told him he must have arrived at an inopportune time. His heart fell.

''I'll set it down wherever you like,'' he said when she made no move to take the mail from him.

''I don't want it,'' she said.

"But I promised Joe Clutter that I'd deliver this to you personally." He grinned at her. "If I don't, I'll be in violation of Postal Regulation Number One Thousand Six Hundred and Twenty-eight Point Two. And you know what that means."

What in the world was wrong with her? She was staring at the mass of envelopes and packages in his arms and made no move to let him in. If his large frame hadn't been blocking the door, he would have bet she'd have bolted past him out into the woods someplace. From the cornered expression on her face, he was positive that she was considering it.

"Is there really a postal regulation like that?" she said, missing the joke he had been about to make. He had been about to say that anyone in violation of such a postal regulation was required to take a beautiful woman out to dinner, but it had fallen flat, that was for sure.

"No, there isn't any such regulation," he said, and the kindness in his voice made her look at him, startled.

"Just...just toss it all on the chair over there. And...and thank you." She avoided looking into his face; she didn't recall his eyes being this blue before.

"You don't sound as though you want to thank me. You sound as though you'd rather curse me. What do you have against mail? Do you realize that you're missing all the sweepstakes entries, chances to win a new boat or a new house or maybe a hundred thousand dollars a year for life?"

She continued to stare at the mail, not even acknowledging that he'd spoken. He'd fallen flat again. Either she had absolutely no sense of humor or he'd interrupted something very important, although he couldn't for the life of him figure out what. A piece of paper and a pencil were on the table, an orange tiger cat snoozed on the hearth rug, and the skunk, thank goodness, was not in evidence.

"Well, time for me to be going," he said reluctantly, zipping the warm-up jacket he wore and stuffing his hands deep into its pockets.

No reply.

"See you around, Cassie," he said, giving up on her at last, and he wheeled and ran down the porch stairs, jogging toward the cabin.

Good grief, what was wrong with the woman?

One thing, whatever it was, there was surely nothing wrong with her looks. She was gorgeous, even in a state approaching catatonia.

But how in the world was he ever going to get her to respond to him?

CASSIE FLOPPED DOWN on the floor next to the chair and picked her mail up in clumps, letting it sift through her fingers to the floor.

"Another letter from Morgana. I'd recognize her half printing, half writing anywhere," she told Tigger the tomcat, who yawned and stretched and looked totally bored.

There were magazines, which she chucked into a wicker basket. The latest issues of *Billboard* joined the other magazines in the basket. There were ads, sweepstakes entries, more letters, typed envelopes and also the kind of envelopes that contained wedding or graduation invitations, all reminders of the life she had given up when she'd come here. None of these correspondents believed she planned to stay on Flat Top Mountain.

She meant to stay here. Her life was here now, and every time she began to understand her life and where it had been in relation to where it was going, something from the outside intruded. Mail was the worst intruder of all. She owned no television, no radio, no stereo, nothing that could pull her out of herself.

And now not only the mail had intruded, but John Howard bringing the mail had intruded.

Those eyes sparkling at her, wanting to make jokes, and his immediate kindness when he realized that her mood was not conducive to joke making. That showed both understanding and patience, she grudgingly admitted to herself as she tossed aside some of the unopened letters to use as tinder for the fireplace and stuffed others in the bottom of Gran's old chifforobe. She threw the rest of them over near Bertrand's box.

"You can make short order of those," she said when the skunk poked a curious black nose up from his blanket of wood shavings. Bertrand just loved to tear up paper.

Slowly Cassie stood up and went back to her paper and pencil, delving inside herself for inner peaceful feelings. She'd almost been in touch with them, had almost been ready to commit them to paper and thus make them real for her. But that was before John Howard had arrived.

Cassie dropped her pencil with a clatter and buried her head in her arms. She was all too aware of her attraction to John. Today, seeing him in those brief running shorts, each muscle of thigh and calf clearly defined beneath a furring of soft hair, his rugged sensuality had teased her dormant senses.

She was used to being in charge of her own sexual feelings. Being celibate meant being in charge; it meant you didn't feel weak when a man looked at you in a certain way, or go gaga when he touched your arm.

So why, when his eyes had merely smiled at her, had she gone definitely gaga?

Oh, John Howard, she thought, not ready to reexperience the wealth of her body, or to discover the wealth of his. *Go away. Nothing can come of this. Nothing. Nothing.*

HE BROUGHT THE MAIL every day. She saw him sometimes from where she hid behind Gran's ecru crocheted curtains, but all he would do was put her mail down on Gran's old cane-bottom hickory rocking chair and jog away, whistling a tuneless tune. If she happened to be outside, he'd try to strike up a conversation, but on those occasions she took the mail from him with as few words as possible and disappeared into the house as though to read it.

"My phone's not working yet," he told her, and "I didn't realize I would have such a hard time finding a good local restaurant." He told her that he liked the way she wore her hair and told her that he'd enjoy her company on his forays into the countryside to photograph plants.

She told him nothing.

Cassie tried with all her willpower not to think about his teeth, so square and white when he smiled at her, about his lips that were so wide and generous, or about the way he towered over her when they occasionally stood face to face. She willed herself not to measure his charm and his appeal, or to think about his brilliant energy, which threatened to sweep a woman off her feet.

"Not me, of course," she informed a totally uninterested Tigger. "My feet are firmly anchored to the ground."

So strong was his effect on her that she knew she couldn't afford the time and energy to fend him off, so she didn't even let him get close enough for her to have to do that. She kept her distance. She remained reticent, vigilant, watchful and elusive.

And in the meantime, John stewed. Now that he had met her, seen her, touched her, Cassie was no longer a hazy figure to whom he felt an obsessive gratitude for a good deed that she had probably forgotten. She was more than that now; she was a real-life flesh-and-blood person with whom he found himself totally fascinated.

TWO WEEKS AFTER THE ARRIVAL of John Howard, Cassie waded carefully into the bed of mint in her garden, through the mint leaves strewn with the golden pollen of the nearby roses. The weather that morning was clear and dry, perfect for harvesting mint now that the dew had evaporated.

She gathered the skirt of her shift into a catchall for the leaves, baring her brown legs even more than usual, and she was bending over to pluck yet another leaf when she heard John Howard hailing her from the path through the woods.

She straightened, unused to anyone approaching from that direction. John usually approached from the direction of the road, on his way back from getting her mail.

"Cassie," he called, and their eyes met.

Oh no, she thought with dread. He had caught her with her guard down for once, when she wasn't expecting him. She'd been enjoying her solitude, had been absorbed in the task at hand. And now here he was, and inexplicably a quotation blipped through her head like words on a Goodyear blimp: "We glide past each other...because we never dare to give ourselves." Who had said that? It was someone famous, someone—but why should she think of it now?

John knew in that moment, when their eyes meshed, that he would never forget the way she looked, slightly bent over and vulnerable, tiny green mint leaves ruffling around her brown ankles, her hair shot through with the morning sun and her eyes rippling like the depths of a silvery mountain pool. And she was thinking of something, something that had arrested her thoughts, he could tell by the expression in her eyes.

"The phone people came out to hook up my phone yesterday, and this morning there's no dial tone," he said. "Not only that, there's a black wire hanging down the side of the cabin."

As he spoke he was walking so rapidly toward her that she left behind all thoughts of gliding past each other and thought instead, in a burst of shyness, of dropping her skirt and running. This morning John Howard carried himself with an all-too-sure knowledge of his sexuality, a sexuality that seemed too much in tune with the lushly seductive sounds and smells of summer on the mountain.

He stood before her now with his hands resting below his hips, unwittingly drawing her attention to his low-slung jeans and the body within them. The jeans were faded; the body was clearly defined by the pliant material. *The male form,* she thought wonderingly, as though seeing it for the first time. *I had almost forgotten.*

At least he hadn't hooked his thumbs under his belt and tilted his pelvis forward in that self-conscious macho swagger of a man on the make. John Howard, despite the wholesome appeal of his sensuality, was not a man on the make—of that she was certain. His eyes were too sincere, and he never tried to mask that sincerity.

"May I use your phone? I think I'd better report it right away. I don't trust that hanging wire." His eyes on her face were friendly, and he seemed unknowingly surrounded by an electromagnetic field so highly charged that it received as much energy as it sent.

Determined to let him know that she was not about to respond to his sexually oriented signals, she picked her way gingerly through the bed of mint, clutching her skirt to her body. A faint minty odor surrounded her.

"I don't have a phone," she told him. "So I'm afraid I can't help you."

John found himself captivated by the tinselly tone of her voice and the whispery quality underlying it; she sounded as though there were a little girl inside her, hoping to be heard.

"You don't have a telephone?" He smiled pleasantly. "I can't imagine getting along without one, especially up here."

"You'll have to drive into town and use a pay telephone," she said. "That's where the nearest phone is. Now if you'll excuse me." She brushed past him, heading for the house.

This had happened once too often. He refused to be squelched.

"Cassie, wait," he said, and his hand on her arm sent a shiver through her. "Go with me. I don't fancy driving all the way down the mountain alone. We could...we could have lunch together."

Her startled eyes found his. "I don't go into town unless it's absolutely necessary," she told him. "And I don't ever eat lunch there."

"After eating one of the Hungry Cafe's greasy hamburgers, I can understand why. Never before have I heard of anyone putting coleslaw on a hamburger the way they do there. See, it's absolutely necessary that you go with me," he raced on, talking fast and hoping against hope that she would respond this time. "It's your neighborly duty to help me find a decent hamburger around here. And anyway, why shouldn't you be treated to lunch once in a while?" He addressed the loneliness in her eyes.

"I—I can't," she said, ducking her head and fleeing from him.

He followed her. "Cassie, wait!" he called in exasperation. He wanted her company, and this wasn't a ruse. His phone really was out of order and there really was a worrisome black wire hanging down an outside wall of his cabin.

But by the time he reached her door, she had shut it. *Slam,* right in his face. Nonplussed, his blue eyes shooting sparks at the sturdy wooden door, he took two steps backward and cursed under his breath. She didn't reopen the door, and he heard no sound on the other side. She'd never done anything like this before to him. No one had ever slammed a door in his face. Who the hell did she think she was?

He resisted the impulse to plant a well-aimed kick right in the center of the door and stalked furiously back through the forest to his own cabin, a small three-room place shingled in gray bark. The cabin was entirely adequate but nothing special after the standard of living to which John was accustomed; the bathroom roof leaked and the mattress was lumpy. He'd only rented the cabin because it was close to her, and its discomforts suddenly seemed like a lot to put up with when she wouldn't even talk to him.

Easy, man, he calmed himself as he scooped up the keys to the car from the dresser. *Her friend Morgana tried to warn you, didn't she? Cassie wanted nothing to do with you, and you knew it before you so brashly insinuated yourself into this situation. So take it easy, play it cool. There's time, plenty of time before you have to leave.* They wouldn't be looking for him at the office until September; thanks to competent managers, he could handle all the details of running AirBridges Cargo Transport by telephone. Once the telephone worked, that is.

John headed his car down the winding road, wondering what he could have done to convince Cassie to come with him today. He knew little about her past tragedies, certainly not enough to know what troubled her so deeply and so long that she'd chosen to bury herself here on this godforsaken mountain, working so hard in that garden of hers, putting herself at the disposal of people who thought nothing of riding up the mountain for her remedies day and night.

Oh, yes, he'd heard the slamming of car doors, the hollered good-byes at all hours. Not everyone felt the same compunction he did about disturbing Cassie when her lights were out for the evening. Hell, no wonder she went to bed so early. She was likely to be disturbed almost every night by somebody with chest congestion or an aching joint or dandruff or who knew what? From what he could tell, Cassie offered remedies for everything from morning sickness to hangnails. She gave unstintingly of herself to others; why would she give none of herself to him?

He slowed down at a particularly rough patch of road. The mountain road was treacherous, with curves and switchbacks. Where it leveled out for the first time, he had to slam on his brakes when a chicken skittered across the road with a child in full pursuit. The child—boy or girl, he couldn't tell—captured the chicken and stood staring after his rented Chevrolet sped past, as feathers fluttered up in the wake of the car.

The kid must belong to this tumbledown shack on the right, thought John, consulting his rearview mirror for one more look at it. Why, the place didn't even have inside plumbing—a dribbling old hand pump stood in the side yard, and a half-moon house perched precariously on the edge of a cliff in back. The windows of the shack were broken and mended with polyethylene film, and the door hung lopsided on its hinges. The people who lived there were Cassie's nearest neighbors, besides him.

Which made him wonder again for the eleven-hundredth time: What in the world was a classy lady like Cassie Muldoon doing on Flat Top Mountain?

Cassie was such a puzzling entity that John decided to do some snooping around Scot's Cove. The logical place to start was with Ned Church, the prosperous proprietor of the town's gas station and its adjacent minimarket. Ned also owned the cabin John rented.

"Say, Ned," John said when he stopped to fill his car with gas. "I've been seeing a lot more traffic on Flat Top Mountain than I'd expected. What's going on up there?"

"Oh," Ned said, his mouth working on a wad of tobacco, "that's just folks going up the mountain to see Cassie Muldoon. She gives 'em medicines she makes from herbs. Her grandma used to do the same thing, years ago."

"She pretty friendly? Easy to get to know?"

A spark lit Ned Church's eyes. "What you got in mind?"

John laughed, man to man. "I thought I might ask her to go to dinner with me. It gets lonely up on the mountain, you know."

Ned Church snickered, then became more serious. "Cassie's not the friendly type, if you know what I mean. Doesn't see anyone much except the people who come by for her remedies. I heard she gets along with the oldest Ott girl okay. But Cassie, she keeps to herself. Don't think you'll get anywhere with her." He spat a brown bullet of tobacco juice toward the highway.

"You know her long?"

"She used to visit her grandma in the summers. Then she came back a couple years ago, after her grandma was dead and gone, and she's been living up there ever since. I see her when she comes into town, which ain't often. No, Cassie's kind of a hermit."

"Mmm," said John, thoughtfully. Unfortunately, he had learned nothing that he didn't already know.

Reaching this Cassie Muldoon was proving to be an arduous task indeed, but, John reminded himself, he had come this far. For him, there was no turning back.

He'd crossed the continent to find her, and he wasn't about to be discouraged so easily.

Chapter Three

At the very moment that John was prodding information out of Ned Church, Cassie was lying across her bed crying her eyes out.

Why, *why* had she shut the door in his face? John Howard had only meant to be nice to her, had only been offering her a chance to go out for lunch. Why couldn't she have refused him more graciously, why had she had to run?

Oh, but he was too much. Too worldly. Too outgoing, too hail-fellow-well-met, too damn likable. Too sexy by far. He was the kind who was proud of himself, of who he was, and he wanted others to approve of him as much as he approved of himself.

That was part of the trouble. They weren't anything alike. She sure as hell wasn't proud of herself.

Blotting her eyes with the ruffle of the embroidered pillow sham, she picked herself up. Bertrand rambled past, brushing up against her ankle, which was dangling off the edge of the bed.

"Oh, Bertrand, there's no end to the guilt." Why was it in her nature to feel guilty about everything? Had she been that way before?

"I don't think so," she said out loud. She had been carefree and ambitious and loving and...but what was the use? She was a different person now.

She got up—or, more accurately, down—from the tall old-fashioned brass bed, Gran's bed, and straightened the coverlet with its embroidered bluebirds of happiness.

Gran's bed was one of her favorite things about this house. It was the most elaborate brass bed she had ever seen, with its gleaming spirals and curlicues culminating in four massive bedposts that flared at the tops like the ends of tubas.

Cassie remembered arriving on Flat Top Mountain one summer from the small Piedmont North Carolina town where she'd lived as a child. It must have been shortly after the Fourth of July celebration, when the big brass band marched down Main Street; and since Cassie had been only three or four at the time, she'd thought Gran was calling her bed a "brass band." To the tiny Cassie, awestruck at a piece of furniture, the likes of which she'd never seen before, the bright brass bed had in fact looked like a whole brass band. She'd fully expected loud oompahs to come crashing from the bedposts at any moment.

She smiled at the memories. Gran's brass bed. How she wished there'd been time to show it to Rory. He would have loved it.

Just then Bertrand scuttled into the closet and reappeared with a pair of panty hose in his mouth. One nylon foot was caught on something in the closet. He tugged at the panty hose until it ripped.

"Bertrand," she said reprovingly. It was her last pair of panty hose.

The skunk laid the shredded panty hose at her feet and licked her bare toe. She bent over and affectionately scratched him behind the ear.

"Trying to make it up to me, are you?" she said as she smiled, but her words gave her pause.

"As maybe I can make it up to John," she murmured thoughtfully. She straightened as Bertrand skidded around the room, his toenails clicking on the wooden plank floor like castanets gone wild.

She stood thinking until Tigger interrupted her thought processes. Yawning, the big marmalade cat stretched out from under the bed. He hopped on her pillow and began to wash his face with one tiger-striped paw. Tigger ignored the cavorting skunk, his usual practice. Skunks and other such creatures were below his lofty dignity.

Cassie's behavior toward John had been inexcusable. She was ashamed of the way she'd acted; there had been no need to get nasty.

"It was the way he looked," she explained to the animals. Tigger blinked up at her, then switched his attention and his tongue to one of his elegant rear legs. At least he didn't pass judgment on her. Cassie was grateful for that.

She chattered to Tigger, who jumped down and followed her to the kitchen, where she consulted the freezer. "What do you think, Tigger? I've got two or three casseroles of frozen shrimp Newburg. I could take one to John as a peace offering later. The cooking facilities in that cabin are substandard, I'm sure." Cassie kept her freezer fully stocked and only went to town to refill it when her supplies were depleted.

Tigger stared at her inscrutably and jumped up on the kitchen counter, which was his habit when he wanted attention. Absently Cassie scooped Tigger from the counter and sat down with him on the floor, scratching the cat under his chin until he rewarded her with a happy, guttural purr.

"I'll drop the casserole on John's doorstep with an apologetic note, knock on the door and run," she said, thinking out loud. Tigger opened one eye briefly, declining to comment as long as Cassie continued to scratch.

What Cassie failed to realize was that this sort of play wouldn't work with a man like John Howard.

A FLUTTER OF MOVEMENT caught John's eye as he inexpertly fumbled with the Nikon. The damned thing was beyond him, with its apertures and its f/stops and all manner of lenses long and short.

"Why didn't I tell Cassie I'm a—well, a biologist, for instance?" he mumbled to no one in particular. There must be a number of things a biologist could do on Flat Top Mountain. Classify plants or something—yeah, that would be good. Crawl around peering at leaves with a magnifying glass. A magnifying glass he could handle.

He caught another glimpse of something in the woods and set the camera aside, moving to the window. He was amazed to realize that it was Cassie. Despite the limp, she moved like a wood nymph from the shadows of the forest into the soft lemon-yellow sunset of the clearing. Her hair did not wisp or waft but swirled up and out and around her, a crisp frame for a face that looked tense but determined. With a certain detachment and a raised eyebrow, he let her set the basket she carried on his doorstep. Then he yanked the door open.

She stared openmouthed.

"Come in," he said.

"I—" She whirled to go.

He was too quick for her. He was down the steps in less than a second, his strong hand circling her wrist.

"Let me go!" she said, outraged.

"Not until you tell my why you're creeping through the woods so quietly, and what's in the basket. What are you, Little Red Riding Hood?"

She glared at him. "Yes, and you must be the wolf."

He laughed. "You get two points for a quick comeback." He stopped laughing when he realized that she wasn't laughing with him.

"I'll let go of you if you promise not to run. Better yet, come inside the cabin," he said.

"I can't," she said, looking inexplicably frightened.

"Oh, you *can't*!" he mocked, his anger renewed by thoughts of the morning. "Don't you think you owe me an apology for slamming the door in my face? You're the only woman who's ever done that to me."

She blinked at him. She was sorry she'd slammed the door in his face—wasn't that why she had come here, to atone for that mistake? Now even that had gone wrong.

John kept a firm hold on Cassie's wrist and slid his other arm around her waist. He felt bones, ribs scarcely insulated by fat. There was no roll around her waistline; she was slim and firm and delicate. She let him ease her up the steps and into the house. They both stepped over the wicker basket.

Once she was safely inside, he turned around and picked up the basket, which he now saw contained a casserole, salad greens and a loaf of bread neatly wrapped in a cloth napkin. An envelope was taped to the casserole lid. It was addressed to him.

She stood watching, her bottom lip caught between her teeth.

"Relax. I'm not going to molest you," he told her, tearing the envelope open.

"Well, at least that's something."

"Grandma, what sharp claws you have," he said as he unfolded the note. His sharp eyes noted that Cassie looked unaccountably crushed at his words. Didn't she understand teasing at all?

He read her note. It was simple and to the point, apologizing for closing the door in his face. That was all, except for instructions about heating the shrimp Newburg in his oven.

"Good," he said succinctly. "You'll stay to eat dinner with me, of course, since you cheated me out of lunch."

"I didn't..." she began, then thought better of it. No use in belaboring the subject. It would be best if she dropped it.

"I'm having the worst time with this gas stove. Help me get the pilot light lit," he told her, appropriating her wrist again.

She tugged her arm away. "You don't need to put on a big he-man act," she said. "You don't have to haul me around."

He looked at her levelly, seriously. "You're right, you know," he said quietly. "It *is* an act. And I don't want to act with you. I want to be real and honest." The sooner he could be honest, the sooner he could drop this ridiculous fiction that he was a photographer.

His deep blue eyes were so sincere that Cassie dropped her own eyes in confusion. They landed on a tightly curled tuft of dark chest hair. He'd left the top two buttons of his navy-blue shirt unbuttoned.

"And," he went on, tipping a finger under her chin so that she was again looking at him, listening to him whether she wanted to or not, "I want you to be equally real and honest with me." This he spoke with the air of a command, but she only blinked. She wasn't used to anyone telling her what to do.

John removed his finger from her chin and turned to the stove. She watched his hands as he struck a wooden kitchen match and held it to the pilot light. The first match went out.

"Can you give me any tips about using a gas stove?" he asked in exasperation. "I've never had one before."

"Neither have I," she said. "Mine's electric."

He struck another match. His hands were big and sinewy and capable, with long fingers and squared-off fingernails.

She let her eyes drift up his arms, to his shoulders, so square and so masculine, and down his chest, with its well-defined pectoral muscles. Below that, she noted the flat, solid tautness of his abdomen. His shirt disappeared into jeans that were well worn, swelling with the lanky curve of his thigh and tapering trimly to calf and ankle. He wore a pair of expensive running shoes. He appeared to be in fine physical shape for a man of his age, which she judged to be mid-thirties or so, just a few years older than she was.

Her unobserved study of him ended when the pilot light lit with a *whoosh!*

"Finally," he said in relief. With a smile of satisfaction, John set the oven temperature and turned to her, his face bright with anticipation.

"Now, while the oven preheats, I have a bottle of—" he took a bottle from the refrigerator "—well, it's nothing special," he admitted with appealing sheepishness. "Just an ordinary Chablis, the kind you can get in any supermarket. I found out that the town of Scot's Cove doesn't have much of a selection of good wine, does it?"

Cassie shrugged and turned away from his gentle persuasion. She wished she were home, eating her solitary dinner. This man was looking at her expectantly, wanting some sort of response. Well, she wasn't used to being social anymore. She'd forgotten how.

"We'll sit out on the porch and watch the sun go down over Magnus Mountain. Okay?"

She shrugged again, sad about this man, his obvious attraction to her, and what he wanted from her. She suddenly wished she could be what he wanted her to be. It was impossible.

John installed her in a chair on the porch and pulled another chair up close to hers. They didn't talk, just sat in the deepening twilight inhaling the fragrance of the honeysuckle vine in the woods. In the distance a small plane glided soundlessly, too far away for them to hear the sound of the engine. Cassie averted her eyes from it and focused on a bumblebee circling a rosebush before heading home to the hive. She saw so few airplanes up here, which was a blessing.

The sun slipped down, shooting a golden aureole up from the peak of the mountain. The wine sent relaxing signals to her elbows, her knees, her fingers, her eyelids. Her lips.

"I'm going to go in and put that casserole in the oven. You'll be here when I get back, won't you?" His voice was smooth, sweet. He had a sweet voice for a man.

She nodded. While he was gone, she rubbed a finger curiously against her bottom lip. The lip was slightly numb, the way it felt when she had just come home from the dentist's office after having a tooth filled.

John stepped out the door as Cassie was rubbing her finger across her lip. Her mouth had relaxed, and her face in the glow of the sunset was stunning in its irregularity. He wished he really were a photographer, because he would like to have a photograph of her, of each half of her face flip-flopped so that he could see what she would look like if her whole face was the same. Which side would he like best? The left or the right? They were both equally beautiful.

She jerked her finger away from her mouth and shot him a guilty look. Why guilty? Was she embarrassed that he had caught her in the act of doing something so sensual? He longed to touch her lips with his own finger. But no, he reminded himself. His attraction to her wasn't sexual. At least, it hadn't been. Now, at this moment, his former attitude toward her seemed to blur into an indistinct pattern.

When they saw the first mosquito hovering in wait, humming its song of the hunt, John took her hand and led her into the house.

"You can make the salad," he said, whipping a large salad bowl from a cupboard and setting it down with a clatter. "Those greens look wonderfully fresh. Did you grow them yourself?"

She couldn't stop herself from warming slightly to his enthusiasm. "Yes," she said, tearing up lettuce, slicing crisp baby scallions, quartering the first of her early tomatoes. "I brought them in from the garden this afternoon."

"I've always wanted to have time for gardening. It fascinates me, the idea of watching live things growing." Whistling, he set the casserole and the salad on a table in the small alcove that served as a dining room. The wide windows overlooked Pride's Peak, its long shadows purple and lavender in the deepening twilight.

John helped Cassie with her chair as though they were sitting down to dinner in the most elegant restaurant instead of the rather plain mountain cabin. *He's used to nice places,* she thought. *He knows how to act.* Her mind shot back to other places, other times. Being handed out of a limousine; walking, head held high, through a maze of beautifully set tables, the candles glowing on the faces of the customers, the fine crystal tinkling daintily, the silver gleaming in the light from the golden chandeliers. Oh, she had known that sort of place, too, once upon a time. Once upon a long-ago lifetime.

"Well," John said, "will you?"

She pulled herself back to the present and stared at him. She had no idea what he'd said.

He saw the lost expression on her face and knew at once that she had been somewhere else, not with him. Pity stabbed through him. He'd have to remember, have to force himself to remember that something sad had happened to her. He'd have to remember that if it weren't for her, he wouldn't be here. Wouldn't be anywhere, for that matter. His gratitude to her washed over him in a giant wave, like the biggest wave he'd ever ridden in the Pacific Ocean back in his surfing days. The gratitude filled him up, emptied his lungs, hit him stronger than any other emotion he had known.

He fought for control. Her confused expression touched him.

"If you don't want to talk," he told her gently, "we don't have to."

"I—I'm not used to being with other people," she said unhappily. "It makes me nervous."

"I make you nervous?"

"No, not you. Just...being with somebody." *A man,* she thought. *Being with a man.* She looked down at her plate. She'd barely eaten anything.

He slid his hand over hers where it rested on the table. "I don't like making you nervous. But I enjoy your company."

She shook her head and shoved the chair back from the table, knocking it over in her haste. It fell with a jarring crash.

"I'm sorry," she said in anguish. "I shouldn't have come here. It was a bad idea." Her eyes were huge and sorrowful.

He was up and after her before she made it halfway across the room.

"Cassie!"

"Please leave me alone," she said desperately, the words falling out in a rush. "You have no idea how it is with me. Leave me alone." She struggled clumsily with the rusty door latch, but it wouldn't budge.

Her words tore at his heart. "I want to know, Cassie, if only you'd tell me."

But here eyes were wild and her fingers on the latch were frantic, so, hoping to quiet her, John wrapped her in his strong arms.

With one arm clasping her waist and one girding her shoulders, Cassie felt his warmth through her loose shift. His warmth and his hardness, the strength of a male member of the species.

She swallowed and squeezed her eyes tightly shut, unable to breathe. His forearm, the one around her waist, barely brushed the bottom curves of her breasts. Her heart battered against it.

"I won't hurt you," he said softly into her ear. His breath fluttered the springy curls. "I'd never hurt you." His hand left her shoulder and slid under her hair. She drew a rapid intake of breath as her bones liquefied beneath his touch.

Reluctantly, despite the telltale leap of her pulse beneath his fingers, he took his arms away.

"Unlock the door so I can go," she whispered, not daring to look at him. One look at him and she'd shatter, like fragile hand-blown glass. "There's no point in our getting to know each other. None at all." She wanted to cry so the tension would go away, this terrible and awful tension that *he* had started, for which *he* was responsible.

Slowly he released the latch, and the door swung open. Like a ghost, like a figment of his imagination, she flitted away, and the woven shadows of the woods enfolded her.

Suddenly exhausted by the effect of Cassie's sheer terror, John massaged the bridge of his nose with his thumb and forefinger, and when his eyes closed, Cassie was there. He flicked his eyes open again, startled, wanting beyond all reason for her to be there, *really* there.

His shoulders slumped as he turned away from the door, wishing he had not scared her so. He'd tried to be kind and gentle, had let her lead the way. Obviously, that wasn't enough. But he had never expected her to be somebody like this, so vulnerable, so frightened, so in need of comfort. So in need of touching, and that was obvious. The way she'd jumped when he'd touched her neck, the tightness in her like a coiled spring.

So what would he do about it?

First of all, he'd have to let go of the fiction once and for all that his attraction to her wasn't sexual. If this compulsion to be near her wasn't sexual, he didn't know what was. It hadn't started out that way, but now…

Now, with that premise scuttled, he'd go on from here. Somehow.

Chapter Four

Cassie's hair blew free in the salty wind of the bay, and when she turned to look at Kevin at the wheel, a wayward strand flapped in her eyes. Laughing, she plucked it away with her fingers.

The speedboat curved, plowing bedazzled blue water into white-bright froth as they sped toward the green islands in the distance. Rory grinned at her when she pointed out the wind-furled sail of a catamaran; Rory loved sailboats and played with his own toy sailboats in the swimming pool for hours at a time.

The bitter taste of salt rimmed her lips, and she licked it away. Then, without warning, their boat spun around, dizzying her, and plunged sharply beneath the sunstruck water, now turquoise *(a Navaho charm?)*, now sapphire *(my mother's ring?)*, now navy *(a sailor I once loved?)*. The boat dissolved in a spurt of misty bubbles, and she was swimming desperately, trying to keep up with Kevin and Rory, who were tumbling down, down into the depths of the cool, quiet water. The deepest shade of blue is black. Cassie tried desperately to follow them into the darkness, straining to keep her eyes on them, but it was no use. She couldn't sink no matter how hard she tried, even though her mind screamed, "Wait! I'm coming!" Her lungs burned hot and hotter, finally igniting, and the fire propelled her violently to the surface again, a human rocket, and she was borne bursting through the watery skin into the bright daylight screaming their names.

Abruptly she awakened to find herself sitting up in Gran's bed. The salt water on her face was her own tears.

She let her head fall limply on her upraised knees as she waited for her erratic heartbeat to slow. Another of those dreams. And she'd thought she was over them, so well over them that she no longer drank chamomile tea at bedtime. It had been one of Gran's favorite remedies for nightmares, "drinking the cham." Well, she'd be sure to drink it from now on.

When Bertrand pawed at the side of the bed she got up and padded into the kitchen, where she poured cat food into his dish and let Tigger in from his night-long romp and poured cat food into his dish, too.

It was the unsettling arrival of John Howard, she thought to herself. She had been getting along fine, occupying herself with her garden and the preparation of Gran's remedies, and the bad dreams had stopped. And now he had arrived, with his sweet voice and his kindness and his body, his body talking to her body with no need for words; and nothing was the same.

She nibbled distractedly at a thin slice of toast spread with butter and homemade preserves for breakfast, accompanied by her own special blend of herbal tea. As she sat at the table, staring out the window, she saw John's car pass her house on its way down the mountain road. He didn't look in her direction.

Well, after yesterday, he would think she was crazy. And perhaps she was, a little. But she was fighting her own way back to normality, and she would make it, too, John Howard or no John Howard. She could have done without the complication of sexual attraction. She had enough problems to solve without dealing with that, which was why she had adopted celibacy as her way of life.

Oh, she had visited Morgana's psychiatrist afterward, when her leg had healed enough for her to go out. Dr. Westwood had been a round dumpling of a man, jolly and clever and sympathetic. But when Cassie had realized that he didn't have a magic cure-all, an incantation that would make everything all right, when she had understood that the work had to be done inside her where it counted, she had decided not to go back to jolly Dr. Westwood.

If she had to put the jigsaw puzzle of herself together on her own, she could do it better in the peace and quiet of Flat Top Mountain than she could in Los Angeles, with its too-frantic pace and its too-frantic people. She could center on herself, find her own harmony, once she was away from Morgana and her oddball friends. And so, over Morgana's objections, Cassie had fled to Gran's, to the little house her grandmother had left her when she died, the same house where Cassie had spent so many pleasant summers in her youth.

"Cassie?" A hesitant tap at the screen door, a slight shadow against the light.

"Oh, Sharon, come in. I haven't seen you since you stopped by on your graduation day, and that was over a week ago."

The girl who entered was young, only seventeen, but a woman full-grown nonetheless. Her curves filled a pair of blue jeans cut off at the knees and a pink blouse, faded from too many washings.

"I know. It's been hard for me to get away, what with Ma's new baby and all. My hens have been laying, though, and I thought to bring you some fresh eggs." Sharon set a carton of eggs on the table.

"Good, I'm glad to have them," Cassie told her warmly. Sharon's eggs came from chickens she kept herself at that miserable shack down the road, where she was the eldest of an innumerable brood of children. Cassie had befriended Sharon early in her stay here, and the girl was Cassie's friend—really her only friend—on Flat Top Mountain.

Cassie stood up and took her dishes into the kitchen, taking time to stow the eggs in the refrigerator egg-tray.

"I thought I'd play and sing for a while, Cassie, if you don't mind," said Sharon, following along.

"Of course I don't mind. You know better," said Cassie in a fondly chiding tone. "Let me get out the dulcimer. Goodness, Sharon, it's been too long since you've been here."

Cassie preceded Sharon into the front room, where she lifted her dulcimer case down from its shelf and ran her fingers over the handcrafted leather. It was her own special case; Kevin had had it made to order for her when they were on vacation in Italy. The leather was butter-soft, and the inside was padded with moss-green velvet.

As always, Sharon's brown eyes brightened as she unzipped the leather case. She lifted the instrument with reverence and strummed softly.

"I'm going to try using a Popsicle stick as a plectrum today," Sharon told her, producing one from a pocket in her jeans.

"That's good," approved Cassie. She plucked the dulcimer strings with a goose quill herself, the way Gran had. But during the past year or so that Sharon had been her pupil, she had encouraged Sharon to develop her own distinctive style, to try new techniques, and to her satisfaction, Sharon had.

This dulcimer was one of the best, a one-of-a-kind instrument created by a skilled mountain craftsman of beautifully grained black walnut wood, its surface smooth as silk. It was a mountain dulcimer, a plucked dulcimer, which some believe is a distant relative of the German zither. Its shape was an elongated oval, something like a stretched-out violin.

Many of the old-time players, Gran among them, had played the dulcimer by plucking it. Cassie, however, had learned, in addition to plucking, to strum it much as she would strum a guitar or banjo. It was a more complicated way of playing, but it gave a different sound.

Sharon strummed experimentally with the Popsicle stick, humming "Little Turtle Dove," which was one of the old-time regional Appalachian songs for which she and Cassie shared a similar affection.

"I like the way this sounds," said Sharon with pleasure, and then she went on to sing the whole song in her low, full-throated voice. Watching and listening to Sharon, whose eyes reflected spirit and intelligence, Cassie found it hard to believe that this girl was a member of the disreputable Ott clan from that shanty down the road.

Not many dulcimer players survive in the Great Smoky Mountains; the skill of playing the dulcimer was one passed from generation to generation, like the art of healing with plants. Both arts had suffered from the encroaching of civilization into even the most backwoods hamlets, and like herbal healing, dulcimer playing had become almost passé. This was one reason that Cassie had felt the compulsion to pass her knowledge along to someone else.

She felt fortunate to have found such an apt pupil. Sharon had a languid way of movement, easy and relaxed, and as she held the dulcimer on her knees and moved her hands so gracefully across the strings, she seemed to become uniquely one with the instrument and the tune.

The vibrating strains of the last chord filled the room. "Much as I'd like to," Cassie told her pupil, "I'd better not stay and listen. I want to gather chickweed this morning before the sun gets too hot."

"Need some help?" Sharon looked eager, but Cassie knew how much Sharon valued her time to practice playing.

"No, I'll enjoy listening to you play as I work." Smiling, Cassie lifted a burlap bag from a peg on the wall and went outside.

As she worked swiftly to gather the weed, Cassie reflected on Sharon's spunk in standing up to her parents and insisting on finishing high school over their objections. Most Otts dropped out of school after the eighth grade or even before if the truant officer didn't complain, and usually he didn't because no teacher wanted an Ott in his or her classroom. Not only had she finished high school, but Sharon earned her own spending money by selling eggs laid by the few chickens she raised.

Cassie was startled out of her thoughts as John Howard's car unexpectedly zoomed past on its way back to his cabin, stirring up a cloud of gray dust. Again, he did not look her way. She bent her head over the burlap bag, hiding her face in case he glanced back. He didn't.

She continued her task as the strains of Sharon's "Careless Love" drifted across the mountain, and it was almost as though Cassie were traveling back in time, to when Gran would send her out on a morning to gather chickweed and she could hear Gran's sweet songs wafting from the house.

The memory made her feel more secure, as though everything was the way it had been back in those long-ago summers when she'd been happy here with Gran, before—well, before everything. And as far as John Howard was concerned, her fear concerning him seemed to be unjustified. She need not worry. John Howard was going to keep his distance.

Later, when Cassie went back into the house, she told Sharon, "You can take the dulcimer home with you if you like."

Sharon caressed the smooth surface of the dulcimer lovingly.

"Oh, no, Cassie, you know I couldn't do that. The other kids might get hold of it and break it."

"I know," said Cassie, setting the bag of chickweed down as she smiled at Sharon. "But people are more important than things. I could always get another dulcimer."

She meant it; she loved the instrument, but she also wanted Sharon to have it whenever she needed it. She, Cassie, had little use for it now.

"No, I'll come over here when I get a yen to play," Sharon said firmly, replacing the dulcimer in its case.

"But you haven't been coming often," Cassie pointed out. "What's wrong? Are you still looking for a full-time job?"

The girl hung her head so that her strawberry-blond tresses curved under her cheeks, masking her expression. "Yes, I'm looking, but I can't find one. In the first place, I don't have reliable transportation into town. In the second place, Ma needs me to look after the kids. And in the third place, no one wants to hire an Ott."

Cassie's heart went out to the girl, who would have a hard time making her way in this town, where the Otts' reputation was not of the highest caliber.

"Tell you what, Sharon," Cassie said after a moment's thought. "I'm going to be needing help with my garden. And it'll be a busy summer, gathering the herbs and preserving them while they're at the peak of freshness. I'll pay you to work for me. That is, if you'd like."

Sharon stared at her, delight swimming up from the depths of her velvety brown eyes. "If I'd *like*! Why, Cassie, it would be heaven!" Then the smile faded. "But I don't know when I'll be able to get away from home—regular, I mean."

"You come when you can, and I'll have work for you, I promise. And if you want to, you can use my station wagon to look for a full-time job." Cassie seldom used the nondescript station wagon anyway, and she never remembered to start it up regularly to keep the battery from going dead; it would benefit from Sharon's use.

Sharon threw her arms around Cassie. "Oh, Cassie, thank you so much. You're so kind to me." She stepped back, and her eyes became serious. "I can't tell you how much I need to get out of the house. The new baby cries a lot, and Ma is so tired, and the little ones fight all the time. Bonnie is some help, but most of the responsibility falls on me." Bonnie was Sharon's sister, two years younger.

If she allowed herself to, Cassie could work up a case of anxiety over the Ott family. What can you say about a mother who accepts having a baby every year as part of her sad lot in life and a father who is, as often as not, falling down drunk? How much could you do for children whose parents refuse any and all overtures?

"Does the baby have colic?" Cassie asked. The parents might turn down her help, but she and Sharon were good friends. The two of them often exchanged small kindnesses.

Sharon shook her head. "I don't know if it's colic or not. He just cries a lot, poor little thing."

He's probably crying over being born an Ott, thought Cassie, but all she said was "Try chamomile tea," and she sifted a bit of it into a plastic bag. She instructed Sharon in the use of the tea for infants, and then the girl left, swinging happily down the road with her own slow, distinctive gait, the bag cradled loosely in her hand.

"Sharon Ott," said Cassie despairingly to Bertrand. "What am I to do about her?"

The girl had talent, a strong natural presence, and was uncommonly lovely with her strawberry-blond hair and deep brown eyes bright as polished walnut wood. But Sharon seemed destined, unless she met with a stroke of rare good fortune, to slide back into the morass of failure whence no Ott ever escaped.

Cassie sighed in frustration. "Face it, Bertrand," she said to the inquisitive skunk, who was nudging his nose against the leather of the dulcimer case. "We can't cure the whole world from the top of Flat Top Mountain."

Can't cure the whole world, or even Cassie Muldoon, she mused, thinking with embarrassment of John Howard. She didn't think she'd ever be able to face him again. Perhaps there would be no need. From the way he'd driven so fast past her house both times that morning, refusing to look in its direction, she guessed that he wasn't any more interested in continuing their acquaintance than she was.

For the next couple of weeks, that appeared to be true. Cassie saw John Howard jogging past on the road every morning. She was unable to resist watching his leg muscles working so effortlessly, his lungs apparently undaunted by the thin mountain air. He still delivered her mail every day without comment, and if he knew she was peering out at him through the crocheted curtains, he made no sign. Cassie felt a twinge of guilt at those times and every time she saw his blue Chevrolet rocket past, but since he seemed to take no notice of her, she finally relaxed. She had put him off that night with her histrionics, no doubt about it.

If only she didn't find herself thinking about John at odd times! The peculiar expression on his face when she'd told him Bertrand wasn't descented, his eyes as blue as the summer sky, his tall and ruggedly masculine form, the kindness in his expression. And when she was through thinking about John, when she had exhausted her limited repertoire of scenes in which he appeared, everything appealing about him boiled down to that one thing above all—his kindness.

Lacking real-life memories of John, Cassie began to create artificial ones. At first he crept into her thoughts unnoticed—for instance, when she was weeding her garden. Then she would begin imagining him there with her, watching her with those warm blue eyes. And then she began to wonder what it would have been like to have him with her in the house as she went about her daily tasks, listening to what she had to say, occasionally contributing to the conversation.

She was lonely. She'd depended on the animals to alleviate her loneliness, but suddenly they weren't enough. Her loneliness had been a secondary factor in her life, but now, with John within reach just a short walk through the woods, and yet out of reach because she couldn't feel comfortable with the sexual feelings he stirred in her, she minded being lonely.

One night, when the ache in her leg all day told her that it would soon begin to rain, and when the sky turned grayish green at dusk and the leaves in the forest began to tremble on their stems in anticipation of the coming storm, Cassie reluctantly let Tigger out at his regular time.

"Find a dry place," she warned him, but he only winked at her in the mysterious way of cats and disappeared, tail held high, into the forest.

"No, Bertrand," she cautioned the skunk, barring him from the open door with her foot. "You're not quite ready to take on the world."

Because her leg hurt, Cassie climbed into bed early and waited for the pitter-patter of raindrops on the roof. She read *Billboard* for a while, even though it was an old copy. She didn't know why Kajurian kept sending *Billboard*. She almost never read it; she just chucked the copies into the wicker basket or the bottom of Gran's old chifforobe with all those unanswered letters from that persistent fellow who wanted to meet her and all the other fan mail for which she now had no use. Including letters from the redoubtable Kajurian, who kept begging her to come back to Los Angeles. Kajurian was the kind who never gave up—which was a quality she had appreciated in her agent, but which she appreciated considerably less in her former agent, who clearly resented what her departure had meant to his agency in terms of dollars.

It was still early when Cassie fell asleep with the lights on. She was dozing when the wind began to howl around the corners of her house, and for a moment in her half sleep she thought the pounding on the door was hail rattling the windows or the clatter of a shutter torn loose by the storm.

"Cassie! Open up! It's me, John!"

She rolled from her bed and ran to fling the door open to find John Howard standing on her porch, his clothes plastered to his body, his blond hair soaked with rain, gingerly cradling an inert and soggy bundle of fur in his raincoat. For a heart-stopping moment she thought he held Tigger, and her eyes widened in alarm.

Then with great relief Cassie saw that it wasn't her marmalade tomcat after all. It was a raccoon, drenched and unconscious, but breathing.

John stepped inside and kicked the door shut against the storm. His blue eyes burned into her, taking in her hastily donned bathrobe. Anxiously she smoothed her wild hair, made even more unruly by the night's humidity.

She had not realized how he had haunted her all this time, but it was true. There was his smile, one corner of it lifting before the other in a sort of delayed reaction; his sandy-blond hair, darker with the wet, sculpted neatly to his well-shaped head. Bright, she hadn't realized he was so bright, a cheerful sun of a man whose rays warmed her and cheered her and whose presence hung a shimmering rainbow there in the small house. He had haunted her, but the images she hadn't been able to banish from her mind were only that—images, a pale substitute for the real thing. The real thing was here now, smiling at her so that the cold, rain-drenched night seemed suddenly warm.

Quickly he explained. "I was driving home in the storm and this raccoon ran right out in front of me. I couldn't avoid hitting him."

"Put him on the table," she said, and he liked the way she spoke, so coolly and quietly, even though he had surely startled her out of sleep. Her eyes looked drowsy and deep, cupped by the lower eyelids, shadowed by dark silky lashes.

Without further comment she tossed towels on the table; he spread them out and laid the unconscious raccoon on top, gently tugging his wet raincoat from underneath. Cassie bustled around the room, collecting supplies, ointments, bandages. She spared John a quick glance. His teeth were chattering.

"You're chilled to the bone, aren't you?"

"Yes," he said, seeing no use in denying it.

"There are towels in the bathroom. You can dry off in there." She had no dry clothes to offer him.

John went in the bathroom and closed the door. He was soaked to the skin; mountain storms could be ferocious. The bathroom was small but scrupulously clean. Not a single telltale gray spatter marked the shiny white porcelain washbowl. There was a simple wood-framed mirror, probably left over from Cassie's grandmother's day, and a rusty blotch in one corner indicated that it needed resilvering. There was a modern rectangular bathtub enclosed with the kind of white gold-flecked Formica kit you order from Sears, and white vinyl tiles, the kind you install yourself, on the floor. The shower curtain was clear, no frills, and the towels were old and soft and made of one hundred percent cotton, the way towels used to be. Pine-scented soap in the soap dishes scented the room, and a single toothbrush hung in the chrome holder. It was a bathroom of bare necessities, and another interesting insight into Cassie's life.

In the front room Cassie bent over the unconscious raccoon. Bertrand jostled noisily around the table legs and finally ran into the spare bedroom to play with an empty spool. She shut the door on Bertrand and began to rub the injured animal with a towel. It was a fairly young raccoon, Cassie judged, although she knew little about them. She couldn't tell how badly it was injured. She was afraid that the animal would panic if it revived and found itself in a house with two humans and a skunk for company.

"Well, is he going to be all right?" John sounded worried as he reappeared from the bathroom, still toweling his hair dry, and she slid a quick glance in his direction to see if he was faking his concern. He wasn't.

He let the damp towel with which he'd dried his hair fall loosely around his shoulders; his hair stood up from his head in wavy peaks, and his eyebrows were knit across his forehead in concern. The pale hair of his eyebrows curled with the damp, and Cassie was surprised to see a narrow white scar bisecting his left eyebrow. She had never noticed it before.

She swabbed the raccoon's only visible injury, a scrape on its left side, with one of her favorite ointments, goldenseal blended with the inner bark of the slippery elm.

"This ointment is known to promote healing," she explained in reply to John's questioning glance. It was amazing to her that she was able to talk to him, to face him. She thought she would never be able to carry on an ordinary conversation with him again after that night at his cabin.

He was still shivering. "You need a hot drink," she said, and, asking him to keep a watchful eye on the raccoon, she hurried into the kitchen and prepared her own special blend of elderberry tea. John was sitting at the table when she returned. She handed him the cup and saucer and sat down in a chair across from him.

"Any sign of life?" she asked, gesturing with her head at the raccoon.

He shook his head. "He hasn't moved," he said. He took a sip of the tea and rolled it around on his tongue. It had an unusual taste. "This is good, but I can't place the flavor," he said, inhaling the steam rising from the cup. "What is it? Licorice?"

"No, it's anise. I make the tea from elderberry blossoms and flavor it with anise seeds." Despite the hot tea, she saw a shiver ripple through his body. "You're still cold, aren't you," she said sharply.

"It's nothing," he said.

She pulled her eyes away from his taut biceps, which were so clearly outlined by the wet shirt he wore. She couldn't believe the absurd thrill she felt at seeing him sitting at her own table. She'd imagined it so many times that he didn't seem real.

"Nonsense. I keep a fire laid in the summer; I'll light it." She hurried to the fireplace, the hitch in her walk more pronounced tonight than he'd ever seen it.

"Why do you keep a fire laid?" he asked her. "Does it get that cold here in June?"

"Sometimes. It rains a lot in the mountains. With the rain comes cold and damp. The damp bothers me, so—"

Instantly, she regretted saying this, even though she was always self-conscious about her leg whenever it ached so much. Why did she feel as though she should call his attention to her leg and her limp? Why did she want him to know all the things that were wrong with her? She had an inexplicable urge to tell him how she had nightmares, how it had frightened her when he had touched her that night in his cabin, how and why she had retreated from society to live in solitude on Flat Top Mountain. If he thought she was seriously neurotic, maybe he'd go away. And yet that wasn't what she really wanted, for him to go away. It was just that his commanding presence, his very virility, made her so uncomfortable.

The tinder caught easily, and then the kindling. Before long, yellow flames licked at the big logs and the fire radiated a pleasant warmth.

"You can sit over here," she said, pulling an old-fashioned settle closer to the hearth.

He stood up and tenderly lifted the raccoon in his arms. He stared down at the funny, furry masked face for a moment, the firelight flickering across his features. "I hope it doesn't die," he said, and there was a wistful note to his voice. It touched Cassie that this big man cared so much about an injured animal.

Cassie walked over to him and studied the raccoon at close range. The ringed tail and paws with their prehensile fingers hung limply, and the eyes remained closed within the distinctive black mask. Nevertheless, he seemed to be breathing well enough. "I think the best thing to do is leave him alone right now," she said. "He's not bleeding, and I don't think he has any broken bones."

"Maybe he's in shock," John said. He fluffed the towels up and gently laid the animal on the hearth. His big hand caressed the still-damp fur, smoothing the stiff black guard hairs flat. "Perhaps the heat from the fire will help," he said.

John sank down on the old settle. Cassie stood uncertainly, not knowing whether to excuse herself to go to bed or to sit here with him, keeping vigil over the raccoon. Cassie didn't think it would be wise for John to leave, to be soaked again by the vicious lashing rain. And there was lightning now, too. But how should she behave?

"Sit here with me," he said, and when she stood undecided, caught by surprise, he pulled her down beside him.

Neatly, she folded her left leg under her—and it wasn't difficult, since that leg had a tendency to fold even when she'd rather it wouldn't—and arranged herself at John's feet on the fur hearth rug, her face level with his knee.

"That's not exactly what I had in mind," he told her, his eyes twinkling.

Her hair grazed his knee as she tilted her head upward to look at him. His mouth curved upward into a smile. He looked her over, his eyes halting momentarily on her hands clasped demurely in her lap, at her breasts straining against the folds of her robe, then moving on to her chin, lingering with interest on her lips, studying her nose, and then, finally, drinking in the expression of her eyes with an earnestness she didn't understand. She arranged her robe more carefully over her knees, then drifted her hand up to check the front of it to make sure the two sides of the bodice overlapped without a gap.

The pleasure in John's eyes was unmistakable. The fire burned her face; they were sitting too close to it. Or perhaps it wasn't the fire that made the blood run hot beneath her skin. Was it too late to ask him to leave?

"So tell me," he said easily, propping his heels on the raised stone hearth as though he sat there all the time, "how did you learn all the things you needed to know to become an honest-to-goodness practicing herbalist?"

It would be easy to talk about this. She drew a deep breath of relief. "Am I an herbalist? I hadn't ever thought about it." In her own mind she had always thought of herself as simply carrying on Gran's work.

"Of course you are. People earn a living at this sort of thing, you know."

Cassie shrugged. "I watched Gran in the summers when I visited her. I worked with her in her garden. Then when I came here to live, I found Gran's recipe book. People started coming up here to Flat Top Mountain, looking for help when they knew I'd moved in, so little by little I picked up what I needed to know. I managed to put what I read in her book together with what I'd learned by helping her when I was a child, and slowly, it became a full-time occupation."

"Have you ever thought about living in town? Or maybe in Asheville or Linville and charging money for your services? More and more, people are becoming interested in herbal medicine as part of an approach to holistic health practices."

She shook her head. "No. No, I couldn't take money for what I do," she said tersely, chilling slightly. She had no need of money, would never need any more money, and the very thought of charging money for helping people was anathema to her. She owed and she never forgot it.

John softened toward her. He thought she had frozen up on him because he had mentioned leaving the mountain. She did that every time. She was scared to death, frightened.

Wanting nothing more than to reassure her, he placed his hand on her shoulder; she shrank. He almost made the mistake of taking his hand away.

But then he thought, *No, no! This is the way it is going to be between us.* It was not possible that their relationship was going to remain chaste, given their easy proximity and the way he felt about her. Sexually he was curious, more than curious, having imagined in the long, lonely evenings since he'd last seen her exactly how her body, exposed to his gaze, would look and feel. And what it would do when he touched it intimately. And what he would do when she touched him.

She let his hand remain on her shoulder, and soon he spread his thumb very tentatively so that it touched her collarbone, and after that she let him massage her skin through the fabric of her robe. Her collarbone felt unusually delicate and fragile beneath the tip of his thumb, and he longed to move his hand even lower, but he was afraid that she would run away if he did. So he contented himself with that. For unless he was able to get close to her, how would he tell her what he had traveled all this way to tell her? And he had to tell her, because he believed now that what he had to say would heal her as well as him.

"Oh," she said. "Look. Our raccoon is stirring." She stood up, all in one fluid motion, and bent over the animal.

The raccoon raised its head, then let it slump back onto the pile of towels where it lay. It looked dazed, and its eyes, which should have been as bright as black beads, were dull.

"I don't know what to do for it," said Cassie, shrugging helplessly. The movement slid the neckline of her robe to one side; for a moment John caught a titillating glimpse of brown upon brown, but the smooth curve of her breasts was quickly hidden once more when she straightened. "I could try barley water," she said. "I often give it to invalids, and it's a wonderful restorative."

"Can I help?" he called as she disappeared into the kitchen.

"Keep an eye on that raccoon," she answered. "If he suddenly pulls himself together and starts running around the room, we're likely to have a problem with Bertrand."

"Bertrand? You mean he's in the house?"

"Yes. In the guest bedroom. Can't you hear him scratching around in there?"

John listened. Over the crackling of the logs in the fireplace, he did hear something. Sharp little claws skittering across bare wood. Something rolling. A scamper every once in a while.

"What's Bertrand doing in there?" he said edgily. He had no desire to remain in the same house with a fully equipped skunk who didn't like men.

"Playing with empty spools and dragging around a couple of old pairs of panty hose. He's very playful, you see."

Cassie rustled back into the room with liquid in a baby bottle.

"I thought—hoped—that by this time Bertrand had rambled off into the sunset to be with his friends."

Cassie laughed. "No, he's still not feeling up to par, I'm afraid. And I'm attached to him. I hate the idea of giving him up." She shook the bottle and expertly dribbled a few drops of the barley water on her wrist. "This is a nice lukewarm temperature. Why don't you hold the raccoon's head up while I try to ease a bit of this barley water down his throat."

John knelt beside her, feeling sadly inexpert at this. "You mean like this?"

"Sure. Slide your hands under his neck—that's right. I think his swallowing reflex will be intact if he was conscious enough to open his eyes and lift his head a few minutes ago."

"What if he wakes up? Have you seen the size of his teeth? I don't have any desire to find out how sharp they are." John looked distinctly uneasy, as though he would drop the raccoon's head at the slightest motion on the raccoon's part.

"I think he's much too weak to do anything but lie there, to tell you the truth." Cassie inserted the nipple of the bottle between the animal's jaws. A couple of spoonfuls of the sticky liquid finally slid down his throat, but much more ran out of the animal's mouth and over their hands. The raccoon's eyes flicked open again and then closed peacefully. His breathing was steady. Cassie tunneled her hand beneath his foreleg and let her fingers rest for a few seconds on the soft downy hair of the raccoon's chest.

"The heartbeat seems regular," she announced in satisfaction. "I think he's going to be all right, John. In fact, maybe we should give him a name. I'm going to have to keep him around a while."

"How about Rupert? It's a name that seems to fit in the same general category as a name like Bertrand."

Cassie broke into a wide smile, and the tension too often noticeable in her face disappeared. "Rupert it is, then. Rupert Raccoon. I like it." Smiling like that in the dancing firelight, Cassie looked beautiful, golden.

The two of them exchanged a look of satisfaction, a look of sharing. They were experiencing a sense of working together to accomplish something worthwhile. Saving the life of another living thing pulled them together, drawing them closer, giving them something in common. The feeling felt good to both of them.

We're going to be all right, too, thought John in surprise and with a sense of elation. But of course he didn't say the words out loud.

Chapter Five

"I'm glad Rupert is going to pull through," John said heartily, wiping barley water off his hand on the towel where the raccoon lay and feeling garrulous with the headiness of their success in saving it. "I felt awful when I knew I'd hit him. His frightened eyes, red for a moment in the glare of my headlights, and then that awful *thunk!* when I tried to stop in time."

"You're lucky you didn't skid off the side of the mountain in this rain," said Cassie.

"I know. I jumped out of the car and scrabbled around in the ditch until I found the poor thing, and I didn't know what else to do but bring him to you. I'm sorry if I interrupted your evening."

"You did the right thing," Cassie answered, at ease with him now. It pleased her that John was not the type to leave an injured animal to die. "Come on," she said, standing up. "You need to wash your hands. We both do."

John followed Cassie into the kitchen, intrigued by the slope of her shoulders. All that hair, and he knew from the one time he'd touched it that her neck was delicate and graceful, a flower stalk of a neck, and it flowed fluently into her shoulders, which were now not hunched in anger or tensed in fright. They swung ever so slightly as she walked, loose and easy. She looked faintly puzzled when she glanced back at him and saw his eyes upon her.

In the kitchen she handed him a pink bar of soap—homemade, from the uneven look of it. When he held it under the running water, the bar released the scent of roses.

"I make the soap myself," she explained, taking the slippery soap from him. Their hands touched, and suddenly Cassie felt as though she couldn't catch her breath. Hip to hip they stood at her kitchen sink, and thoughts and images strobe-flashed through her mind like a psychedelic dream—his blue eyes, his hands, his hands cool from the running water upon her hot body, her body tight against his, mouths moaning, his body knotting around hers, slicking her skin, finding her rhythm, letting her go, letting her *go*!

The water running unheeded over her hands, the soap slithering around the bottom of the sink and draining away with the wasted water, her wasted life, and "Cassie, do you have a towel?"

She blinked her eyes to see John's hands dripping water all over the countertop, and to cover her confusion she whipped open a nearby drawer, not the one that held the towels at all, and slammed the drawer closed again with a clatter of cheese cutters and can openers and potato peelers, until she could say in an almost-normal tone, "You'll find a towel hanging on the back of the kitchen door."

He found it, she turned off the water, and she dried her own trembling hands on a paper towel. They stood staring at each other in the green fluorescence of the overhead kitchen light. After the mellow fire glow, Cassie felt overrevealed in the light's harsh glare.

"I suppose I should be going back to my place," said John reluctantly. He peered out the kitchen window into the howling night. If anything, the storm had increased, not abated. "How long do you suppose this tempest will go on, anyway?"

Cassie found her voice. "I've seen storms in the mountains go on for hours. All night, perhaps." Oh, no, she had said the wrong thing. He would see this as a half-veiled invitation to stay the night. She wiped her palms, so soon damp again, on her robe behind her back, where he wouldn't see.

A white-hot flash of lightning rent the distant sky, echoing and reverberating from mountain to mountain.

"I could wait a few minutes and see if it dies down," he said.

Cassie was silent.

"Of course, if you'd rather I go, I will," he went on.

"I—well, suit yourself." The words came out too tartly. She brushed past him and went back into the front room, where she made a show of checking the raccoon. John stood in the doorway between the kitchen and the living area and wondered what to do. He hadn't survived all he'd survived to be fried by a stray bolt of lightning, that was for sure.

Cassie was shivering as she stood with her back to him, her slight figure limned in the firelight. They had come closer tonight to friendship, to the intimacy of friendship, and she'd run from it again. Her behavior confounded him. He couldn't figure out how to connect with her.

"Cassie, I'm going," he said decisively. He didn't want to cause her whatever anguish she was undergoing now, and he knew he was the cause of it.

"You don't have to leave," she said, her voice no more than a murmur. She turned to look at him, her eyes wide and dark. "You could stay in the guest room overnight if you'd like."

Was this an overture, or was she offering because her back was to the wall? The latter, probably. He forced a smile. "With Bertrand? I think not."

She looked startled for a moment. "I'd close Bertrand in the kitchen. I do that sometimes anyway."

He shook his head. She was trying pathetically hard, making too much of an effort to fight the sexual tension strung tight between them, and it showed. His heart went out to her.

He forgot to worry about how she would react. He was a toucher, a man who loved to touch and be touched, and it seemed natural at that moment to gather her into his arms. It wasn't until she was actually there, shivering against his chest, that he recalled what had happened last time he had tried this. He half expected her to pull away this time, too, but she did not. Instead, she stiffened; then went totally passive, not taking anything, but not giving, either. He expected her to twist away at any moment. Perhaps it was different with her now that they were on her own turf and not his. Perhaps being in her own house made her feel more secure. Whatever it was, she stood within the circle of his arms, waiting.

"No, Cassie, I won't stay," he said gently. "I don't know exactly how it is with you, but I want to know. If you want to tell me, that is. If you don't that's okay, too."

She lifted her head and stared up at him, her eyes bottomless pools of pain. Her eyes shouldn't look like that, he thought, not now. Not if she wanted him for any of the right reasons. And the right reasons did not include using somebody else's body to exorcise demons. Yet how was he to get close to her with those demons between them?

He pulled her down on the settle beside him and kept his arm curved around her. She huddled against him, as though seeking shelter. Oh, he would shelter her with his body, all right. But not hide her from herself.

"Cassie—Cassie, what is your real name? Not Cassie, surely?"

"Cassandra," she whispered.

"Cassandra. A beautiful name, and I will call you by it when I want you to know that what I say is important and real and true, and when what I am going to say is meant only for you."

Why was she sitting here with this stranger, listening to him shape these words that fell so strangely upon her ears? She should be lying alone in Gran's big brass bed, raindrops whispering on the roof, thunder shaking the house. Not flattened against John Howard's shoulder, with his words raining upon her ears, her own thoughts shaking her as no thunder ever had.

"Cassandra, you don't need to hide from me. I won't hurt you. Do you believe that?"

He spoke to her as he would to a child, but she didn't take offense. She felt protected when he held her.

"All right," he went on, taking her silence for assent. "Then we can be friends, you and I. I don't want to be lonely. There is no reason for either of us to be lonely. You're a fascinating woman, and you're beautiful to me."

Beautiful? No man had called her beautiful, not since Kevin. She didn't deserve to be called beautiful. She didn't deserve anything. She most certainly did not deserve the dream of happiness that curled cautiously upward as she heard those words in John Howard's kindly voice. She tamped the happiness down, and when it wouldn't die, she reamed it out with memories. Kevin. Rory. Wrench out the happiness by its fragile roots; let it wither, let it die.

"I'm not beautiful, and I'm not fascinating," she said forcefully, pulling away from him and setting her face in what she knew was a cold, uncompromising expression. "You'd better go." She leaped to her feet and gathered the folds of her robe about her so that no part of it touched him.

John fell back in surprise. Things had been going so well. He'd had her attention, he'd managed to calm her. It was his touch that had calmed her, his words that had gained her trust. And now all that had fallen away. As soon as he'd told her she was fascinating, which was true, and beautiful, which was also true, she had clamped down on the feelings that he knew without a doubt she felt.

His perception of her popped into a new dimension. It was as though a light bulb flashed on above his head like those light bulbs in a hundred clichéd cartoons. Cassie resisted anything that would make her feel special, desirable, all right. If anyone tried to build her up, she immediately tore herself down again. She felt herself unworthy. Unworthy! Why hadn't he seen it before? The signs were all there—the withdrawal from her previous life, her reclusive existence up here on this godforsaken mountain, her resistance to being admired by a man. To being touched by a man, to allowing herself that ultimate pleasure of all—the pleasure of being loved by a man.

Stunned by this realization, he stood up, too. His troubled eyes took in her defiant stance, the stubborn set of her jaw, and the look of her that was somehow still so frightened.

"Cassandra," he said compassionately, aching for her. Tentatively he reached for her, and amazingly she accepted his hand at the nape of her neck, and then his other hand curled into the curve of her waist. Then he reached up with both hands and buried his fingers in the rich outburst of hair, raking his fingernails through its vibrant depths until his fingertips met her warm scalp and her head, so small under all the hair, was cupped in his palms. The rosy scent of the soap lingered on his hands, and it was the roses he smelled as he drew in his breath sharply before he lowered his mouth to connect with her parted lips.

They opened beneath his, surprising him in this woman, who found it difficult to open her thoughts or her mind or her life to anyone. The sighing sound of her breath first, then the warmth of it on his cheek, and the cushiony flesh of her breasts pushed now against the hard muscles of his chest, and downward the pulse in her abdomen thrusting against his, and the length of their thighs muscle to muscle. But no time to reflect on bodies when mouths had so much to do, to smooth, to soften, to seek and search and swim with the wet until stroking with the tongue was not enough and sucking was, and then that was not enough either.

Her hands firm on his chest, then his neck, the cords straining against her palms, and then her fingers around his chin tentatively so that she could feel the machinations of his mouth from outside as well as in;

and then she wanted strength as well as softness and found it in the muscles of his back, working as he intensified their embrace, making her close to him, wanting her to be one with him, and she wanted it, too—oh, no, she'd thought she never wanted it again, but she did now. Was it she who trembled, or was it the earth?

But what was he to do, he wondered. John had never been one to take the sharing of another's body lightly. Intimate body contact was a privilege, and being naked together was a gift. And the rest of it—the passion, the letting down of one's guard—was what made a man and a woman completely and utterly real to each other. If one or the other partner harbored reservations about being together, the act became meaningless, and that sort of thing left him feeling depressed and empty.

He had already decided that the sexual act would not be right for them yet. If she wanted him because she wanted him, that would be different. But he sensed that was not the case. She didn't want him for himself, or because their sexual congress would be a joyous communication of two souls. He'd made up his mind that he wouldn't hide her from herself, and at the time, just a few minutes ago, that had seemed honest and good. With infinite gentleness he pulled away from her shuddering eagerness.

But she surprised him again. He did not know what to say when she took his hand and led him into the bedroom.

He watched as she slowly unwrapped the tie to her robe and let the robe slip from her shoulders to the floor. The rain drummed on the roof, or was it his heartbeat pounding in his ears? His mouth went suddenly dry.

In a split second she had made up her mind how to handle the betrayal of her body, which was eager to open to him the part of her spirit that she had so successfully locked away. Cassie didn't want them to glide past each other because they never dared to give of themselves. She could not give him all of herself, but she could give him a part of herself and thus assuage her sudden hot hunger for the sharp, secret things she had thought were best forgotten. And he was kind and good, and she knew he would be kind and good to her.

For her, it seemed utterly natural to be standing with him in Gran's bedroom, the covers turned back on the brass bed, caught in a circle of lamplight like two intimates. All her imaginings, all her daydreams had placed John Howard here a hundred times at least. Did he know? Could he guess that he'd been here before? He looked faintly surprised and strangely reflective. What was he thinking?

He thought, *I know her and yet I don't know her. How well do we know each other? How well does anyone know another person?* Cassie had denied him entrance to her tortured mind and thoughts, but now she was preparing to allow him entrance to her body. Her body was brown and glowing in the lamplight, her legs shadowed into a dusky V through her thin nightgown by the light behind her. She was offering her body and he would not refuse. Not because he needed a body, but because her body could be the portal through which he could reach her. And to reach Cassie Muldoon would be the utmost in kindness.

He touched her cheek with a tentative finger. She closed her eyes and let it wind into her—one touch and she tightened and twisted inside, spinning at the end of a cord of longing that he could reel in if only he would.

"That feels good," she whispered, wanting him to know it.

"And this—how does this feel?" He slipped the strap of her gown down over her shoulder and rested his hand, all gentleness, on the top curve of her breast.

"Lovely," she whispered, quieting inside. "Just...lovely."

"I'm not going to stop," he said, dropping his face to the curve of her neck, fragrant with the faint scent of rose soap.

"I don't want you to," she said, pulling his head down so that his lips touched her nipple. This startled him, and he pulled away, not wanting to move too fast. But her great silver eyes, dark-rimmed, deep with the patina of trust, were urgent upon his face.

"Please," she said. "Please."

The question in his expression didn't go away. He was unbelieving that she had dropped her reticence, that she was so open.

She said, "I want it to happen, I want." The words all ran together, as though she couldn't control them.

He needed to be sure. "You want what?"

"You," she said, pulling his head down again, the upward movement of her arm tilting her breast upward. The curve of it was lush, irresistible. With a low moan he opened his mouth and surrounded the nipple until it tickled the roof of his mouth, a hard, ripe, swollen berry.

She felt the heat of him through her gown, smelled the rain in his still-damp hair, and let her body respond. No time now to evoke the protection of her own special ghosts, and she pushed the thought of them into the outer reaches of her mind. There would be time enough later, later when it was over, after the flood of weakness had passed.

She could no longer stand. She slid down through the circle of his arms, her breasts against him all the way down, against the flat muscles of his stomach, against the rise beneath, his belt buckle twisting one nipple in passing so that she winced in sudden pain. His hands on her shoulders pressed her face to him so that his urgency felt hot against her cheek.

Then he knelt in front of her, caressing her breasts, lifting the other side of her nightgown away so that she was exposed to his gaze, and he could scarcely keep his eyes off her body as it was revealed bit by bit as she shifted so that he could slide her gown over her hips, then her knees, to leave it pleated around her feet.

He touched her slowly, reverently, beginning at her lips, his finger lingering at the corner of her mouth and picking up a thread of wetness, feathering his fingertips down, swirling them slowly across her shoulders, spreading them flat on her sternum, then spiraling them around and around each breast, reverently touching each nipple and kissing it, too, and down to the silvery marrings on her abdomen, leaving them to slowly tip the mossy growth below and quest there, seeking what he eventually found.

The bright spreading ache started in her abdomen, radiated in waves to her legs, her arms, her breasts. How long it had been! How had she forgotten what it was like?

She fell back on the rumpled lavender-scented sheets of the bed, fumbling with his shirt until he pulled it out of his pants so that it was easier then for her to work the buttons through their holes. And he somehow shed his other clothes until he spread over her naked, and they caught their breath at the magic of it, and she raised her lips to his to be kissed.

Cassie felt skinful, full in her skin, as though she had never filled her skin so completely before. And his fingers tingled her, burned her, found her, filled her. *Ah, the pleasures of the skin,* she thought, and his skin pleasured her as much as her own. The textures of it—soft and crinkly around his eyes, full-muscled in his upper back, downy with hair on his chest and tight abdomen, hair that ranged splendidly from black to brown to blond to black again. She focused on his body, became totally involved in his body, the way it responded, changed and consumed her own.

Their lovemaking found its own rhythm, now faster, now slower, not fast enough, then, for him, reaching a shuddering crescendo, leaving him gasping above her.

And when he calmed, he nestled his head against her shoulder and said in a low voice, "I should have waited."

"No," she said. "No."

But before she could say anything else he had begun again, slowly, carefully, lovingly retracing the pattern, determined to bring her the same joy. And he kissed her nipples, and he made his mouth do exquisite things, and he wrought excruciating sensations with his fingers, but still she did not release herself to him.

She knew what he was trying to do, and at first she simply floated along on the ecstasy, delighting in the wonder of it, feeling it all, feeling the beauty of one body responding to another.

All night, she thought dreamily. *We will make love all night*. She returned measure for measure, and when he climaxed again she rejoiced, but still it did not happen for her.

"Cassandra," he said, his mouth against her hair, "can't you?"

All the beauty, all the joy of giving, all the happiness he had brought her was not enough. Not for him, and not for her.

She remained silent, but she wanted to cry. This wonderfully thoughtful man wanted for her what she could not do. And she did not want him to think he was less than he was, for in truth, she was the one who was less. She was unable to give herself over to a man in the way he wanted.

"It's not your fault," she said unevenly, swinging her feet over the side of the bed.

"Cassie," he said as he grabbed for her hand, but adroitly she twisted away from him, bent swiftly and picked up her robe and slid her arms into it. Before he could speak again, she left the room.

He got up and went after her, not bothering to pull on his clothes.

She bent over the raccoon on the hearth. "He looks fine," she said briskly. She pulled a cardboard box out of a cabinet in the corner. "I'll put him in this box for the rest of the night. I'll leave him by the fire so the coals will keep him warm." She lifted the limp raccoon and placed him carefully in the cardboard box.

John stared at her. She felt his eyes upon her, and she spared him a glance. He was a Greek god statue, stone-naked and glowing in the light from the dying embers.

He shook his head, trying to clear it. He'd always regarded all women as mysterious, with their cycles like the moon and the secret processes that went on inside their bodies, not to mention inside their heads. But this woman with her silences and her capriciousness and her frightened withdrawals must be the most mysterious woman of all.

"Cassie, come back to bed," he said, thinking that if he were to find out anything about her, it would have to be there. It was the only place where she even halfway let down her guard.

"Oh, I think that would be a mistake, don't you?" She melted at the sight of him, so real, so beautiful, so *there*. Her mouth filled with saliva, and other places ran warm, then wet.

"No, I do not," he said firmly. And then, without warning, he unceremoniously picked her up in his strong, sinewy arms and strode with her into the bedroom, where he placed her on the bed.

He slid under the covers next to her, holding them up so she could slide under them, too. She hesitated for a moment, then rolled close to him and lay on her side, facing away from him. He tucked the cover comfortably around both of them, and they lay for several minutes listening to each other breathe. Outside, the rain still pattered on the roof, but there was no more thunder.

"How long has it been, Cassie?" he said finally.

"How long has what been?"

"How long without a man?"

"Aren't you overstepping your bounds?" she shot back.

"I don't think so. No, I don't think so. Because I'm not just a one-night stand, you know. I'm going to be around for a while. And I don't just want a warm body to lie with on cool mountain nights. I want an honest-to-goodness intimate relationship. Which we can't have if we go on the way we've been doing. So, how long has it been?"

"Since I've been here," she said in a small voice. "Almost two years."

"Didn't you want—?" His voice was gentle.

She considered this. "Yes, for a while," she said.

"A little? A lot?"

She shifted uncomfortably, and the soft fabric of her robe brushed his abdomen. They were lying spoon-position.

"A lot at first. Then not so much. Then nothing. As though that part of me had withered and died."

"I'm going to help you bring it to life again," he said, tracing the whorls of her ear with a fingertip. She loved the whisper of his finger on her ear overlaid with the sweet mellow tones of his voice.

"Not possible," she said, her voice muffled by the pillow. "Definitely not possible."

"Well, I'm going to have a hell of a good time trying," he told her, and then he was shifting himself across her, lying on the other side of her, gazing into her eyes.

"Would you mind taking off that robe?" he said politely. "I very much prefer making love to naked ladies."

She couldn't help smiling as she slid out of the robe. He tugged it out from under the bedcovers and threw it across the room.

"Why did you do that?" she asked, liking him as much for himself as for what he could do to her.

"So I can watch you walk across the room in the morning, nude," he said.

She cuddled up to the strong, solid bulk of him. It seemed strange to feel sexual again. Strange but comfortable. And nice.

"And now, shall we try it again?" Beneath the covers she felt him unfurling against her, and above her, he shone bright with desire.

Let him do with me what he will, she thought helplessly, slipping her arms around him.

And so he did.

MORNING. Gray fingers of light climbing the far wall, because they had never pulled the curtain across the window. Tigger meowing to come in the house, and Bertrand scratching to be released from the guest room. Memory also knocked, and Cassie opened the door.

She lay flat on her back in the early-morning quiet and pictured Kevin. She always thought of Kevin first thing in the morning. And Rory. Kevin, his dark hair tousled over his forehead, the morning growth of his beard stubbly against her breasts. Rory, waking earlier than they did and running in rosy from sleep in his pajamas with the feet and pouncing on their bed, knocking pillows to the floor. Laughter. Tickling. Giggling. So different from now, and so long ago.

But this was John. His body depressed the mattress on his side of the bed. She wasn't used to anyone else being there. Oh, Kevin. Oh, Rory. *Oh, Cassie, what have you done?*

Trying not to roll over on his side of the mattress, she slid carefully out of bed and retrieved her robe across the room. John hadn't seen her walk nude across the room after all. It occurred to her that she should have had some feeling about that, but she felt no humor, no sadness, no anticipation of next time, nothing.

She closed the bedroom door behind her and went to the hearth to check on the raccoon. It was asleep. She nudged open the guest-room door and Bertrand shot out like a rocket, and she put the box with the raccoon in the guest room and closed the door. Then she let in Tigger, who wound furrily around her feet and almost tripped her. Finally, she went into the bathroom and washed her face and brushed her hair and teeth. She slipped on a plum-colored shift, hanging her robe up on the hook on the back of the door, the scent of last night's lovemaking wafting from its folds. And she went in and fed the raccoon barley water, washed out the bottle and rinsed her hands.

Then she took her dulcimer down from its shelf and sat with the soft leather case in her lap, thinking longingly of Kevin and his thoughtfulness in having it made for her, stroking the fine leather and watching the sun come up over Pride's Peak.

It came to her in bits and pieces, the song. A chorus first, a rhythmic cadence. Then a word or two about the way people live their lives in tiers—tears, a possibility of a play on words here—one tier as a child, the next highest as a husband or a wife, the next as a parent and finally as a grandparent. Before she could lose it, she whipped the dulcimer from its case and strummed a few chords. She rummaged in Gran's desk for a piece of paper, just a scrap, really, and jotted down the words in almost indecipherable chicken scratches. The chords she would work out later—no, now, it would have to be now, because later she might not remember.…Oh, it had been so long since she had been able to write her music.

John heard the notes from the bedroom. Groggily he reached for Cassie's warmth, but she wasn't beside him. Then the fog of sleep halfway retreated, and he thought, *That's Cassie making that music.*

Puzzled, he pulled on his jeans, dry now since he'd hung them over the back of a chair last night, and shook his hair out of his eyes. He opened the bedroom door slowly, so he wouldn't disturb her. And when his eyes fell upon her, he saw her in profile, silhouetted against the sunrise over the mountain. He was staggered when he realized what he should have realized long ago.

But he couldn't have known, he couldn't have, because he had always considered her face as a whole, two different but beautiful sides to it, a highly individual kind of face. In her photographs, on television, she had always been photographed from one side, the right, because with each side of her face so different, she had always been considered a "problem" to light. And her face had been rounder two years ago, without those lean planes beneath her cheekbones.

Cassie stopped strumming the dulcimer when she saw John standing there. She had been so involved in the creation of her song that she hadn't noticed him when he stepped out of the bedroom. She caught her breath at the astonishment on his face, and in that moment she knew that her secret was out.

It all fit: the mountain dulcimer, the goose quill, her retreat to a place where virtually no one could find her.

"Cassandra," he said unevenly. "You are—you *must* be—Cassandra Dare!"

Chapter Six

"After the accident," Cassie said matter-of-factly over blueberry pancakes, "I couldn't work. I didn't want to go on tour. I couldn't write songs anymore. Nothing anybody said about it made the slightest difference to me. I didn't have the heart to go on. So I left L.A. in that old station wagon out there in the shed. I just walked into a used-car lot and told the salesman to sell me a car that would carry me as far as the Great Smoky Mountains, and I paid cash for it. And here I am."

"Your song—the one about homeless people—was a tremendous hit, but you were nowhere to be found," said John. "Every time I turned to the entertainment channel on the cable network, someone was talking about the mysterious disappearance of Cassandra Dare. You vanished into thin air after your accident. You could have had a worldwide concert tour, your picture on the cover of *People* magazine, all of it."

John studied her soberly and with a sense of unreality, still unable to believe the truth of it. Cassie Muldoon was none other than Cassandra Dare, the multitalented singer, musician and songwriter with the international reputation, the same Cassandra Dare who over the past decade had captured the public's attention with her whispery soprano voice and her mountain dulcimer. The idea that this quiet, frightened Cassie Muldoon and the poised and confident Cassandra Dare were one and the same was so incredible that John could scarcely grasp it.

Cassie shrugged. "I've had worldwide concert tours before, and my picture has been on lots of magazine covers. And 'Where the Heart Is' was only a hit because Morgana Friday used it as the title and theme song in her documentary *All the Way Home*." She stood up abruptly and carried her plate into the kitchen; John, not willing to relinquish the subject, followed her.

"I've seen Morgana Friday's film," he said. "It's a striking statement about the plight of homeless people. *All the Way Home* won several awards, and it's been nominated for several more. It's an unusual film, and unlike most documentaries, it has a chance at becoming a commercial success. That's mostly because of your song, Cassie."

"Morgana's a great filmmaker. I doubt that my song had much to do with it," protested Cassie.

"Don't sell yourself short," John retorted. When he saw the frozen expression on Cassie's face, he was afraid he'd been too abrupt. "*All the Way Home* is a film that deals with the issue of homelessness with great sensitivity," he continued more gently. "You should see it."

"Maybe someday I will," said Cassie, but she doubted that this was true. She was pleased by Morgana's success with her documentary, but her song's success—well, success wasn't one of the things that mattered to Cassie anymore. She'd had her fill of fame.

"And Cassie," John told her earnestly, "I meant what I said about not selling yourself short. Your song is wonderful. The film wouldn't be what it is without the song."

But Cassie's only response to his compliment was a quick evasive smile, and she began to rinse their plates and silver with a great clatter while John tried his best to comprehend her. He understood now that Cassie had retreated to this place to lick her wounds, and yet he didn't know why she had stayed. She should have healed by this time; instead, she seemed dedicated to healing everyone else, but not herself. It seemed to fit in with his perception of her last night: She felt unworthy. And so she was somehow denying herself the inner healing that should have taken place long ago.

Sensing that John was becoming too thoughtful, Cassie said on impulse, "Let's leave the dishes and go for a walk in the woods. Just after dawn is the most beautiful time."

So together they crossed the clearing, which was damp and cool in the morning mist, and entered a trail that twisted through the verdant forest on the mountaintop. Rough-barked gray-brown tree trunks glistened with moisture. Here and there dead fallen branches blocked their way; John bent and tossed these aside. Green edged upon green, downy soft moss and lichen contrasted with glossy leaves, and gently uncurling fern feathered against gnarled tree roots. Birdsong sparkled in the thin morning air.

They walked separately until John took her hand. Cassie didn't object. Their entwined fingers seemed natural and right.

"So when are you going back to L.A.?" he asked.

She shook her head with certainty. "Never," she said.

His heart plummeted to his heels. He hadn't realized until that moment how much he wanted Cassie to be a continuing part of his life. But that would be impossible if she insisted on staying on Flat Top Mountain.

"Why?" he asked very quietly.

Her eyes held a faraway look, as if she were seeing scenes that he couldn't. "Here, I have a life of honesty and simple values. There, the world gets complicated."

"It wouldn't have to be complicated," he said. "You could change it."

"No," she said, and John sensed a vast silence in her. He treasured the stillness of her spirit, and yet, he felt—no, he *knew*—in his heart that she was capable of retaining that stillness, no matter where she lived.

"You're lonely here," he said softly. "You can't deny that." He half expected her to deny it now, but she surprised him.

"There was a time when the loneliness didn't bother me," she said, her eyes fixed steadfastly ahead on the trail.

"When was that?"

"Before you came."

"And now?"

"It's different," she admitted.

He curved his arm around her shoulders and pulled her close. "It's going to keep on being different," he told her.

"For a while. Until you have to leave."

"No, Cassandra. Longer than that."

She darted a quick disbelieving glance up at him. "You're not thinking of moving here permanently?"

He shook his head. "I can't do that. But you could go with me."

"I don't even know where you live."

"I live near Los Angeles." There, it was out. Would she make the connection? He almost hoped she would.

But she shook her head forcefully. "I'd never go back there. I've already told you that. I'll never move off this mountain."

Their circuitous path had taken them back to the clearing where Cassie's house stood, to the area behind it where her gardens were planted. Here the sun, higher now in the sky, had melted away the dew and the moisture from last night's storm. John found a shady place to sit on a moss-trimmed rock wall and watched Cassie as she moved surely among her plants, deftly nipping off a dead leaf here, pulling up an offending weed there.

"Tell me the names of the plants," he said, taking pleasure in watching the natural grace of her movements.

"Over there—" she pointed "—that's marjoram, with the soft little green leaves. And that's the thyme flowering, and on the other side of it, sage. The sage has already gone to seed."

The silken profusion of her hair crinkled around her in the sunshine. No wonder he hadn't recognized her before this morning—as Cassandra Dare, she had always worn her hair convoluted at the nape of her neck in a chaste knot, and her fingers, clasping her goose-quill trademark, had blossomed with rings. This ethereal and yet earthy creature no more resembled the famous singer and songwriter Cassandra Dare than he did.

John loved the way Cassie looked that morning, carefree and at ease. Had last night done that for her? He'd thought at the time that his heartfelt lovemaking hadn't done enough. His feelings for her rose like a lump in his throat; suddenly he wanted to touch her more than anything in the world.

"And this—this is lavender," she was saying from the midst of the lavender bed, its plants low and bearing pale purple flowers. She didn't know he had walked up behind her until she felt his arms go around her, holding her firmly.

"And this—this is Cassandra," he murmured lazily into her ear, his breath tickling her earlobe.

She laughed lightly. "Thank you for introducing me," she said.

"You have a lot to learn about yourself," he said.

"And you're going to teach me, right?" She could hardly breathe, hardly talk. His abundant energy folded around her protectively, like a cloak.

"It's a rotten job, but somebody has to do it," he said solemnly, but she could hear the smile behind his words.

She closed her eyes as his hands moved to her breasts, touching lightly. She leaned into him, lifting her weight off her left leg, the injured one that always hurt a bit, and she arched her neck to give his lips access to the long sensitive tendon in her neck. Her eyelids drooped sleepily, heavily, unresisting, and as his hands slid lower, down the warm curve of the abdomen, a new rhythm arose within her, an exquisite pulsing along her veins.

And then, down, down, he was lifting her and turning her so that they glided smoothly into the lavender, and she sank unresisting into the young shoots. Their thighs and shoulders and buttocks crushed the tender leaves beneath them so that the rich sweet aroma perfumed the air. Overhead, the sky shone so piercingly blue that it hurt Cassie's eyes to look at it.

His hands went around her face, his wrists meeting under her chin, enclosing her face in a heart. The silence around them was crystalline in its purity. Cassie lifted her lips to his. Now, at this moment, the perfume of the flowers was the scent of youth and hope. Her world burst with hope, and her heart overflowed. Anything was possible if John Howard could be here on this isolated mountaintop, if he could be gazing at her with such a beatific expression, if she could be accepting his tenderness.

It amazed him how acquiescent she was, this fearful woman who had always fled from his touch. He inhaled the scent of her hair, gently skimmed the tip of tongue across her lips in wonderment, then hungrily closed his mouth over hers. And he was moaning into her mouth, and she was rocking against him, and her dress rode up over her hips, and then her nipples sprouted beneath his fingers.

"Take the dress off," he whispered as he helped her, bunching it into a pillow for her head. And then he took his clothes off, so that it was just the two of them in the lavender, free in the wind-washed mountain air, with the bright blue sky above.

She found his body absolutely beautiful, his golden-bronze skin, his blue eyes gleaming with pleasure, his sandy-blond hair, which, in the sunlight, she discovered, was here and there threaded with silver. She looked at the colors of him, the ones she could see when he had his clothes on, and the ones she could see now that he had his clothes off, the variety of his colors in the bright sunlight, the bronze, the pinks, the browns, the mauves. Much has been made of the beauty of woman, but too little has been made of the beauty of man. She wanted to explore every part of him, first with her fingers, then with her tongue, to see and touch and feel and taste.

John examined Cassie closely in the bright sunlight, allowing himself a luxury of time and of feeling that he hadn't had time for in the heat of last night's passion. His fingertips lingered over the mole above her waist on her right side and briefly feathered along the silver stretch marks on her abdomen, reminders of the child she had borne. His fingertips explored the solid flesh of her thighs and paused at the back of her knees, and he turned her over so he could etch the faint blue tracery of veins there with his gentle fingers. When his fingers reached the long hollow scar below her knee, its hard surface white against her tan, he looked at her questioningly, but she only smiled a faint sad smile and in a burst of desire spun around and captured his lips fiercely with her own.

She wanted to bury the agony of old scars; she wanted oblivion to be born out of this new sensation in her life. Her pleasure in their mating was intense. His body engulfed her, quickened her with feeling, loosed her and warmed her. It did not even matter that he reached his peak and she didn't; her delight in his body was enough.

Afterward, ardor spent, they lay side by side on their backs, inhaling the heady scent of crushed lavender and watching puffs of clouds scudding across the searing blue sky. Their skin shimmered silvery in the sunshine, dewy and moist.

"What were you like?" John asked curiously, lifting her hand and tracing the curving line across the width of her palm as though it were a map of her previous life. "What were you like back then, before the accident?"

She knew what he meant. She smiled, picturing herself in her mind's eye, looking at herself from the perspective of space and years.

"I was fluffy," she said, remembering her round face, devoid of planes, bare of experience.

"What do you mean, 'fluffy'?" He turned his head slowly and looked at her, amused.

"You know. Fluffy. Frothy. Unserious. About as much substance as that cloud up there. For me life was just a bowl of cherries. Until all I had left was the pits." Her eyes hardened momentarily, then became soft again.

More silence while he digested this. "You're not still frightened of me, are you?" he said finally, his hand now toying idly with a lock of her hair.

"No," she said, "but I—" Here she stopped.

"You what?" he said, his eyes keen upon her face.

"I'm afraid you're disappointed," she whispered.

He raised himself on one elbow and stared at her. It was her inaccurate idea of her own unworthiness again, rearing its ugly head to rob her of the beauty of their experience.

"No, I'm not disappointed," he said fiercely. "Never. I want everything to be all right between us because of *you*, not me. You have to understand that right now, Cassandra."

The fervor in his words not only startled her, it also convinced her. She felt something akin to awe at the intensity of his feelings. "All right," she said uncertainly. "But maybe you're expecting too much, John. I don't think I'm capable of—"

"Cassie, you've had a lot to deal with. Be patient with yourself. And kind to yourself, too."

She mulled this over in her mind. "Kind? I don't deserve my own kindness, John. Or anyone else's, for that matter." She hid her face in the feathery soft hair on his bare chest, but he was suddenly alert.

"You and your negative thoughts!" he exploded. "Listen to what you're saying, Cassie!"

He had frightened her with his outburst. "Forget I said anything," she said, wrenching herself from his arms. Her expression harsh, she sat upright and fussed with her shift, pulling it over her head and twitching it straight.

"No, I think this is the key. You don't deserve, you said. You don't think you deserve kindness, or happiness, or pleasure. You're tearing yourself apart with unworthiness, Cassie Muldoon, and for no reason." He began to pull on his jeans angrily, jerkily, standing up.

She turned her face away from him, but before she did, he saw that her expression was a tableau of grief.

"What do you know about it?" Cassie stumbled blindly to her feet. John grabbed for her arm and locked onto her. She stared up at him, her chest heaving. She wished he'd let her go; she had a right to her feelings. Who was he to tell her how she should feel?

Just because she had shared her body with him she was not going to share her life. No way. Because she'd been imprisoned in places John Howard had never known, dark caverns of the heart and of the mind, places you didn't just dance away from but fought your way out of bit by bit, heartache by heartache, until you were bleeding and battered and had no taste for life. Oh, she could tell John Howard a thing or two.

"I know plenty," he said, and his eyes struck upon hers like blue flint on gray granite.

"Talk to me," he said, and she didn't half understand what kind of hold he had on her, why she listened. She only nodded numbly and let him lead her to a sheltering maple where sunbeams streamed through the heavy foliage, and she sat down with him in the dappled sunlight, limp now from the strength of her emotions.

"Trust me," he said, and oddly enough she did.

To her own surprise she began to talk, the sentences running into one another as though it were a recitation. In a way, it was. She had repeated the words over and over to herself for years.

"I killed them. I killed Kevin and Rory. Oh, I didn't hold a gun to their heads or stab them with a knife, but I might as well have. I loved them, and I killed them, my husband and my son, and how does a person live with that?"

Gently, his anger dissipating in the face of her abject grief, John drew Cassie into his arms and listened to her heart beating, felt her breath against his throat.

"I remember the write-up in all the papers when it happened," he said against her hair. "The three of you were flying home in your plane to your place north of San Francisco, and the plane crashed when you attempted an emergency landing. Your husband and son were killed, and you survived. Cassie, you didn't kill them. The crash did."

She lifted her head, and her face was ashen, her expression lifeless, her lips taut and bloodless. Her eyes were silver mirrors that reflected all the tragedy in the world.

"There are ways to keep the whole story out of the papers, if you have a good public relations man," she said haltingly. "That story is the one that was released, but it wasn't the whole truth. My agent wanted to protect me."

She swallowed and placed her square hand flat out across his hard pectoral muscles. He folded his hand over hers, burrowed his fingers under her fingers. He was so strong. She drew strength from him.

"Do you want to tell me what really happened?" he said gently.

She began to sob softly against his chest, the way a baby whimpers when it is exhausted from crying. He cradled her head in his hands, murmuring soft words. Her tears spilled over the hair on his chest, where the droplets winked in the leaf-dappled sunlight like sad, lost diamonds. John stroked her hair tenderly.

When she could speak, she said, her voice hardly more than a whisper, "Kevin passed out as we were flying somewhere south of San Francisco, just fell forward, and I couldn't wake him up. And Rory was frightened and started to cry, and I couldn't think what to do. So I turned to the emergency frequency on the radio—Kevin had made sure I knew which frequency it was—and tried to contact a control tower, another plane, anybody...." Her voice trailed off, her eyes glazing in remembrance of the horror of it.

John's arms tightened around her. "God, Cassie, do you want to tell me these things? You don't have to if you don't want to." His heart ached in her behalf.

She swallowed and shook her head. Then she drew a deep breath and went on.

"Finally a voice came over the radio, and he said he was a pilot and he'd talk me down out of the sky. He told me where I was, and he carefully explained just what I had to do and what the instruments were and everything. I knew a little bit about flying from watching Kevin and what he had taught me, but I'd never taken the pinch hitter's course. That's a brief course of instruction that doesn't lead to a pilot's license but helps you to know how to handle an airplane if there's ever an emergency. Oh, John, Kevin always wanted me to take that course. But I never had time! There was always a rehearsal or a concert date or some reason why I couldn't do it or thought I couldn't do it! Why, why didn't I take that course?" And her sobs ripped through his heart.

"You never dreamed anything like that would happen to you," he said quietly, kissing away the tears.

Cassie sat up straighter and visibly tried to quiet herself. "I guess I didn't. Who does?" With an effort she pulled herself together enough to go on.

"The pilot on the radio was on the ground at a small private airport less than five miles away, and so I followed his instructions until I saw the runway. They'd lit it all up with lights, making it easy for me to find it. And I did everything he said, everything, and Kevin was still unconscious and Rory was in the backseat holding his breath and I was hanging on for dear life, thinking I had it made—and I lost it. About ten feet above the ground, I lost control of the plane. And we hit so hard that the plane flipped over and Kevin was thrown out on impact, still buckled into his seat, and Rory was, too, and they died, they died! And it wasn't fair, I should have died, too. But I didn't. I wasn't thrown from the plane and I lived."

"You were hurt seriously, as I recall," said John, shaken by her narrative and the agony with which it was told.

"I had bruises and cuts and a compound fracture of the tibia. I was in the hospital a long time, but not long enough. I was afraid to get out and face things again. Fortunately, I didn't have to face things at first."

"What did you do?"

"I went to stay with Morgana. Morgana Friday, my friend from the early days when we both had just arrived on the West Coast. It was during the time after the accident, when I stayed with Morgana in her Century City apartment, that I gave her permission to use a song I'd recorded but had never released. She was directing *All the Way Home*, which she described as a really terrific documentary, trying to get me interested in something, anything. That's how my song became so famous, I guess. It would never have been released if it hadn't been for Morgana." She closed her eyes and rested her head against John's broad shoulder, taking comfort from his sympathy.

John had Morgana to thank, too. She was the one who had finally given him Cassie's address. But Morgana had been maddeningly evasive, protecting her friend's privacy at all costs. John hadn't had an inkling that Cassie

Muldoon was the lost entertainer Cassandra Dare, nor had he known the complete details of the accident.

She was tough, Morgana was. It had taken him months to convince her to tell him where he could find Mrs. K. J. Muldoon. He'd never once connected the Muldoons with what had happened to Cassandra Dare; he'd never known what kind of accident the Muldoons had had. Only that they'd had one, and that it was his salvation—no, Cassie's generosity was his salvation—and he was obsessed from the beginning with finding her and thanking her no matter what happened. It had become a quest of honor, finally.

And now that he'd found her, and now that he knew who she really was, and now that he knew that the saving of his sight was due to the generosity of this woman whose husband was also a pilot, it all seemed to make some kind of sense, as though destiny had brought them together. Thoughts whirled inside his head, but Cassie was talking, and he forced himself to listen.

"Ours was a good marriage, one of the few I know of that was good," Cassie was saying softly. "Kevin and I met when I'd been in California barely a year, and he understood show business because he had been around it all his life. He became my manager, and if it hadn't been for him, I wouldn't have been a success. After all, who wanted to hire a girl who sang folk songs and played a mountain dulcimer? But Kevin knew the people to see and how to get in to see them, he protected me from the harsher realities of the business, and he made it easy for me. We showed them that I could sing other kinds of songs, too, and, well, you probably know the rest."

"Only the public part," John said. "Pictures of you in the tabloids, in the newspapers. Public relations articles. You kept a pretty low private profile."

"Kevin and I decided early in the game that we didn't want to be part of the glitter and the glamour of Hollywood and Beverly Hills. So we did the things we had to do to advance my career, and the rest of the time we spent as a family, hidden away at our place in northern California. We had such a wonderful life. I don't know why it had to end."

John backed away from her a little, taking in her large, sad gray eyes, her slightly parted lips, the unusual and beautiful face he loved. The face Kevin had loved, and which he, because Kevin had died, and because his own corneas had been irreparably scarred, saw now quite literally through Kevin's eyes.

Chapter Seven

John had been in love three times and in "like"—for want of a better term—more times than he could count. Each time he'd been in love was different.

There was that first memorable college romance—stormy, chaotic and fraught with anguish over whether or not marriage would be the end result. It wasn't.

His second love, who embodied every quality he had ever sought in a woman, dropped out of his life without warning just when he thought their relationship was at its peak. "I'd rather leave while I'm in love," she explained, echoing a Rita Coolidge song. John had never been so depressed in his life.

And then he'd met Charlene. Moneyed and mad about him, she talked him out of his depression and into marriage within six weeks of their meeting. John had never been so happy in his life.

Then he found out that, like Robert Browning's "My Last Duchess,"

> she liked whate'er
> She looked on, and her looks went everywhere.

When Charlene's looks, not to mention certain parts

of her anatomy, lingered too long on her karate instructor, John walked out. The divorce had been neat and uncomplicated, but he hadn't been in love since, a circumstance that John considered a blessing.

That left being in "like."

He'd known starlets trying to make it in a no-go world, secretaries who had figured out that the best way to become upwardly mobile was to marry a man like him, and a corporation type who spent a lot of time speculating what would happen to their relationship when she was transferred to Houston.

He'd been invited to coke parties and driven himself home early and alone; to dinner with business contacts who brought along their voluptuous daughters and dumped them on him; and on a memorable trip to Hawaii with a woman who in midair developed a crush on the male flight attendant and had moved into the flight attendant's hotel room in Waikiki, leaving John to hang out morosely in the hotel bar and debate the true meaning of life with the sympathetic bartender.

John's last girlfriend had lived in an apartment tented with bargain batiks, booby-trapped with low-slung fretted tables, and dominated at one end of the living room by a huge brass coffeepot in which no coffee ever perked. There had been spears and gourds and other oddities too ominous to mention, many of them situated in uncomfortable places. A wild boar's head, stuffed, fixed any occupant of the king-sized waterbed with a baleful eye, not to mention a well-honed tusk when one got up to go to the bathroom in the dark. John had eased out of the relationship, just short, he was convinced, of being paralyzed by a poison dart and being mounted like the trophy he was.

Which was just before a Mack truck mowed into him on the freeway. His head bashed through the windshield and the glass ground into his eyes, injuring his corneas, those fragile transparent outercoats of the eyeballs. His view of the world was scarred, but he would regain his vision, the doctors said, if he would undergo corneal transplants. John waited almost a year before they found a donor.

The donor had been one K. J. Muldoon, killed in an unspecified accident. His wife had signed the permission papers that allowed Mr. Muldoon's corneas to be used. Within weeks after the cornea transplants, John, his eyes made new by another's generosity, could see again.

And he knew he had to speak with Mrs. K. J. Muldoon to convey his heartfelt gratitude. Only he hadn't been able to find her.

He'd written to Mrs. K. J. Muldoon after getting the name from a nurse who was leaving the hospital's employ the next week and thought it something of a lark to pass along forbidden information from the hospital records. His letters to Mrs. K. J. Muldoon at her northern California address had never been answered, and of course, he'd never connected this Muldoon woman with Cassandra Dare. He'd written more letters, and they'd been sent back marked "Return to Sender." Frustrated, desperate, knowing he could not rest until he thanked her, he'd driven up there in his BMW once his recuperation time was over, to the estate called Wildflower near Occidental, north of San Francisco.

And he'd arrived at the big walled retreat, noticing the airplane runway and small hangar in back of the house, close to the woods, noticing because he was a pilot himself and if he'd known there was a runway, he probably would have flown one of his planes instead of driving. But the runway and the hangar hadn't made any particular impression on him. He knew a number of wealthy people in Los Angeles who owned their own planes and who owned other houses in other parts of the country, each with its own runway, convenient for when they chose to visit.

He hadn't been able to raise a soul at the house, even though he'd pushed his way in through an open back gate and pounded on several doors and shouted until he was hoarse. A curious gardener had finally peered around the corner of the house, convinced that he was confronting a madman.

A couple of twenty-dollar bills convinced the cautious gardener that it would be in his best interest to tell the madman where he sent the monthly bill for his groundskeeping services, and John had driven his cream-colored BMW away toward Los Angeles with a Century City address in his pocket.

The Century City address had led him to Morgana, eventually, and finally to Cassie.

He was a tenacious man. He had, after all, taken a small cargo airline that was about to go bankrupt and built it into a multifaceted organization serving many cities on the West Coast and now Hawaii. He was the kind who perceived a problem, defined the solution, and hung on until the solution was reached. He was not about to give up just because the long process of finding Mrs. K. J. Muldoon turned out to be more than he bargained for. Finding her became a point of honor to be pursued, no matter what the difficulties.

And when she turned out to be Cassie, a real-life person who touched his heart and his mind and his body in a way no one else ever had, he fell in love with her. He intended to bring her down off the mountain and marry her no matter what it took.

When he decided that it was love, there was no going back. He would learn her moods, erase her sorrow, earn her love, and be everything in the world to her. He would exorcise the devil of guilt that rode screaming on her back.

He never thought it would be easy, nor was it.

Chapter Eight

Cassie and John rested in a green-shadowed glade beside a wide stream. Here and there, the racing water of the creek foamed into swirling knots around low brown rocks. Cassie leaned back against a poplar trunk and raised her face to a shaft of sunlight. So warm it felt, so peaceful. *She* felt peaceful. She savored the feeling, keenly aware of John's presence as he lay beside her.

Lambent light highlighted his rugged features, flickered across his wide, generous lips, picked out the warm blue depths of his eyes, half closed and lazy now. With that bronze skin of his and the sun-streaked hair, he looked as though he should be wearing crisp tennis whites rather than the jeans and T-shirt he wore. His hand, firm and sure, reached out to interlace with hers on the leaf-strewn ground between them, a casual gesture bespeaking the intimacy the two of them shared.

She knew him now, knew him well. She knew all the warm configurations of him, convex, concave, as though she had sculpted him with her own hands. She knew the silky texture of his hair threading through her fingers, the downy sweetness of his earlobes, the honeyed wetness of his mouth. She knew the flat satiny skin of his abdomen, knew the coarse softness of the hair below and the carven perfection of what it sheltered, knew how to make him bloom at her very touch. She knew John Howard.

"Sleepy?" he said, rolling on his side, his voice rich and low and tender.

She shook her head. "Somehow a walk in the mountains always invigorates me," she told him.

"I feel that way early in the morning, when I run. But now I feel dozy, relaxed." He squeezed her hand.

"Flatlander," she accused affectionately. "Everybody knows flatlanders take time to adjust to the altitude."

"I'm feeling pretty high all right," he agreed with a teasing look. "High on you."

She laughed, used to his joshing. She had forgotten how good it could be to have someone to laugh with, to tease with, to make things light and fun. Their morning had been delightful; the mundane became exciting when she and John shared it.

They'd gone in search of ginseng that morning. Cassie used the rare ginseng root as a tonic, and she kept Gran's old ginseng patch in a secret place in the woods. She only harvested the 'sang in the fall, but she liked to check on the plants occasionally during the summer. John had asked to accompany her. They'd taken a picnic lunch with them, and on their way home they'd stopped beside the cool stream to eat.

"When will you finish your work here?" Cassie asked him unexpectedly.

"In September," he told her, his eyes widening with the impact of her unforeseen question.

Cassie averted her eyes. During the past weeks John had carved his own special place in her heart. She wished they didn't have to say good-bye so soon.

"I'd like you to come with me when I go," he said quietly.

She stared at him. "I've already told you I'll never leave this mountain," she said.

"Only for a visit?"

"Oh, John, it wouldn't work. My place is here," she said gently.

"You're afraid to go back, aren't you?" His eyes, ever understanding, probed hers.

She didn't know whether to answer this or not. She was used to John's directness as well as his kindness; she didn't remember ever knowing any other man who had this same directness. Even Kevin, whom she had loved so much.

"I don't like Los Angeles," she said finally. "I don't know if it's a matter of being afraid anymore. I'll admit that when I left I was running away, but I've found peace on this mountain and a way of life I can manage."

"You're strong enough to leave Flat Top Mountain now, Cassie."

"Maybe. But maybe I had to be strong to come here in the first place. Don't you think it was a brave thing to do, coming here all alone to confront my own shortcomings?"

"Your shortcomings are fewer than most people's," he said.

"Oh, John, you've made me feel better about myself, and I'm grateful to you for that."

"Look, I know I'm tampering with a tender area, but it seems to me that you're forcing a punishment on life by withholding yourself from it. What's the point?"

Cassie inhaled a deep breath. The air was rich with the scent of trees and water. She hated to argue with him, and arguments about this had become entirely too frequent. How could she make him understand that she had planted herself here much as she had planted the plants in her garden, that she was now coming to fruition and was ready to gather herself in to preserve what she might? At least that had been her purpose before he'd arrived on the scene, plucking at her, shaking her, demanding that she separate herself from her security, her very roots, and prematurely, too, before her full ripening had taken place.

"Come to Los Angeles with me, Cassie. Just for a visit. We could fly there, maybe take a long weekend during August. I could show you my house, and we could fly back on a Monday. Would a visit be so bad?"

Cassie began to toss plastic cups and forks and knives into the picnic satchel. She was near tears; he must see that.

"Cassie?"

"I don't fly. I can't." She choked back the pain in her throat.

The silence lengthened. A dragonfly flitted by on cellophane wings, hovering over the water. A dragonfly didn't know, thought Cassie, of the dangers of flying. For dragonflies, flying was necessary to living. For people, it wasn't. The dragonfly zipped away, ignorant of the risks. Lucky dragonfly.

"I didn't know," said John quietly. "I should have guessed."

"That's why I couldn't go on tour. I would have had to fly, you see. And after—after...well, I couldn't get in an airplane. My heart would pound at the very thought, and I'd get dizzy and...Oh, I can't even stand to think of someone I know getting in one." Her sentence ended on a note both high and tense, and John felt helpless to confront such terror. He was also dismayed.

"Have you tried counseling?" he asked carefully.

Cassie told him about her visits to Dr. Westwood. "I finally quit counseling, and Morgana was always hopping on a flight here or there, and every time she'd leave the apartment I'd think I'd never see her again, and I lived in terror until she came back. Because I knew I couldn't stand to lose Morgana, too."

John looked grave, but his mind was racing. What would happen when he told her that he was not a photographer at all, but a pilot? What if he told her that he made his living by flying cargo from one place to another along the West Coast and in Hawaii? Although as president of AirBridges Cargo Transport, he was now concerned mainly with administrative duties, he still loved nothing more than to climb into the cockpit of one of his planes and take it up. And, too, there was his Mooney, the four-seater private plane that he kept exclusively for his own use.

If he revealed himself to Cassie as a pilot now, wouldn't that convince her that continuing their relationship was impossible? Flying frightened her, not only for herself but for others, and he could understand why. But flying was his life, had been his life since he'd first flown for the Air Force in Vietnam.

He knew, with a sharp pang of regret, that he should have told Cassie the truth about himself to begin with. Lying to her had gone against his grain. He should never have started this innocent fiction that he was a nature photographer, though at the time it had seemed only an easy and reasonable explanation for his presence on Flat Top Mountain and one that could be disposed with readily as soon as he got to know her. Unfortunately, nothing had turned out as planned.

Sick at heart with his deception, he helped Cassie gather the picnic things and hoisted the satchel over his shoulder. What Cassie wanted and how she felt was important to him, but he wanted her with him, and he was convinced that being together would be good for Cassie, too. How was he going to bring it about?

THE WOMAN STRODE UP AND DOWN the earthen path in front of Cassie's house, tossing her long pale hair impatiently behind her shoulders much as a sprightly thoroughbred mare would toss her mane when miffed. She was dressed totally in black, a black silk jump suit with a stand-up collar and black leather high-heeled boots, and she wore a hammered silver belt slung slanted across her hips. In her boots, she stood over six feet tall.

Cassie stopped stock-still at the edge of the clearing, unable to connect the figure with reality at first. Then, startling John, she dropped the canvas tote bag she carried and ran laughing to envelop the waiting woman in a joyful embrace.

"Morgana!" exclaimed Cassie, blinking happy tears from her eyes. "You're the last person I expected to see on Flat Top Mountain!"

"Believe me, darling, I feel like the last person in the whole world. I've been waiting *hours* for you to come home. This place is so isolated! How do you stand it?" Morgana assessed Cassie with anxious eyes, but her friend looked whole and well and tanned and happy and much healthier than the thin and woebegone wraith who had left Los Angeles almost two years before.

"The isolation is what I like about it," retorted Cassie. She noticed the black Cadillac parked at the side of the house, and she regretted not being home when Morgana arrived; Morgana hated to be kept waiting.

"Whose car is that?" she asked her guest. "And please say you're planning to stay."

"I had a ghastly time trying to rent this car at the Asheville airport, and I *am* planning to stay, although not long. Why didn't you answer any of my letters? And why don't you get a telephone like any civilized person? And who *is* that over there? Why doesn't he come out from behind that tree?"

Not knowing which question to answer first, Cassie looked in the direction Morgana was looking and saw John hesitating, their picnic satchel on his shoulder, his camera hanging from a wide strap around his neck.

"Oh, John," she called, holding her hand out toward him. "Morgana's here. Morgana Friday, my friend who directed the documentary you admire so much."

John walked forward slowly, cautiously. Apprehension filled him. Morgana could ruin this, could destroy his tenuous relationship with Cassie. He'd met Morgana before in Los Angeles, had kept hammering at her over the phone for months until she'd agreed to meet him for a drink, and after they'd polished off most of a bottle of twelve-year-old Scotch, she'd written down Cassie's address for him. Morgana knew how he had sought Cassie ceaselessly so that he could thank her, and he still had not thanked Cassie, because to do so would be to reveal himself. Morgana would not know that, however. *Please,* he thought desperately, *pretend that you don't know me. Please.*

Morgana took in Cassie's breathlessness and her face alight with love as the two of them watched John walk in their direction. And she sensed the worry in John, caught the message in his eyes. Morgana was shrewd and wise; she was no fool. Her native intuition told her that the pair were lovers.

"Morgana, this is my friend John Howard," announced Cassie with obvious pleasure.

Cassie had arrived here in pieces, and now she seemed whole. Morgana didn't know what part John had played in Cassie's wholeness, but she suspected he had something to do with it. Morgana had known from the beginning, as Cassie had known, that John was a decent man. She would do nothing to tear down whatever he and Cassie had built.

John stood before Morgana, his blue eyes clouded with doubt, waiting for her to loose the sharp words that would slice his relationship with Cassie to pieces.

Morgana gazed at him unblinkingly, her face expressionless. He thought it was all over.

And then, "How do you do?" Morgana said coolly, extending her hand as though she'd never laid eyes on him before in her life.

"MY GOD, CASS, what is this? A zoo?" Morgana stared at Bertrand the skunk as he waddled to and fro in the kitchen, waiting to be fed; then her startled glance took in Rupert the raccoon peering through his black goggles around the edge of the bathroom door and finally came to rest on Tigger curled up on a chair.

"Don't worry, I'll put the cat out when it gets dark," said Cassie. John carried Morgana's luggage into the guest room, and Cassie whispered as soon as he was out of earshot, "What do you think of him?"

Morgana fixed her eyes on Tigger. "He's a delightful animal, I'm sure," she said loudly and deliberately.

Tigger preened, and John shot her an unfathomable look on his way back out to the Cadillac.

"Not the cat, Morgana. You were never dense." Cassie smiled. It was so good to have Morgana here.

"Only when I choose to be, darling. And I think anyone who puts a house cat out and keeps a skunk inside at night should start counting her marbles to see if any are missing."

Cassie laughed. She'd forgotten what it was like being around Morgana.

"John, why don't you uncork a bottle of that wine?" said Cassie when John returned.

Morgana raised an eyebrow. "Wine? What kind of wine?"

"I make it myself," said Cassie, "out of—"

"Please," groaned Morgana. "Spare me. I don't want to know if you make it out of dandelion stems or porcupine quills or some godawful root you dug up in the wilderness. Just pour me a large glass and I'll try not to think about what's in it."

John grinned. He poured them each a glass of the amethyst liquid and they gathered on Cassie's front porch to drink it, Morgana sitting on Gran's comfortable old rocking chair, Cassie perched on the porch railing and John comfortably ensconced on the steps.

"So how did you two meet?" John asked after the first few sips of wine.

Morgana and Cassie exchanged a look and laughed.

"Well, we were looking for an agent," said Cassie.

"And we found ourselves sitting next to each other in the William Morris Agency waiting room," supplied Morgana.

"And I had found a place to live—remember that awful apartment, Morgana? On impulse I asked Morgana if she wanted to be my roommate, because she mentioned that she didn't have a place to stay."

"Hah—I not only didn't have a place, I'd been thrown out of my last room just that morning for non-payment of rent. I was still dashing and flashing my way to stardom in those days," said Morgana. "I thought I'd lost my big chance when I didn't nab the Wonder Woman part that Lynda Carter got. We were the same size exactly, but they didn't want a blonde." Morgana tossed her hair in that distinctive way of hers. It was hard to pinpoint the exact shade of it; her hair ranged somewhere between palomino and platinum.

"I cried for days. I would have dyed my hair, I could have worn a wig," she went on. "But if I'd been Wonder Woman, I probably wouldn't be directing documentaries these days. Great Hera, it's funny how things turn out." She held her glass up to the light and narrowed her eyes at it. "What's in the wine anyway, Cass? It's making me unaccountably mellow."

"Scuppernongs," said Cassie.

Morgana shuddered. "I won't tell anyone if you won't."

"And what was Cassie like?" John prodded before Morgana stopped feeling reminiscent.

"Cassie? She was this shy little folksinger fresh out of the South," said Morgana. "She rode into town with a funny-looking instrument no one had ever seen before and she played it with a goose quill, for God's sake. All she had to do was pull out that dulcimer and start tickling it with a feather, and people would fall out of their chairs laughing."

"It's true," agreed Cassie with a smile. "My first year on the Coast was the most awful year of my life, except for Morgana. I knew I couldn't come back home to the little Piedmont North Carolina town where I'd grown up. My future would have been what my mother's was—eking out a precarious living as a shift worker in a paper mill. My dulcimer—Gran's dulcimer, really—was all I had. I knew I had to succeed or it was back to Conco."

"Conco?" said John, puzzled.

"Cone Company of the South," explained Cassie. "Yarn for the looms in the South's textile factories is wound on disposable paper cones, and Conco makes ninety percent of them. In those days L.A. looked like paradise to me."

"That's understandable," said Morgana with irony. "I can hardly picture you stacking cones for a living. But then, I can't imagine you staying here and mixing up herbal remedies for the rest of your life, either. When are you coming back, Cassie?"

The question hung in the air, ready to fall, and John held his breath.

"I'm not, Morgana," said Cassie.

"Not? How can you not?" Morgana frowned at her.

"Oh, I don't want to talk about it now," said Cassie abruptly, jumping down from the porch rail. "I think I'll go see if those butter beans are cooked." Quickly she went inside and slammed the door.

"Well, well," said Morgana, talking to the liquid in her wineglass. They sat in silence for a moment. A horsefly droned against the screen door behind them.

John drew a deep breath. "Thanks, Morgana," he said.

"Whatever I've done, you're welcome," she returned. "Whatever *you've* done, it had better be in our Cassie's best interests. I don't want her to get hurt."

Morgana tipped her head and fixed him with a warning look.

"Neither do I," said John quietly, his blue gaze never wavering from Morgana's face. "I'm in love with her, for whatever that's worth."

Morgana looked startled. "These days it's usually not worth much, at least from most people. But with you..."

She let her words trail off, assessing him. There was that sincerity; it was the reason she had trusted him enough to tell him where Cassie was when he had come searching for her, looking as though he were driven. She'd taken a chance on that, but from what she could tell about Cassie, it appeared that the chance had paid off. John had reached Cassie—that was obvious. She had not been able to reach Cassie, nor had Dr. Westwood, nor had anyone else she knew.

"She doesn't know I'm a pilot," said John, speaking softly and hurrying to get the words out before Cassie returned. "And I haven't told her that I'm the recipient of her husband's corneas. It's taken me this long to earn her confidence, and—" he lifted his shoulders and let them fall helplessly "—I can't ruin it. Not yet. I love her and I want her to come back to L.A. with me. But there are so many things I'll have to convince her about, so many things we need to talk over."

Morgana nodded somberly. She would never forget Cassie, so broken and empty, hurting so much over her guilt about Kevin and Rory in those months she had stayed with Morgana in Century City. Despite her rough exterior, Morgana never liked to see anyone suffering, and most particularly not the people she loved. John loved Cassie, too. Morgana trusted him.

"Go to it, fella," Morgana said softly before tossing down the contents of her glass. "And good luck. You're sure as hell going to need it."

THE NEXT MORNING, Morgana prowled up and down the length of the front room, gleaming inappropriately in gold lamé lounging pajamas with a deeply slit neckline. She and Cassie had breakfasted on fresh eggs and whole wheat bread that Cassie had baked herself.

Morgana watched Cassie as she sat on the hearth, brushing Rupert's long hair with a stiff-bristled brush. The raccoon had almost completely recovered from his semicomatose state the night of the storm. He'd proved to be a sociable pet, becoming immediately housebroken and driving Cassie crazy with his penchant for stealing shiny objects such as spoons and thimbles and hiding them away in his own secret places. Rupert and Tigger and Bertrand edged carefully around one another for the most part, adopting a pragmatic policy of live-and-let-live. Bertrand, however, still seemed to take perverse pleasure in threatening John with his scent glands whenever John appeared on the scene, a fact that amused Morgana immensely.

"Haven't we lazed around long enough?" asked Morgana anxiously.

Cassie released Rupert, who immediately disappeared behind the sofa. "Laze? You never laze, Morgana. You only stride."

"What I mean is, what are we going to do today?"

"We're doing it."

Privately Cassie was amused. Life in Morgana's high-powered world was fast-paced and reckless, interrupted by the ring of countless frantic telephones and seasoned by an array of characters so bizarre as to boggle the mind. No wonder Morgana was bored after only one quiet night on Flat Top Mountain!

Morgana arranged herself dramatically on the old settle as she watched Cassie clean the raccoon's hair out of the brush.

"Kajurian called me," she said, without preliminaries.

"Oh?" said Cassie, expressing only mild interest.

"He wants to know why you never answer his letters," said Morgana.

"I don't answer *any* letters," Cassie pointed out. "Gran's chifforobe is stacked high with letters I haven't answered. So tell Kajurian he's not being discriminated against—I'm simply not interested in bookings."

"Cassie, you're a fool. Thanks to your hit single—and, I might add, thanks to me, because I used the song in my documentary—you could be making a million dollars. Kajurian's sore, and I can't say that I blame him. You were his top moneymaker, and you ran off to this mountaintop without any regard for what might happen to him or anyone else. Lord knows my documentary could use the publicity generated by your comeback."

Cassie rocked back against the stone of the hearth. "Oh, Morgana, from what I've heard, *All the Way Home* doesn't need me to be a commercial success. And as for Kajurian, what's he been doing—losing money at the racetrack?" Unmarried and childless, Cassie's former agent was known to have a penchant for the ponies.

"Well," said Morgana, "how would I know? He didn't discuss *that*. Who knows anything real about anybody in this industry? I've heard rumors that things are not going as well for him as they might be, but—hell, Cassie, if you want to know, call him up."

Cassie thought for a moment about the man who had taken her on only because he'd owed Kevin a favor and who had stuck with her when she was a nobody. She'd liked Kajurian and he'd liked her. She hated the idea that her old friend might be having financial problems, but Kajurian and everything he represented were part of a past that she had left forever behind.

"I don't have a telephone. And Morgana, you're a manipulator," said Cassie, but not unkindly. "Stop trying to play on my emotions. I've already told you that I've parted company with Los Angeles for the last time. Believe it." She started to get up, but Morgana began to pace the floor in great sweeping strides.

"I suppose it doesn't even mean anything to you that your song 'Where the Heart Is' had been nominated for two awards? That the American Academy of Film Arts may very well bestow on you its top honors? That—"

Cassie shook her head, trying to clear it. "Wait a minute, Morgana. Slow down. What awards?"

Morgana looked flabbergasted. "The AAFA awards, you idiot. Don't you read *Billboard*?"

"Not very often."

"Then I have the honor of informing you that 'Where the Heart Is' has been nominated for the best theme song by a female vocalist, and you, Cassandra Dare, have been nominated for best songwriter." Morgana stood, hands on her hips, one eyebrow cocked skyward, and waited for a reaction.

"I—I'm stunned," said Cassie at last.

"Well you might be," Morgana shot back. "As you know, the nominations were just announced. Surely you're not planning to send regrets to the AAFA

Awards Spectacular Committee? No one, my dear, but no one, does *that*."

"When is the Awards Spectacular?" Cassie was still so amazed that she couldn't think. She'd won awards before, for her albums and her single records, but this was different. This was tied to a very special kind of documentary, a documentary that made a statement, just as her song made a statement. In the old days such an award would have meant a great deal to her.

"It's in October. That gives you a couple of months to slide down off this mountain, dust yourself off and buy some decent clothes." She scanned her eyes none too admiringly over Cassie's customary loose shift. "I hardly need to tell you that short, shapeless sacks are hardly considered haute couture this year, darling."

For a moment Cassie wavered. Thinking about it, about sweeping into the Awards Spectacular on John's arm, of his delighted pride in her, and then of actually winning—but the scene frosted over and faded away. Creeping in to replace it was the stark, awful fear, the anguish of spirit that accompanied the very thought of setting foot in an airplane again. The only other way to get to the West Coast from here would be by train or car, and Cassie couldn't face the idea of that, because the automobile trip here from L.A. had been long and debilitating and fraught with emotional turmoil....No, she could not go. She simply could not.

"It's out of the question," she said, removing Gran's sunbonnet from its hook on the back of the door and whipping the ties into a bow under her chin. She lifted an empty bushel basket off the floor and cradled it in the curve of her arm. "I'm going to work in the garden, Morgana," she said, clipping her words off short and, turning her back on her friend, she hurried outside, the expression on her face remote and sad.

From the window Morgana watched Cassie bending low over the straight green rows of tomato plants in her vegetable garden, and she swore softly under her breath.

"In that case, Cassandra," she said out loud, "it's time to send in the rest of the troops."

Chapter Nine

On the following Sunday, shortly after Morgana had left for the airport and her flight back to L.A., Cassie hurried back from her house where she had gone to present an unexpected guest with a bottle of Gran's famous rheumatism liniment. John lounged against the rock wall near Cassie's garden while Sharon Ott sat on a tree trunk and strummed the dulcimer. The golden notes of Sharon's rendition of "Careless Love" faded away as Cassie flung herself down on a velvety cushion of moss beside John.

"What did I tell you?" said Cassie triumphantly with a sideways look at John. "Can Sharon sing?"

"Beautifully," said John, impressed. "I didn't think anyone but Cassie could coax such round, full notes out of a mountain dulcimer. But you're good, Sharon, really good."

"I'll never be as good as Cassie," said Sharon. "Not in a million years."

"Keep at it and you'll be better than I am," Cassie told her seriously.

"Since I haven't been able to get a job, do you think they'd take me on at the Juniper Inn, singing for tips? They've hired college kids before as singing waiters."

"It's an idea," said Cassie. "You know you can use my station wagon to drive over there any time you like."

"I thought I'd ride over tomorrow morning. The owner is usually around on Mondays to check over the menus for the coming week."

"If you could get in at the Juniper Inn, it would be good experience," mused Cassie, liking the idea. "It might help you get a professional job later on."

The Juniper Inn was a seasonal restaurant on the highway toward Asheville, and it catered mostly to tourists. But working there, even if only for tips, would be exposure for Sharon. The girl was becoming more discouraged about job prospects every day, and Cassie knew the chances were slim to none that Sharon Ott would ever be employed in the town of Scot's Cove. The Juniper Inn was about a forty-minute drive from Flat Top Mountain, but that meant that the restaurant was located far enough away that the Ott name might not be a problem for Sharon. Better yet, Sharon could use a professional name. Cassie asked Sharon if she'd ever thought of it.

"Why, no, I never have. Cassie, do you think it would be a good idea?" Sharon hugged the dulcimer to her chest, considering.

"Why not?" said Cassie. "What do you have to lose?"

"Nothing," agreed Sharon ruefully. "Nothing at all."

"Okay, then," Cassie said. "We'll christen you—oh, I don't know. What's a good stage name for Sharon, John?"

He laughed. "I'm the wrong one to ask. Sharon, what do you think?"

Sharon shook her head. "I'm not good at names, I've no imagination," she protested. "Cassie?"

"What's your middle name?"

Sharon blushed furiously. "Oh, Cassie. I've got the strangest name."

"What is it? Come on, Sharon, it can't be that bad."

"Every time I tell anyone what my name is, I have to explain it," said Sharon, growing visibly more reluctant by the second.

"Out with it," demanded Cassie, grinning at her friend's discomfort.

"All right," said Sharon unwillingly. "But don't you dare laugh." She drew a deep, steadying breath. "My ma didn't go to the hospital to have me. She had me right at home, in our house. And on the bed was this quilt her ma had made her for a wedding present."

"And this has something to do with your name?"

"Uh-huh. The name of the quilt pattern was Rose o' Sharon. Ma thought that quilt was real pretty, and she kind of concentrated on it when she was having the pains. So when I was born she named me—"

"Rose o' Sharon Ott," chorused Cassie and John.

"Right. You see, I don't think that's going to help us pick out my stage name."

"But it's lovely," objected Cassie. "You could be known as Rose o' Sharon. No first name, no last name, just Rose o' Sharon. People would notice it and remember it. And it's important to have a gimmick—my goose quill was a gimmick for me, though I never intended it to be—and you could wear a rose in your hair whenever you perform."

"Oh, Cassie, I could never—"

"You'd better listen," said John in a mock stern voice. "Rose o' Sharon was good enough for John

Steinbeck to use as the name of one of his characters in *The Grapes of Wrath*, and Steinbeck knew what he was doing. So does Cassie. She understands better than both of us how show business works."

"Come over tomorrow morning before you go to the Juniper Inn," Cassie told her. "We'll pick a rose from one of Gran's rosebushes. It'll have to be just the right delicate shade of pink to pick up the tone of your skin and your hair, and maybe I even have something you could wear."

"What song should I sing if the owner asks me to audition?" Sharon asked anxiously.

"The one you just sang was lovely," John said.

"That one and 'Darling Cora,'" suggested Cassie. "I like the way you let go with 'Darling Cora.' You put so much zip into it." "Darling Cora" was about a mountain woman not to be trifled with: She wore "a .44 buckled around her and a banjo on her knee."

Sharon zipped Cassie's dulcimer into its case. "I'll come over tomorrow morning around nine," she said. "Is that all right, Cassie?"

"Sure. Say, how's the new baby?"

"Riley's doing fine. The chamomile seemed to help."

"Good. I'll send some more home with you."

The three of them walked slowly back to the house, John's arm flung easily around Cassie's shoulders. When they got there, Cassie went inside and counted out the money Sharon had earned working in the garden that week and prepared a small bag of chamomile for little Riley, while John assured Sharon that she should feel free to use his telephone in her search for a job. The Otts didn't have a phone.

"Sure appreciate the help," said Sharon, sparkling under all the attention. Cassie and John watched as she walked away down the path, her strawberry-blond hair bouncing around her shoulders.

As Sharon disappeared around the curve in the road, John took Cassie's hand and pulled her down on the porch steps beside him. "Do you really think Sharon has a chance for a job at the Juniper Inn?" John asked thoughtfully.

"I hope so," said Cassie. And then, because she never wore a watch, she asked John urgently, "What time is it?"

He glanced at his slim gold wristwatch. "It's seven o'clock. Why?"

"Morgana," she said in obvious agitation. "Her plane is due to take off from the Asheville airport at seven-thirty."

"Oh, Cassie. Must you worry so?" He spoke with deliberate gentleness, but though she usually found it soothing, his mild manner only set her on edge now.

"Yes," she said helplessly. "Yes."

"It's irrational, this fear you have," he said, and his bland tone belied the tension in the air.

"It may be irrational, but it's real to me," said Cassie in a small voice.

"You and Morgana enjoyed your time together," said John, pressing the matter. "You're ruining it by being terrified about something over which you have no control. Don't you know that most of the things we worry about never happen? It's true."

Suddenly Cassie realized that she was not being allowed to feel her own fear but was being forced to face her phobia. And she didn't want calm reasoning. In her fear she was beyond it. Her heart began to beat with an irregular rhythm, and her breath froze in her chest. Her eyes went suddenly dry, felt achingly cold. Before he could say anything more, she lurched to her feet and ran into the house, but John followed her.

She didn't think he would let her off so easily, so she said too brightly, "I thought I'd cook hamburgers for supper," and she threw open the refrigerator door and slapped the meat down on the oak counter. "Do you want to stay?" The effort to get the words out almost choked her.

"Sure," he said evenly, casually. Too casually.

Cassie didn't look at him, but she knew John was watching her carefully and much too alertly. She didn't like squirming like a bug under his magnifying glass; she didn't like her emotions being raked over John Howard's judgment. What did he know about it? He'd never suffered through anything remotely like she had.

With great determination, she managed to calm her rapidly beating heart. It slowed to a dull thud against her rib cage, its heaviness filling her insides like a stone.

When she couldn't stand it any longer, she shot John a fleeting look. It was her undoing. It was impossible to stay angry with him. He was altogether too handsome, she thought; his looks did her in every time. Those blue-sky eyes, their gentle light, their laser-beam probing that plunged to her very depths just when she didn't want to reveal what she was thinking. The size and shape of him, which brought to mind the feel of him, which made her go weak with sudden longing.

"Maybe you could set the table," she suggested lamely, clattering the plates and glasses down from the cupboard, and in her hurry one of the plates slipped through her nervous fingers and bounced on the floor into fragments with a resounding crash.

"I'd better clean up the debris first," John said dryly, bending over and picking up the pieces.

Cassie turned away quite deliberately and steadied herself against the counter, hanging on to the edge of it for dear life. Was it seven-thirty yet? She closed her eyes, picturing the wing-swept silver bird that would bear Morgana aloft, soaring away into the blue-gray twilight, up and up, trailing lofty plumes of jet vapor in its wake. At the very thought of Morgana being on that flight, a cold wave of nausea washed over her, and retching suddenly and violently, she leaned over the sink.

"There," said John efficiently, dumping the pieces of plate into the garbage can. "That should—" And then he realized something was wrong.

He was across the kitchen floor in two strides. His hands, so strong and sure, gripped her shoulders with warm strength.

Cassie fought the churning of her stomach. The world tipped for a moment, washing away on a dizzy tide, slinging itself back into focus for a moment, then catching her in the backwash. Her mouth filled with a sick, sour taste, and she tried to swallow it. Tears squeezed from her eyes and hung like dewdrops on the tips of her long curved lashes.

And then she was bound tight against John's broad chest, the teardrops spilling onto his blue cotton shirt, her nose pressed into his shoulder and his hands stroking her head.

"Cassie," he soothed, his breath stirring up her hair, his voice vibrating with concern. "Cassandra." Without a word he swung her into his arms, lifting her without strain, carrying her to Gran's huge bed. He laid her carefully on top of the coverlet. His hands hovered over her head, smoothing her hair, brushing the tears from her cheeks, grazing her lips, checking out all the parts to make sure that she was all right, that she was whole.

Ah, but his hands couldn't soothe the darkness in her soul, the place where she wasn't whole. The darkness didn't show, it didn't reveal itself until something like this happened. Her self-loathing rose to engulf her and she rolled away from him, turning away. *How,* she thought miserably, hopelessly, *how can John Howard want a wretch like me?*

But want her he did, and he was pained to think that he had brought this upon her. He didn't want to hurt her, he would never hurt her, not willingly. He shouldn't have made such an issue about her fear for Morgana; he should have realized how his remonstrances would affect her. He knew Cassie was a gentle, caring person. He understood her affection for her friend. He even understood why she felt the way she did about flying. Remorse twisted inside him, spread to his gut, stung between his eyes so that he had to consciously steady himself.

Helplessly he reached out for her, touching her back with tentative fingers.

"Please leave me alone," she said, and the emptiness in her voice hollowed him out until he felt like a shell of a man. He wanted more than anything for her to turn to him with outstretched arms and pull his head to her soft breast and fill him up again with warmth and love.

But it did not happen. His hand fell lifelessly to the coverlet, where it rested on embroidered bluebirds of happiness stitched upon it by Cassie's grandmother, bluebirds representing a happiness that seemed at this moment quite unreachable.

Was happiness unattainable with this woman? As he sat there, he thought about it, his mind flashing back to the many times they'd made love, her openness with him, her selflessness and simplicity, her gray eyes so soft with caring or bright with laughter or glistening with emotion.

Yes, by God! He loved her. And because he loved her he would fight for her and with her against this fear that held her in thrall. In days gone by, knights had fought dragons for their ladies, and her fear was his dragon! He was no less than those knights, and Cassie was more, much more, than any mythical fair maiden. She was real and warm and loving, and she was needy. She needed him. And he owed her, he never forgot that. But that wasn't why he would joust with her enemy. He would do that because he loved her. He loved her.

So much time went by that Cassie, fraught with the violence of her emotions, thought that he had left, had crept away with the twilight, leaving her alone in the dark room. And so when his voice touched her in the night, it seemed disembodied and unreal, and she jumped at the sound of it.

"Cassandra," he said clearly and urgently, and after the shock of it passed, she remembered that he only used her full name when what he was going to say was important and real and true and meant only for her.

"Cassandra, you and I are going to tackle this fear of yours. You're not going to have to struggle through it alone anymore. I'm here, my darling. And we're going to win. You'll see, Cassandra. We're going to win."

Startled, unbelieving, she turned to find him staring at her through the darkness with eyes so intense and so compelling that she was taken aback. Something fierce and unyielding stiffened his gaze, and she wondered,

How can it be? How can he care so much what happens to me? And what does he want of me? Can I measure up? Can I? Oh, what if he's asking more than I can give? Because I'm not a strong person, I've already proved that, I've already failed enough, and I can't take another failure. Another failure, and I'll lose whatever peace I've gained, and I've worked hard for it, so hard. Oh, I wish he would go away and leave me alone, just leave me alone the way I was before he came, because I was getting to be all right then, wasn't I? Wasn't I?

But she didn't want John to go away, she never wanted him to go away, and she knew that this feeling was truer than her wanting him to leave. Mutely she held out her arms, acknowledging him with silent acceptance, and he folded her close and pressed her against the lean length of him. Slowly she relaxed in his embrace, inhaling the familiar masculine scent of him and trusting him enough to slide wearily into a deep dreamless sleep.

THE NEXT MORNING Cassie awakened when she heard Tigger meowing outside. She struggled against the bedclothes, trying to separate herself from them with no luck at all. When she finally freed herself from the lavender-scented muslin sheet that was wrapped around her legs, she became aware that someone else was letting Tigger in. There was the rattle of cat food on Tigger's aluminum pie-plate dish and an equal rattle on Bertrand's dish. There was a murmured "There, that ought to keep the two of you busy for a while," and then the barefoot sound of John's feet slapping against the wide wooden floorboards.

Cassie sank back into a warm nest of pillows. John. Last night came back to her in a wave of emotion. The way he had carried her in here, had taken care of her, had gentled her and talked to her, the things he had said. She wouldn't be alone with her fear anymore, he had told her that. She believed him.

"Good morning," he said cheerily. He stood in the doorway, his hands planted against the doorjamb on either side. His hair fell endearingly over his forehead like a shock of cornsilk, and his blue eyes gleamed. He cocked his head at her. "Whenever I see you all alone in that big brass bed, I think you're being devoured by a family of overgrown tubas." He bounded across the floor in three leaps and flung himself upon the bed. "And I have to rescue you," he said.

"Stop, you're tickling me," she gasped as his knowledgeable fingers found the sensitive skin in the curve of her waist. She began to laugh in great whoops, unable to stop.

John rolled off her and sat propped up on one arm, smiling down at her. He reached up and rapped sharply on one huge flared bedpost. "Terrible tone," he commented. "But relax, I've subdued them again."

Cassie stretched luxuriously, her hands above her head, her toes stretched out the length of the bed. "What time is it now?" she asked.

"Seven-thirty," said John promptly. His eyes softened, and his hand separated one strand from her springy mass of hair, and he pressed it to his lips. "Now that you're awake, I'd better remind you that Sharon is coming over before she goes to the Juniper Inn. Which means," he said, lying back on the pillows and pulling her over him so that she was looking down at him, her breasts cushioned against the light mat of hair on his chest, "which means that we could eat breakfast now or..." and the words were lost against her lips as his mouth closed over them. His kiss was dewy and light, but it intensified until she felt the blood pulsing through her veins like singing rivers. When he released her lips she almost couldn't breathe, because his kisses robbed her of breath.

"I think I'll take the 'or,'" she managed to say as his hands traced warm trails down her sides to cup her buttocks. Slowly and languorously, a study in slow motion, he rolled her over so that she was on the bottom, and as her eyes melted into his she was swept with a sensation of overwhelming love.

He saw it; there was no way he could not see it. He smiled down at her, and the smile was still on his lips as they touched hers.

"I love you, Cassandra," he managed to say, shaken by the reality of his words. He had thought them so often, but he had hestitated to tell her. He hadn't known what her reaction would be, before. But now, now that he saw the answering emotion in her face, he could no longer remain silent. Because if he were going to help Cassie conquer her fear, she would have to have the assurance that his love could give her.

Her answering smile was a glow brighter than the white morning sunbeams rising along the far wall of the bedroom, brighter than the radiant faces of the black-eyed Susans beneath the bedroom window, brighter than the luminous sky on a cloudless day.

"I love you, too," she whispered slowly and clearly.

If ever there was a moment when life and love merged to become one, a moment of timeless perfection that could not be any more meaningful, then this was that moment. John could only hope that he could live up to his commitment to her, and he had no illusions about the task he was taking on. Delivering Cassie whole from her phobias was going to be an arduous task; he only hoped he would be equal to it. It would be a hell of a lot different than conquering make-believe tubas. He was well aware that there was no way he could know what he was in for, because he had never tried to bring a troubled woman in line with normalcy before. Somehow he had to heal her scars for her as, unknowingly, she had healed him.

Cassie arched sinuously against him until he let his weight rest upon her, and knowing by this time how to heighten their awareness in secure familiarity, their movements built in intensity until John felt the sun burst inside him, and when he opened his eyes it was to see if she had felt the sunburst, too.

But Cassie lay passively beneath him, her cheeks flushed and her eyes closed, and the tension in her shoulders cupped by his hands beneath her told him that it hadn't been the same for her.

He nuzzled her cheek, murmuring words he only knew the shape of, knowing that whatever good things he said to her were true.

And he knew that Cassie would not truly be healed until she could feel again to the deepest measure, give of herself that which she withheld out of her own sorrow and guilt.

They would have to work on sunbursts, he thought with pleasure. And, as she guided him into her once more and he felt her instantaneous response, he lovingly began to do just that.

Chapter Ten

"You know, John, I'm going to have to let Bertrand and Rupert go back to the woods soon. If you hadn't been gone all day today, I would have asked you to take pictures of them for me," said Cassie one night about a week later as she efficiently spread popcorn kernels in Gran's old wire popcorn popper.

John hesitated. Cassie had always been casually incurious about his photographic work, probably because she was always so absorbed in her garden and with the steady stream of visitors who came to her seeking remedies, and besides, Cassie tended to blot out everything that took place off the mountain. Now was the time to tell her his true profession, if he dared. But John caught himself up short. He couldn't tell her, not until the flying issue had been resolved.

"My errands took longer than I expected" was all he said. He wished fervently that he could stop pretending.

Bertrand hobbled past and twitched his nose in the direction of the popcorn.

"Don't worry, Bertie, I'll give you some, too," Cassie said soothingly.

"Bertrand likes popcorn?"

"He loves it. I hope he'll be all right once I send him back to the great outdoors. He's become much too civilized, staying awake in the daytime and sleeping at night. That's unnatural for a skunk, you know. Skunks are supposed to be nocturnal. Also, I've been thinking that I might have to take Bertrand far away, over to Pride's Peak maybe, so he doesn't keep coming around here."

"That's a wonderful idea," said John with some relief. Bertrand immediately turned his backside on him, hissing a warning and performing the tiptoe dance with his front feet that John had learned, from a dozen or so Disney movies, meant "Beware." John, who had never learned to trust the mercurial Bertrand, leaped up and put the settle between himself and the skunk.

Cassie's hand intervened. "Take it easy, Bertrand," she said, stroking the animal along his wide white stripe. Bertrand subsided, as he always did when he felt Cassie's gentle hand on his back.

John took advantage of this opportunity to plug in the portable radio he'd bought during the week. He'd introduced it as part of his campaign to accustom Cassie to the idea that there was a real world out there somewhere. At first he'd switched on an easy-listening station when they were making love, and then he'd progressed to leaving the radio on during the hourly newscasts. Cassie had accepted it, and it had become natural for them to talk about current events and other topics that the radio introduced.

Having a radio was a small step but a necessary one, he felt. Now, with his help, Cassie was beginning to perceive the world as a nonthreatening place. He had to get her down off this mountain somehow. That would be his next campaign.

Their life, because Cassie adamantly refused to leave Flat Top Mountain, was confined. It didn't feel confining because they found so much to explore in each other, but John knew it wasn't natural to live so far removed from other people.

Cassie, kneeling at the hearth, concentrated her full attention on the popcorn, which was beginning to burst into fluffy white kernels.

"What station would you like on the radio?" he asked her.

"It doesn't matter. Anything you want." She shook the wire popper. "Did you know that there's a trick to popping popcorn over a fire? You have to let the embers die down to a certain heat, and you need to hold the wire popper high enough so that the heat'll explode the kernels without burning them."

"I'll bet your grandmother taught you how to pop corn," said John with an easy smile. The radio poured forth rippling romantic music. He adjusted the volume low.

"She did. Bring me that big earthenware bowl from the kitchen, will you, John?" asked Cassie, sparing a smile in his direction.

"Sure. Do you want more wine?"

"Mmm, no. Anyway, drinking scuppernong wine with popcorn is definitely an acquired taste, and I'm not sure I've acquired it." Cassie shook the long-handled wire popper vigorously.

John found the bowl and brought it to her, admiring the way her hair gleamed so brightly in the fire glow. These peaceful moments were, for him, equal in joy to the passion they shared in their lovemaking. Oh, he loved making love with her, loved her earthy enthusiasm for the act as well as her delicacy and thoughtfulness in the way she pleasured his body.

Aside from the physical, however, there were dimensions to his love for her that he had never found with anyone else: their early-morning walks, when it was just the two of them in the mountain wilderness, when communication came so easily and seemed so right; mealtimes, when her shining, adoring face across from his seemed the closest thing to heaven; lying together in the brass bed after the lights were out when they talked and talked, learning and loving more about each other each and every time.

Cassie heaped the popcorn in the bowl and set aside a pile of it on the hearthstones for Bertrand. Lazily she fell back on a stack of floor cushions, edging to one side so that John could join her.

"Delicious popcorn," he said, munching on a mouthful.

"Mmm," she replied, settling into the golden glow of another pleasant evening with John, liking the way he slid his arm around her so protectively, even though there was nothing to protect her from.

The radio announcer came on with the news, and Cassie and John talked in a desultory fashion about the problems in the Middle East. And then, a complete surprise: The sweet opening strains of one of Cassie's own songs began to play, and Cassie bolted upright at the high unmistakable soprano of her voice.

It was a love song she'd written for Kevin. It was sweet and tender and full of meaning, a gem of a love song, Kevin had told her.

It had been so long since she'd heard the words or even thought about them. So long since she'd sung them, but in a flash of remembrance she could see herself singing them, could recall as if it were yesterday, standing before the microphone in the glass booth at the recording studio and watching Kevin's dark eyes upon her from where he stood in another booth. She'd sung the song to Kevin that day, meaning every word from the depths of her heart, transferring her real-life emotion to the tape. She'd written the song on their third wedding anniversary and the emotion was there for anyone to hear; it had helped make the song a tremendous success, scoring number one on the charts for weeks. How dare John Howard bring that song into her house! How dare he!

She clapped her hands over her ears. "Stop it!" she screamed. "Turn it off!"

Clearly shaken, John flicked the radio switch.

"Oh, Cassie, I'm sorry," he said, stricken.

Her hands fell to her lap. "That song—it's the one song—the one song I can't bear to hear," she said in a whisper.

He opened his mouth to console her, but the words wouldn't come. He'd known she'd eventually hear her own music. But he hadn't expected it to affect her this way. Oh, why couldn't it have been some other song, the one she sang about the children romping in the pinewoods or the funny little ditty called "Watermelon Smiles?"

"I haven't heard a tape or a record of myself singing since I came here," Cassie said brokenly.

"You and Sharon play the dulcimer together. You've sung with her." He knew he had to keep her talking or she might run into her bedroom and slam the door. Cassie, always running, always retreating to the innermost chamber of herself. But not anymore. He wasn't going to let her.

"That's different," she said, blinking at him. She felt numb. The shock of it and the hurt of it had rendered her senseless; she, who had in recent weeks rediscovered the delight of her senses, who had learned to taste and touch and hear and see and feel all over again with John and through John. And now her awareness was gone again, iced over by this numbness of body and mind. Not numbness of the heart—oh, no. Her heart ached as though it had been pierced through with a dagger.

"The old songs Sharon and I sing hold no memories for me except happy ones," she went on, feeling bloodless and cold and sick. "They're not like the ones I wrote myself when I was—when I was—" She stopped and swallowed. She couldn't go one.

"When you were Kevin's wife," said John gently.

She raised her eyes to his. "Yes," she said. "Yes."

John stood up and paced the floor, running a hand through his artfully layered haircut until some of the strands stood out in bas-relief. His strong profile, with the cleft in his chin, was etched in gold against the dark background of the stone fireplace.

Suddenly he knelt before her. "Cassandra, I wish it hadn't happened this way. The two of us were feeling mellow and good about ourselves, and it seemed natural to want to enjoy music at such a time. I guess I knew that someday we'd hear your music, but I didn't expect you to react so strongly when it happened. I love your music, Cassie. So do a lot of other people."

"That part of my life is over," Cassie murmured. His blue eyes shimmered at her in earnestness. She knew he hadn't meant to hurt her. John would never hurt her.

"You're acting as if your whole *life* is over," he reminded her gently. He picked up one of her hands from her lap and raised it to his lips, kissing it tenderly. "Cassie, isn't it time for you to pick up and go on? You should face the fact that you *lived*, you didn't die with Kevin and Rory and you don't have to give up the rest of your life out of guilt."

Cassie withdrew her hand, and something behind her eyes flicked before she subdued it. "No," she whispered. "No. Don't say these things, John."

"I must say them, love. I've watched you doing backbreaking work in your garden day after day, I've stood by while you wore yourself to a frazzle mixing balms and ointments and essences that you give away to any and all who wend their way up this mountain. How long are you going to atone for their deaths?"

The words assaulted her like a physical blow. "That's my business," she said stonily.

"It's my business, too," he said as gently as he could. "It's my business because I love you. You've said you love me, too."

"I do," she said helplessly, hopelessly. "I do."

"If we're going to have any sort of life together, it can't go on like this," he told her.

Her eyes were huge and deep. "Why can't it? I'm happy, John." One hand went to smooth one of the lines that ran between his nose and mouth. Laugh lines, because he had laughed so much, and they had laughed together. He bent his head to her touch, absorbing it.

"Because, eventually, I must leave."

"No," she said, even though she knew it was true.

"Yes," he said.

The silence was terrible, and Cassie thought how illusory life was. Nothing was sure, nothing was forever. Not Kevin, not Rory, not John.

"Please go," she said. "I'd like to be alone."

"Cassie," he said in gentle reproach.

She would pluck him out as if he were a weed in her garden. No use in letting him grow bigger and stronger in her life, no use in letting him strangle her when she was just beginning to flower.

The naked anguish in her eyes made him ache with misery for her.

"We're in this together," he reminded her gently.

For the fraction of a heartbeat she thought, *no*! But then he was gathering her into his arms, and sudden tears flooded her eyes. He was so good to her, and she didn't deserve it. He spent so much time building her up, making her feel and think and do things that she would never have done on her own.

"You're so pretty, Cassie," he'd say with that smile of his, one corner of his mouth lifting slightly before the other. Or, "You mean so much to me, love," at special times when he wouldn't have had to say it. Or, "Thanks for being part of my life," when she least expected him to say such a thing—for instance, that very morning when they were working together in her kitchen, making wild-strawberry jam.

He kissed her tears away now. "Let's not give up," he said softly, "just when we're beginning to make progress. And anyway, if you don't get that skunk away from the popcorn bowl, there won't be any left for us."

Cassie pulled away from him with a watery smile and shooed Bertrand away. She took the bowl of popcorn in her arms and sat down on the floor pillows, patting the pillow beside her.

"Sit down," she said. "But before you do, how about turning the radio on again? I'd like to see if we can start the evening over. This time maybe we'll get it right."

John took his time turning on the radio, and then he eased himself down beside her.

"You've got a lot of spunk, Cassandra," he said, kissing her on the temple. Bertrand sneaked around the pile of cushions and nibbled tentatively at Cassie's hand where it was curved around the bowl.

"A lot of skunk, too," she said wryly, pushing Bertrand away, and even though they both knew it was a terrible pun, John realized that it was the first time Cassie had ever made an attempt at any kind of humor.

And so they went on from there.

"I WON'T JUST BE PLAYING for tips. The manager is going to pay me a salary. And I'm going to work every night but Sunday!" Sharon exclaimed, too excited to eat the proffered biscuits with Cassie's fresh strawberry jam.

The three of them sat on a blanket outside under the black oak tree, John having declared it the perfect day for a picnic breakfast.

"When do you start?" asked Cassie, who was delighted with Sharon's success in landing a job at the Juniper Inn.

"Tonight. And tomorrow's my birthday. A job—what a wonderful birthday present. Oh, Cassie, I'm so thrilled!"

"And rightly so," declared John, who didn't mind wolfing the biscuits the women didn't want. Cassie's strawberry jam was delicious.

"Will you come to my opening? Will you?" Sharon's glance flashed expectantly from Cassie to John and back to Cassie again.

"Oh, I—" began Cassie in a negative tone.

"Of course we will," said John warmly, warning Cassie with his eyes.

Cassie felt indignant that John would interrupt her, but then she realized why he had done it. Sharon in all likelihood had no one else to invite to her opening. The lackluster Ott family wouldn't support Sharon now; they certainly never had before.

"Wonderful," said Sharon, hopping up. "I've got to get home. I want to take up the hem in that skirt you let me borrow, Cassie, if you don't mind?"

"You may keep the skirt," Cassie told her. "The sweater, too." They were the clothes Sharon had borrowed for her audition.

"Now I'll be able to buy some new clothes of my own," Sharon said, the words bubbling over with excitement. "You have good taste, Cassie. I wish you'd come with me to shop."

"I—I'll think about it," Cassie said faintly, aware of John's eyes upon her.

"Okay. See you tonight. Oh, I'm so glad you'll be there." And with a happy wave back at them, Sharon took off at a run.

John stood up and tossed a clinging green caterpillar off the picnic blanket.

"You don't mind going to Sharon's opening, do you?" he asked.

Cassie hesitated. "I guess not. For Sharon's sake."

"What about for Cassie's sake?"

"I haven't been out to dinner for years," she reminded him.

"But things are different now," he told her as they walked back to the house.

She sent him a sideways glance and tucked her arm in his. "I've noticed," she said, and a smile teased the corners of her mouth.

He opened the door for her and they went inside.

"Today maybe you could take those pictures of Bertrand and Rupert," suggested Cassie as she stashed the picnic blanket in the chifforobe. One of the corners of the blanket caught on a piece of paper and the paper swooped to the floor. John bent to pick it up, mostly as a stall. He still hadn't really mastered the Nikon, and as for taking a picture of the irrepressible Bertrand, he'd rather pass.

"Is this anything important?" Then, because he couldn't help noticing that it was a song, complete with notes and chords and scribbled words, he inspected it more closely.

"It's nothing," said Cassie, moving to take it from him.

"Wait," he said, and because of his height he could hold it out of her reach. "I didn't know you'd been writing music again."

Cassie flushed. "Once in a while. When the mood hits me."

"Play it for me?"

"No. Oh, no, John, I couldn't."

"You don't mind my reading this, do you?"

"Well..." Cassie hesitated. Her feelings were wrapped up in the songs she had written, and it was hard to share them. But she and John were so intimate and so open with each other that she hardly wanted to refuse.

"If you don't want me to, I won't read it." His eyes were soft upon her face.

"I want you to read it," she said in a small voice, and suddenly feeling the need to do something with her hands, she rushed into the bathroom and picked up the scouring powder and sponge. She was surprised to find that her hands were trembling. She turned on the water, listening to it gurgle down the drain. What would he think about her song? What would he ever think?

For she had written it with the taste of him still on her lips late on night when she couldn't sleep after their lovemaking, when her eyes wouldn't close for the happy tears that spilled from them. She'd crept from the bed and scribbled it all down, writing quickly and without the dulcimer, hearing the music in her head. She'd titled it "For Love's Sweet Splendor," and it could have been an old song, so regional was its flavor. But the words were honest and true and unmistakably about John and Cassie and the wonder she felt at being loved by him.

Through the door she saw John walk pensively to the window, studying her song.

Let him like it, she thought, because she felt suddenly shy that he was reading the words.

"Cassie," he said quietly.

She dropped the sponge and the cleanser and grabbed the cold porcelain sink, her heart beating wildly.

"Come here," he said.

She turned off the water. Slowly she came out of the bathroom, not daring to look full into his face. When her eyes met his, she saw that his eyes brimmed with wonder and shone in admiration.

"How well you put it into words, my love," he said softly.

She went and stood before him, gazing up at him. "It was written for you," she said.

He slid his arms around her and held her close to his heart; the piece of paper crackled behind her and John's heartbeat thumped beneath her ear. She closed her eyes and was thankful for him and the changes he had wrought in her life and in her thinking. The moment would have become even more intimate had a car not rounded the curve.

"One of your seekers," said John, pulling away before kissing Cassie lightly beside the ear. He had taken to calling the people who came up the mountain for herbal remedies seekers, because Cassie didn't like them to be called patients and he didn't think they could properly be called clients.

This particular seeker drove a deep blue Lincoln Continental, parking it under the black oak tree.

"Let me put this music away," said Cassie, taking the crumpled piece of paper from John. She stuffed it in the chifforobe drawer.

"Wait," said John, seeing other papers in the drawer as well. "Do you have more songs like that?"

Cassie sent him a long, mute look. Since John had entered her life, she had given up keeping her journal. Instead, she now channeled her thoughts and energies into her music, much as she had done before the accident. Only now there was a more serious, introspective dimension to her songs.

"Yes," she said after a long silence. "I'll let you see them if you like."

"I would like. I would like very much indeed." His voice was infinitely reassuring.

But there wasn't time to share her music now, not with the car door slamming outside and someone's footsteps crunching on the gravel drive.

Cassie smoothed her ever-unruly hair and straightened her dress before glancing quickly at her reflection in the oval mirror on the chifforobe. At the knock on the door, Cassie hurried to open it. John was in the kitchen, rummaging in the freezer for ice cubes, then getting a drink of water. He preferred to stay as much out of the way as possible when Cassie's seekers were around.

But Bertrand didn't. The skunk refused to make himself scarce when Cassie had company; his curious nature brought him out sniffing and scampering and making mischief. He seemed to delight in people's shock at seeing a real live skunk running loose inside the house.

Cassie stumbled over Bertrand on her way to the door, but the second barrage of knocks was so peremptory that she didn't take time to remove the skunk to the spare bedroom as she might have otherwise. Instead, she merely nudged him aside with her toe as she slung the door open.

On the front porch stood a familiar stocky figure wearing the perennially rumpled suit with which she identified him. She stood and stared in amazement while a broad smile lit up his face, so that she could see the gold caps gleaming on his back teeth. Bald, snub-nosed, disheveled and stout, he was a funny-looking man who looked as though his vertical and horizontal controls had gone out of whack—but what was her former agent doing here?

"Kajurian!" she exclaimed, and she held out her arms, ready to envelop him in a big welcoming hug.

At that moment, Bertrand, who had managed to slip past Cassie, hissed and stomped his front feet, but Cassie's attention was elsewhere.

And so Bertrand let go.

Chapter Eleven

"Tomato juice," said Cassie stoically. "It's the best thing in the world for getting out skunk odor."

Kajurian looked glum. "I read somewhere the smell lasts for days." He stood, forlorn and reeking, in the middle of Cassie's kitchen as Cassie rummaged through the small pantry, searching for a can of tomato juice.

"It's on the higher shelf," said John, reaching over Cassie's head to get a grip on the big can. He was thankful he hadn't been Bertrand's target, and his sympathies were with Kajurian. The trigger-happy Bertrand had been banished to the shed until further notice.

"What a welcome you give me," moaned Kajurian. "Morgana warned me that you probably wouldn't be overjoyed to see me, Cassie, but I didn't know about your secret weapon."

"Bertrand doesn't like men," said Cassie. "Morgana should have mentioned that. Anyway, did Morgana send you?"

"Not exactly. I wanted to come see you long ago. I talked to Morgana when she came back from here, and she said, 'Kajurian, you go on up that mountain and talk some sense into Cassie.' Now look what's happened. I should have stayed back in L.A. There it's only smog, not skunks. Smog I'm used to."

Cassie held out the can of tomato juice. "Take this in the bathroom and wash yourself in it."

Kajurian looked at her as though she were crazy.

"I mean it. It'll work. Pour this juice through your hair and then wash it out with shampoo. Rub it all over your skin before you take a bath. Tomato juice gets rid of skunk odor, and it's the only thing I know that will."

"You got any vodka? Tomato juice and vodka is okay. I feel like getting drunk, all right. I sure don't feel like taking any bath in tomato juice."

"Go," said Cassie, pushing him toward the bathroom. "You'll find towels in the cupboard. John will bring in your luggage so you can put clean clothes on afterward."

"Here are the keys to the car," said Kajurian morosely, handing them over to John. "My suitcase is in the trunk."

After Kajurian had disappeared into the bathroom, Cassie hurried to fling wide the few windows that weren't already open.

John went outside and eyed Bertrand, who had curled up underneath Cassie's station wagon in the open shed. The rank odor of skunk hung in the air. No doubt about it, Bertrand's stay here would be short now that this had happened. Cassie would surely see the need to get rid of the insufferable creature. She was lucky it hadn't happened earlier. Hell, *he* was lucky that it hadn't happened to him.

John carried in Kajurian's suitcase and handed clothes through the bathroom door in Kajurian's direction. Cassie went out to the shed to confront Bertrand, taking Tigger with her. John watched through a window as she knelt beside the station wagon, talking earnestly to the skunk. John repressed a smile at the sight of Tigger, who was twitching his nose and listening in smug superiority from the hood of the station wagon where he'd perched.

Kajurian emerged from the bathroom, holding at arm's length, the clothes he'd been wearing. His face was screwed into a veritable prune of distaste.

"We'll have to bury my suit," Kajurian mourned.

"I'll bundle those clothes into a plastic garbage bag for now," said John, producing the bag. Kajurian dropped the clothes into it. "Maybe the local dry cleaner can do something about the suit," John said, but he doubted it. Actually, he thought Kajurian would be better off without it. The suit was probably a good twenty years old and looked it.

"Well, Kajurian," said Cassie, coming back in. "You're smelling better."

"Hmph. I'm not the only thing around here that stinks" was Kajurian's disgruntled reply.

"What in the world are you talking about?" said Cassie.

"You. Specifically, you hiding up here on this mountain. Come home, Cassie. Show business needs you. Morgana needs you. *I* need you. More to the point, my agency needs you."

"Why? So you can lose more money at the race track?"

Cassie's knowing remark hit home. "Can I help it if I gamble a little? If I wasn't a gambler, I'd never have survived in this business. Come back to L.A., Cassie. Let me set up a comeback appearance for you. Maybe in Las Vegas. How about it, eh? We'll make millions together, you and me, like we did in the old days."

"I don't need millions. I have more money than I'll ever need, thanks to Kevin's wise investments. I'm sorry, Kajurian, but it's impossible. I hope you'll be able to stay the rest of the week, but when you go home, you go alone."

John interrupted. "Look, I'll let you two hash this over together, all right? I need to get ready for Sharon's opening tonight. Kajurian, we're going to the Juniper Inn for dinner. Will you join us?"

"An opening? What kind of opening?" Kajurian's ears, attuned for more than forty years to show business, perked up at the mention of an opening.

In a flash, it was as though Cassie saw a road unfurling in front of her, a road as gleaming and as inviting as the yellow brick road to Oz. Only this particular road led down out of the wilds and across the country. It led to show business, and on it she pictured Sharon Ott. And at the end of the road Cassie saw not Oz, but Ott, and the name so reviled here in Scot's Cove was shining in lights.

Rose o' Sharon Ott would never have a better opportunity than the one that was standing in front of Cassie now. Kajurian was tops in the business.

"It's a local singer," said Cassie diffidently, belying her eagerness to expose Sharon's talent to the man who could help her most. "She's a pupil of mine. She plays the mountain dulcimer."

"You mean there's more than one dulcimer player? More than one Cassandra Dare? This I do not believe." But Cassie noticed that Kajurian looked uncommonly interested.

"There aren't many dulcimer players with a voice like this girl's," said Cassie. She shot John a look. "Am I right, John?"

John realized exactly what Cassie was up to. "You're absolutely right, Cassie. Sharon can sing."

"Like you? She sings like you?"

"Not like me. Different. She has an amazing range, and her voice is low and—well, why try to describe it? You'll go with us tonight to the Juniper Inn."

"I thought you never went off this mountain. Morgana said—"

"For Sharon Ott I'm going to the Juniper Inn. Come back around six, John. We'll have a glass of scuppernong wine before we go." The wine had put Morgana in a mellow mood; maybe it would do the same for Kajurian.

"Scuppernong wine, she says," complained Kajurian. "Never in my life have I drunk scuppernong wine. What is it, anyway?"

And so Kajurian's train of thought was deflected from Cassie to Sharon to scuppernongs, and after Kajurian had retired to the guest room to dress for the evening, Cassie flipped through the clothes in her closet.

Morgana would be aghast if she could see the meager condition of her wardrobe, decided Cassie. She hadn't bought any clothes in the past couple of years. Finally she selected a loosely fitted but nevertheless classic and sexy silk dress in cornflower blue. No panty hose, so she'd have to go barelegged. But her legs in the strappy sandals were so tan that the lack of hose didn't matter.

Promptly at six, John drove the Chevrolet into the side yard next to Kajurian's rented Lincoln, and Cassie plied Kajurian with scuppernong wine for the next hour. The wine mellowed Kajurian to the point where he was able to laugh off the incident with Bertrand, and Cassie was grateful for that. She wanted him to be in a good mood when he first saw and heard Sharon.

They rode down the mountain, the three of them in John's car, with Cassie sitting up front with John and Kajurian riding in the back. Cassie made no comment when they passed the Otts' tin-roofed shack, and neither did John. Cassie raised a hand to wave at the hollow-cheeked man sitting hunkered over on the porch, but she received no answering wave. The man was Sharon's father. Cassie wondered if he knew his daughter had an opening that night at the Juniper Inn, or if he would even care if he did know.

John glanced over at Cassie. She looked beautiful in that silk she was wearing. It was about time he saw her wearing a dress she could do something for. He had never seen her dressed to go out. He had never seen her with makeup on. They had never ridden in a car together. The things that ordinary people took for granted in a relationship were missing in theirs.

He wondered if Cassie thought about these things, if she herself realized what a big step this was for her. The Cassie he had encountered in his first days on the mountain had been much too afraid to dress up and go out. She had lacked confidence in herself and trust in others. He had given her these things. The thought pleased him, and when she glanced questioningly in his direction, he smiled. She smiled back. It was working, he thought jubilantly. His plan to draw her inexorably back into the mainstream of life was actually working!

The restaurant was crowded with an influx of tourists, and a long line of would-be patrons coiled out the door.

"I called ahead for reservations," said John, shouldering through the crowd. Cassie clung to his hand, almost overcome by the people, their talk, their laughter, their unaccustomed mingled scents of perfume and after-shave lotion.

"Our table is ready," John told them after a conference with the hostess. Sliding a protective arm around Cassie, warming her with a reassuring smile, John guided her smoothly through the crowd as Kajurian followed behind.

The Juniper Inn was a white-frame former mansion, now refurbished and remodeled into a restaurant. Fireplaces, banked with huge sprays of rhododendrons in the summer, graced every room. Walls had been torn out and rooms rearranged so that each dining area opened up into a large central space where there was a small stage. The windows revealed a spectacular mountain view.

The three of them were seated at a damask-draped table near the stage. Cassie inhaled a deep nervous breath and looked around her. The very energy of this place assaulted her senses: The clinking of silver, the clanking of dishes one against the other, the odor of food, the laughing, the drinking, the talking. Cassie clenched her fingers together in her lap, feeling slightly queasy.

She hadn't expected her reentry into society to be accompanied by physical symptoms. But it had been so long, so long! And she was so accustomed to her solitude, her animals. Lately she had reluctantly opened her life to include one other person, John. Now she was out in public, actually sitting among people who might recognize her, for the first time since she'd moved to Flat Top Mountain. And here was Kajurian, grinning his gold-toothed, hopeful grin at her from across the candlelit table, and she knew she'd have to deal with him sooner or later, would have to convince him once and for all that she wasn't going back to L.A. All of this was almost too much to handle at one time.

John's hand clasped hers beneath the table and she clung to it. His knee pressed comfortingly close to her thigh. Kajurian was gazing off into the distance, at the stunning mountain view beyond the windows.

"I love you," mouthed John silently.

"I love you, too," she pantomimed in return.

They smiled at each other, sharing the secret. They squeezed hands. And Cassie felt better immediately.

The waiter was bringing their dessert when Sharon Ott appeared. The girl slipped in quietly from a side door to the stage, where there was a high stool, a floor microphone and nothing else. If Sharon was nervous, Cassie couldn't detect it.

"That's Sharon," she whispered to Kajurian, who immediate sat up and took notice.

Sharon wore Cassie's skirt, shortened to a length not too long and not too short. The sweater Cassie had given her outlined Sharon's curves nicely, accentuating the swell of her breasts without delineating them too clearly. The sweater, a soft shade of coral, emphasized the natural tint of Sharon's strawberry-blond hair, and the full-blown rose with which she'd pinned back her curving locks on one side brought out the pale beauty of Sharon's translucent skin.

"She's a looker, Cassie," said Kajurian admiringly, wolfing a forkful of peach pie without taking his eyes off Sharon. "You didn't tell me she was a looker."

"I figured you'd find out for yourself," Cassie whispered back. Inwardly she was delighted that Kajurian considered Sharon "a looker." Kajurian didn't know the words "beautiful," "exquisite" or even "gorgeous." To Kajurian, you were either a looker or not, and Cassie knew that he considered being a looker of primary importance in promoting young hopefuls to stardom.

The man who introduced Sharon wasted little time with preliminaries. He simply stepped up onstage, adjusted the microphone and spoke into it.

"And now, ladies and gentleman, for your listening enjoyment—the first time on any stage, Rose o' Sharon."

A spotlight switched on, illuminating Sharon's lovely features, and Cassie's throat tightened. Sharon was every bit as beautiful onstage as Cassie had known she would be.

Cassie remembered the first time she herself had ever summoned the nerve to perform in public for pay; it had been at a civic-club convention at Myrtle Beach. She'd been so scared that she'd hardly been able to force out the words of her first song.

But Sharon did not seem nervous. Sharon smiled easily and brushed her hair back over her shoulder in that languid way of hers, and then she bent her head over the dulcimer for a moment so that the lights played off her hair in all its bright glory, and at last she lifted her head and began to sing a John Denver song that Cassie found ideally suited to the occasion, the instrument and the singer.

Kajurian seemed spellbound. Cassie glanced at John, and he lifted his eyebrows. She nodded in silent reply. They were both thinking that Kajurian would not be sitting as he was, his forgotten forkful of pie raised in midair, if he had not been hypnotized by Sharon's performance.

And hypnotized Kajurian was. Not only was this girl a looker, but she could sing. Sharon Ott possessed that rare quality, a quality you couldn't begin to describe, but which anyone worth his salt in the business recognized when he saw it. Charisma, some people called it. The girl was a natural, a natural! Like Cassie had been. Only different. But marketable. Definitely marketable.

The dying chords of the first song faded away, and Cassie, joining in with the rest of the audience, applauded until the palms of her hands ached.

"What do you think?" whispered Cassie to Kajurian, although she knew what the answer would be.

"She's fantastic," said Kajurian. "Why didn't you tell me she was fantastic?"

And then Sharon lit into "Darling Cora" so that the rhythm filled the air and captured the attention of the audience once more, and the applause afterward was even louder than before.

"I had no idea that Sharon would be able to perform so well in front of an audience," marveled Cassie to John.

"She's wonderful," John agreed. "But you deserve the credit for teaching her."

"Not I," objected Cassie. "She's gone beyond anything I ever taught her. Far beyond." She turned her eyes to her pupil, who now sang an age-old mountain ballad with feeling and strength.

"I must talk with her," said Kajurian after the next number. "Would she come to California to work? Or has she got a thing about staying up on that mountain like you?"

Cassie considered this. Lord knows, Sharon *needed* to get out of Scot's Cove if she were to break out of the Ott cycle of despair and poverty. As ambitious as

Sharon had proved herself to be, Cassie was sure that Sharon would be willing to accept any employment that would help her up and out. But then, Sharon was also a simple mountain girl, and although she'd confided to Cassie that she longed to make something of herself, Sharon had strong ties to her younger brothers and sisters and an affection and sympathy for her mother. When it came right down to it, would Sharon leave Flat Top Mountain?

"I don't know," said Cassie finally. "I honestly don't know."

"After she leaves the stage, I'll go to her. You'll come with me, Cassie, won't you? She knows you. You can explain to her, maybe, what it means to sign with a top agent in the business." Unconsciously, Kajurian puffed up with pride. Cassie smiled. But of course, Kajurian was right. He *was* tops in the business.

Sharon sang for another twenty minutes, twenty minutes during which Kajurian sat on the edge of his chair, narrowed his eyes at her speculatively, and jittered his knees up and down, unwittingly shaking the table. The girl was a prize. Not like Cassie. Completely different. But a singer, a good singer.

Not a great singer—after all, her voice was completely untrained. Kajurian thought she'd need a few singing lessons; not many, because Kajurian wouldn't like the girl's naturalness to be beaten and subdued into something artificial. Maybe a few gigs at small clubs in L.A. first, then on to opening the show for larger acts on tour. Maybe some television. She'd look great on TV.

As her closing number Sharon chose Cassie's award-nominated theme song from Morgana's documentary, the song "Where the Heart Is." And as she sang it, Sharon focused her eyes on Cassie, her gratitude to her teacher and mentor shining on her face. Cassie sat spellbound as Sharon sang. The phrasing, the technique—Sharon sang the song as Cassie had imagined it should be sung, with a resonance to her low-pitched voice that Cassie had never been able to achieve with her own soprano. Suddenly, although Cassie was entirely caught up in the warmth of Sharon's rendition, a chill vibrated through her bones. In her heart Cassie knew with certainty that Sharon's life had changed forever. Sharon was going to be a star.

Sharon slipped down from the stool, bowed, then bowed again as the applause rippled anew from the audience. When it seemed as though the applause was not going to stop, Sharon bowed in Cassie's direction and swept a hand in her direction. Cassie felt all eyes upon her, and she heard the surprised voices whispering, "Cassandra Dare, Cassandra Dare."

The applause began all over again, but now it was meant for her.

Cassie blanched. The color drained from her face, and she felt dizzy. All these people, all looking at her, all puzzled and curious. They'd know about the airplane accident and how she'd disappeared from the face of the earth. She wanted to run. She wanted to run without looking back. She could not face those people, could not be Cassandra Dare again. Could not.

But John was smiling at her, squeezing her hand. His eyes on her were intense and blue, and there was a strength in them that communicated itself to her.

"They want you to acknowledge their applause," he urged softly.

Gripping his hand, weak with the effort of having to respond to an audience again, Cassie stumbled to her feet. She bowed slightly, feeling awkward, feeling embarrassed. John held her hand tightly, and he stood to help her with her chair when she sat down again after the applause had finally faded and Sharon had slipped from the stage out the side door.

"Oh," Cassie said faintly, "that was so unexpected."

"They love 'Where the Heart Is,'" said John. "They wanted to show you their appreciation. Look, they've all gone back to eating and drinking now."

It was true. People were eating, talking, laughing. Except for an occasional nod and glance in Cassie's direction, no one was paying attention to her. No one was asking for anything more than Cassie had already given; no one was pressing her or inconsiderately interrupting her privacy. Cassie closed her eyes in relief. She was going to be left in peace. She did not have to be Cassandra Dare again. No one expected a performance out of her. Slowly her grip on John's hand relaxed.

"Come on," said Kajurian. "We must go to the girl. She'll have a second show, don't you think? I must talk to her before that." He stood up and tossed his napkin down with an expectant look toward Cassie. "Cassie? You said you would take me to her."

She shot a look at John. "Will you come with us?"

"No, Cassie," he said firmly. "I don't know anything about the business. You and Kajurian see to Sharon while I see to the check." He grinned at her encouragingly; he was proud of the way she was handling herself, she knew. He released her hand, and she went with Kajurian, sparing one backward glance at John. His eyes were upon her, and when he saw her looking back at him, he winked.

"GO TO CALIFORNIA?" said Sharon blankly.

"Yes. If you sign with me, that's what you must do."

Sharon swiveled her head toward Cassie, her hair arcing out behind her. "Cassie?"

"It's true, Sharon. Kajurian wants to sign you. That means he'll try to get bookings for you on the Coast. It's a wonderful opportunity for you if you choose to take it."

"The Coast?"

"The West Coast," Kajurian filled in. The girl was clearly taken by surprise.

"I never dreamed..." began Sharon, but then she couldn't go on. In her wildest imaginings she had not foreseen being approached by an honest-to-goodness agent who would promise her a career in show business, a career that might take her to the same heights Cassie had reached.

Sharon lowered herself onto a straight chair in the closet that served as a dressing room at the Juniper Inn. "I've just performed in public for the first time," she said dazedly. "I was real excited to be getting a paycheck at last. Now you're offering me this big chance, and, well, I can't believe it. I just can't." Her eyes sought Cassie's.

Cassie sank down on her knees beside Sharon. "Kajurian is being honest with you. He was my agent for years, he helped me get my start. He can do the same for you, if you're willing to work."

"I want to work. I want to be a success. I love singing, you know that, Cassie. But leaving home..." Her voice drifted off. "My ma would have to take care of the kids by herself. That would throw a lot of responsibility on my sister Bonnie. Pa is no help. He's drunk half the time. I'm not sure I can leave Ma and Bonnie." Sharon's eyes swam with troubled tears.

Kajurian was afraid that this wonderful find, this discovery of his, was about to turn him down. He could not conceive of anyone turning down a career such as the one he was offering Sharon Ott, but it had happened before and would happen again. After all, he reasoned, look at Cassie. She made it all the way to the top and then she quit singing in public, quit writing music, quit everything she had worked so hard to get.

"Miss Ott—"

"Sharon," she corrected. No one had ever called her Miss Ott before.

"Sharon," he said patiently. "Talk to Cassie here. She can reassure you, tell you what the life is like, tell you what it's like when you make it big."

"Do I have to decide right away?"

"No, no, my dear. Of course not. You think a little, you talk a little. You ask your mother's advice if you want to. I'm not going to force you to do anything. But I'm telling you, with your talent and your looks, you're making a mistake if you don't sign on with Kajurian." He smiled at the girl kindly. He sympathized with her feelings; he'd been through this with other young kids. Wanting, they all had the wanting to succeed, but sometimes they were unsure if they had the will. And it took will, no doubt about it.

"Sharon, we'll stay for the second show," said Cassie, rising to her feet. "We can talk about it later, just the two of us, if you'd like. Okay?"

"Okay." Sharon smiled gratefully. She looked up at Kajurian. "It's just that I'm so surprised, you know," she said, pleading for understanding.

"I know," he said, patting her on the shoulder in a fatherly manner. "You take your time. I'll be staying here for—" and he paused, because after the skunk had sprayed him, he'd wanted to leave immediately. Now that he was hot on the trail of someone he perceived to be the heir to the Cassandra Dare tradition, however, he had changed his mind. "I'll be staying here until you decide," he amended.

Cassie and Kajurian joined John at their table and saw Sharon's second show which, if anything, was even better than her first.

"A star," mumbled Kajurian during their walk to the parking lot afterward. "That girl could be a star."

They heard a shout from somewhere behind them, and they turned to see Sharon running toward them, her face pale in the glare of the parking-lot lights. "Cassie," she called, and then stopped uncertainly.

"It's all right," said Cassie encouragingly.

"I thought—I mean, if you think it's a good idea—that you and I could maybe ride home together?" It was clear to all of them that she wanted to talk privately with Cassie.

"Why don't you?" urged John. "Kajurian and I will be all right on our own."

"Okay," said Cassie, and the relief on Sharon's face was evident.

"I'm driving your station wagon," Sharon reminded her. "It's parked over this way."

On the way back to Flat Top Mountain, Cassie drove because Sharon declared herself too excited to attempt it.

"Oh, Cassie, tell me what to do! I'm so afraid!" Sharon sank deep into the corner of the station wagon's front seat, nibbling on a thumbnail.

Cassie kept her eyes on the bright red pinpoints ahead on the highway, the taillights of John's rented Chevrolet.

"I can't tell you what to do," she said gently. "I can only tell you what it would be like if you signed with Kajurian."

"Tell me," said Sharon, and she sounded as though she were holding her breath.

And so Cassie told her about the excitement of auditions, the disappointment of learning that you hadn't landed the job, the anger when you thought no one appreciated your talent, the joy when someone finally did. Talking about it made the whole scene come back to her in vivid detail, took her back to the past. Those days had been wonderful days, she realized with surprise. The anticipation of success had fortified her with energy, and joining with Kevin to work toward a common goal had been exhilarating. Until now, she had buried her past so successfully that she had forgotten the past's importance in the overall picture of her life.

"If I don't go, I'll always wonder if I could have made it big," said Sharon wistfully. "Did you feel that way when you started, Cassie?"

"I knew I had to either go for it or work in a cone factory for the rest of my life. I watched a boring, monotonous factory job wear my mother down and wear her out. She had to support me after my father ran out on her, and that's why she worked so hard. Mom told me, 'Cassie, get out of this town. Make something of yourself.' And so I did."

Cassie remembered with love the fierceness of her mother's ambition for her. Her mother had left her own home with Gran on Flat Top Mountain to marry neither wisely nor well; she had desperately wanted something better for Cassie, her only child. She died shortly after Cassie had married Kevin, never to know how her own ambition had fired her daughter's success. Dear

Mom. She had infused Cassie with her optimism, her determination, her longing for something better in life. Without her mother's faith in her, Cassie would never have summoned the courage to leave home.

But Sharon's mother was not like Cassie's. Sharon's mother had never been supportive, had never shown in any way that she hoped for a better life for any of her offspring. Sharon had no one to boost her up and over.

No one, that is, except Cassie herself.

Chapter Twelve

They had made love in John's bed only twice before, but that night, after taking Sharon home, Cassie had needed John, needed to be held by him and loved by him and, most of all, to talk with him. Which they did as they lay peacefully wrapped in each other's arms, the weak springs of the lumpy mattress having rolled them to the middle of the bed.

"I told Sharon the basics about the kind of life she's considering," said Cassie in a troubled voice. "But there are other things I can't tell her, that she'll have to learn from experience."

"Like what?" asked John, his sweet voice disturbing the hair above her ear.

Cassie paused to lift her face to John's and brush her lips gently across his cheek.

"If Sharon signs with Kajurian, she'll be sucked into a demanding life, not to mention a perilous one."

"Perilous? You make it sound like an undertow. I know all about undertows from my surfing days."

"Show business can be like an undertow, John. You're sucked in and tossed out to sea, and sometimes there's no getting back. Oh, there's so much hustle and hassle in show business, and the life-style is, well, freewheeling, and all too often there are pressures to get involved in drugs. I was lucky that I had Kevin to protect me. He made sure that no one used me, John, or set me up or capitalized on my fame or got away with any of the other things that could have destroyed me. That kind of life is a lot for Sharon to deal with, fresh off this mountain. It worries me."

"Let Kajurian worry about it. Let Sharon worry about it. It's her life, after all." He lifted her fingertips to his lips and kissed them gently, one by one, determined to take her mind off these problems.

"Sharon is so innocent. She couldn't know what she'd be getting into. And yet I don't see any other way for her to achieve anything unless it's with her music and her voice. What if Sharon were to end up like all the rest of the Otts? What a waste that would be." Cassie fell silent, thinking about it.

"When you think of the alternatives, then, signing with Kajurian still seems like the best deal for Sharon." John nibbled gently at Cassie's earlobe, and his breath sent delightful tremors rippling through her. She closed her eyes and slid her leg over his, feeling him quicken against her thigh.

"Yes, but it's still a profession unforgiving of mistakes, a life that demands a tithe. So much of you given here, so much of you taken there...ah, that feels good."

"So much of you here, so much of you there," he said lazily, trailing his fingers across her breasts and down her stomach to the soft warm skin of her abdomen.

"So much more of *you*," she said, touching him, giving herself over to the feelings because she knew he thought she was worrying too much. And when he realized he had captured her complete attention, his lips against hers curved into a smile before becoming much, much more serious.

Cassie left later, flitting into the blue-white moonlight of the clearing outside John's cabin, her silk-clad figure shimmering briefly like a muted blue-and-silver moonbeam before she disappeared into the stark black shadows of the woods. She hadn't wanted him to walk her home. It might disturb Kajurian, who was tired from his trip, she'd said.

Always concerned and caring about others, that was Cassie. If only she could care about herself!

But she was making progress. John was proud of the way Cassie had handled herself at the Juniper Inn. He, more than anyone else, knew what courage it had taken for Cassie to venture off the mountain for Sharon's opening. And she had done it out of her love for Sharon. Cassie would go out of her way to do anything for anyone else, but because she still felt guilty, she felt unworthy of even the smallest consideration and therefore would do little for herself.

Eventually this quality of Cassie's, this caring quality, which, conversely, made John admire her and despair of her at the same time, would be the very quality that would save her.

It was, John saw now, the key to Cassie's own deliverance from herself. And now, he would begin to fit the key into the lock that had imprisoned Cassie for so long. When she was free, he also would be free—free at last to tell Cassie the truth about himself.

"YOU MEAN YOU'VE GOT MORE? More of these songs?" Kajurian stood in front of the old chifforobe, clutching pieces of paper with scribbled words, scribbled chords.

"Some," hedged Cassie.

"Some? Many!" Kajurian scooped more papers up out of the drawer. "What do you say I take these and get them written out proper, try to get them published?"

"Oh, but—" Cassie shot a doubtful look toward John.

"They're lovely songs, Cassie," John said gently. "I think you should publish them." He had seen them all by this time, and he understood enough about music to be able to piece Cassie's songs together in his head, to understand how they would sound if played and sung. The songs had been inspired by Cassie's love for him, he knew, and because of that pure outpouring of love, expressed so poignantly and yet with such grandeur, they were very special songs.

Cassie's eyes held John's for a long moment, exchanging a look of utter love and devotion.

"All right," she said to Kajurian with a sigh. "Go ahead. Take them."

Kajurian smiled his gold-toothed grin. "Oh, they will get published," he assured her. "After 'Where the Heart Is,' you could write the alphabet on a piece of paper and sign your name to it, and it would be published. You're still a hot property, Cassie."

Cassie did not reply, but watched silently as Kajurian tucked her songs carefully into his briefcase.

"MRS. OTT, I STOPPED BY to answer any questions you might have about Sharon's signing with Mr. Kajurian."

"Don't have no questions."

"Surely you'll want to know what kind of contract he's offering, the terms of it—"

"Don't know nothing about contracts."

"Sharon asked me to speak to you, to put any of your fears to rest."

"I've got a pack of young'uns here, and if Sharon goes off, Bonnie will have to do Sharon's work. That's my biggest fear. Who's going to keep an eye on Riley when he's big enough to walk?"

"If you'd like to meet Mr. Kajurian, he'd be happy to speak with you. You won't have to pay Sharon's way to California. I'll be more than happy to take care of that expense."

"Sharon ain't got enough money to get to California, for sure. But I don't need to meet your Mr. Kaj—Kaj—"

"Kajurian."

"Like I say, I don't need to meet him. Reckon Sharon's old enough to do what she wants to do. Can't keep her. Can't hold her down. One less mouth to feed."

"Mr. Kajurian wants you to know that Sharon is a talented girl and that she has a wonderful future ahead of her."

"That's good. Maybe she'll send us some money home. Tell her that, will you? To send money to her mother?"

"CASSIE. MAKE SENSE. This is an invitation to sing at the American Association of Film Arts Awards Spectacular. You'll be carried live on millions of television screens all over the country, and all they want you to do is sing 'Where the Heart Is.' What a way to start a comeback! What a chance! A few years ago, you would have died for a chance like that! What's with you, Cassie?"

"I don't want to perform anymore," Cassie said, her lips set in a stubborn line.

"You don't want to perform! You don't want to perform!" Kajurian raised his eyes to the heavens in despair. "What do I tell Morgana? That you don't care about publicizing her documentary? And what do I tell the AAFA committee? That you turn them down? Do you know what the AAFA will do? They'll be so insulted that they will blacklist you forever. What do I tell them, Cassie?"

"Tell them," said Cassie slowly, an idea burgeoning, "tell them this, Kajurian. Tell them that Rose o' Sharon will sing 'Where the Heart Is' at the AAFA Awards Spectacular. Tell them *that*, Kajurian."

"I'M GOING TO DO IT, Cassie, I'm going to sign with Kajurian. But I'm scared out of my mind. Oh, Cassie, I can't go to California all alone! Why, I've never been any farther than Asheville, and that was on my high-school class trip! Cassie, you've got to come with me out to L.A.! Cassie? Cassie!"

IT WAS A GOLDEN-TREE AFTERNOON on Pride's Peak, the leaves on the hickory trees at the edge of the meadow shimmering golden in the bright sunlight. Cassie and John walked hand in hand through a daisy field, knee-deep in a dazzling profusion of flowers. Today Cassie seemed happier, more relaxed, than she had been in the past few days.

"I hope we've done the right thing, John," she said. "Bertrand seemed so unsure of himself when we let him out of the box."

"Don't worry," said John wryly. "Bertrand has proved beyond a doubt that he can defend himself."

"But he was with me for so long. What if he can't adjust? Oh, I shouldn't have kept him; I should have let him go as soon as he was well. I was just fooling myself when I said he wasn't strong enough to go back to the wild. But I was lonely, and it was nice to have the animals in the house."

"You're not lonely anymore. And Bertrand will be all right. So will Rupert. Rupert will be scooping trout out of that brook by nightfall, I'll bet."

"I'm glad you took their pictures, John, so I'll have something to remember them by."

John didn't reply. The night before he had struggled with clumsy fingers to load the film into the camera, and the shots that morning of Bertrand and Rupert were the first actual photos he'd ever taken with the Nikon.

He noticed that Cassie's limp seemed more pronounced.

"Let's stop here for a moment," he said. "I'm ready for a rest." John knew by now never to ask Cassie if her leg hurt. She would always deny it, would push herself to the limit of her endurance to keep up with him rather than admit any pain. So he had learned to gauge her limits and to pace himself accordingly.

They sank down in the middle of the field, which sloped down to a swiftly running stream. In the distance, the sky foamed here and there into billowing cloudlets teasing the mountaintops. A cool, unfevered sun gilded their bodies, and a whisper-soft breeze scattered Cassie's worries away. The problems of what to do about Sharon's career and the pressures of Kajurian's needling seemed far, far away.

"Did you know that the Anglo-Saxons called daisies 'day's eyes'?" John asked as he sifted through the basket of daisies he and Cassie had gathered earlier.

"Mmm, no. I didn't know that," said Cassie lazily, stretching and leaning back until her head rested on his thigh. From this position, she and John seemed centered beneath a blanket of blue sky bordered with daisy lace.

"Well, they did," he said, proceeding to weave flowers into her hair. "Eventually 'day's eye' evolved into the word 'daisy.'"

"What are you doing?" Cassie wanted to know. His fingers felt cool against her warm scalp.

The pungent scent of broken daisy stems hung green and seminal in the air around them, stirring her senses with an unexpected pang of desire; she gazed up at John through heavy-lidded eyes.

"I've spangled your hair with day's eyes," he said, swooping down to kiss her on the tip of her nose.

A butterfly danced by on the air, a monarch butterfly with delicate black-veined wings. For a moment it lit on John's shoulder, and Cassie reached to brush it away. Her fingers lingered on the chambray of his shirt, and, in an abrupt change of mood, John bent over her, his hands gentle against her sun-warmed cheek as he cupped her face and captured her lips in a kiss as warm and as sweet as honey.

Cassie swirled down into the sensation of melting lips, his fingers tangling in her hair. Daisy petals floating across her face as they drifted down in a flurry of white. Time stopped and then started again, slower now, everything rolling along in slow motion as John's fingertips fluttered down her arm, pausing with strong, sure pressure before curving delicately around one breast.

She curled her hands around his neck, the throb of his pulse heavy against one thumb, and then she twined her fingers together behind him. The muscles of his back rippled as he shifted position and pressed against her, the roughness of his shirt welcome against her tingling skin.

It was good, Cassie thought hazily, to be able to lose yourself in this sweet, easy pleasure of the senses, to be able to shut the world away simply by opening the door to exquisite sensory experience, to draw from it a certain solace. John had shown her the way, guided her along the path and made her open that door, and she was glad. Oh, yes, glad, and she had not only opened the door but opened her whole self to him. There was nothing that she could not share with John, no part of her life that was not his to know. His love was healing her, making her whole again. Gratitude filled her to overflowing.

A white-winged bird whirred up out of the daisies a few feet away, so close that the rush of air from its wings burst against their hot faces.

"Cassandra," John said unsteadily, tugging at her blouse until it fell away from her skin, exposing her firm, round breasts, their nipples so large and brown. He pulled at the zipper of the jeans she wore, the jeans she had found somewhere to wear in place of her usual loose shifts, and turned back the fabric on either side to reveal a triangle of tawny fluff. She slid out of the jeans, murmuring his name over and over, sweet music in his ear. She helped him with his clothes, too, until they lay together naked in the daisy-lace meadow.

He would never tire of seeing Cassie this way, he thought, gliding his hands across her warm, silky skin, marveling at her fragility and her strength, at her softness and her hardness, at her flatness and her curves. He would never get enough of kissing her, of their mouths blending first with gentleness, delighting in preliminary explorations, and then tightening as the tempo of their lovemaking quickened, inflaming them with urgency.

Deftly and eagerly he bent his head, his blond hair gleaming in the sun, and took Cassie's brown-berried nipple between his lips and slowly sucked it, savoring its sweetness. She moaned lightly and moved beneath him, guiding his hands to the places where they would pleasure her most.

Today, sensing that she needed a break from the tension in the air, John had convinced Cassie to come with him to Pride's Peak, had thoughtfully and artfully contrived to sculpt his mood to fit hers. And now in return she molded her body to his, her fingers gentle tendrils winding through his hair, her ankle sliding its concavity to the convexity of his calf, her breasts rising to press hotly against the confines of his curved hands.

His tongue traced a damp trail from her breast to her throat and lingered in the hollow, dipping into the salty sweetness before spinning a silver thread of wetness on its way to her mouth. His lips met hers in a kiss that stilled Cassie's moans but did not assuage her rapidly beating heart.

And so they made love again, in that age-old renewal of body and spirit, and Cassie felt loved and desired and contented, but she did not feel any sunbursts.

And John knew once more that it wasn't the same for Cassie as it was for him. But he cradled her close, and he whispered, "I love you" against her hair, because it was true. And he vowed that soon, soon, Cassie would be able to give of herself and take for herself as well.

"AND SO YOU TOLD SHARON you'd think about going with her?" John asked later as he braided more daisies into a wreath.

"Yes," said Cassie hopelessly. "Because I couldn't bear to tarnish Sharon's bright happiness about going to California."

"Cassie, you could do it. I know you could."

"No, John. Not if I have to fly. And I couldn't bear to drive all that way again. It would remind me too much of the last time I made the trip, when I first came to Flat Top Mountain after Kevin and Rory were killed."

"When is Sharon going?"

"Now that she's signed his contract, Kajurian is planning to leave tomorrow. He's getting a voice coach scheduled and some auditions lined up. He's even talking to the committee for the AAFA Awards Spectacular about having her sing 'Where the Heart Is' in my place. Wouldn't that be a lucky break for Sharon? He wants her to meet him in L.A. in two weeks."

"Two weeks. You could be ready to go in two weeks, Cassie."

She shook her head. "No, I couldn't. But you could. You could accompany Sharon."

John dropped the daisies he was weaving and stared at her. She looked lovely in the aftermath of lovemaking, her skin dewy, her blouse still unbuttoned down the front so that one breast was revealed in all its fullness, the other screened by fabric. They had pulled on their clothes in case someone happened upon them, but they hadn't zipped zippers or buttoned buttons yet. That could wait until they were ready to leave.

"Ah, Cassandra," he said tenderly, reaching out and cupping her full breast lightly in his hand. The nipple drew up, responding to his touch. He leaned toward her and kissed her on the cheek. "I can't go with Sharon, love. A young girl in the company of an older man? Surely you can see that it wouldn't be proper."

"You said you wouldn't mind returning to Los Angeles for a visit," said Cassie stubbornly. "You could go when Sharon goes. She trusts you. You and I and Sharon know that it wouldn't be improper."

John sighed and pulled away. He began again to weave the daisy wreath.

"I *wouldn't* mind going to Los Angeles for a visit," he said carefully. "The idea was for you to go with me. Remember?"

"John, you know how I feel about flying." Cassie tentatively rested one hand on his bare chest for a moment, then drew her fingertips through the soft downy mat of hair. "John?"

"I'll go," he said, leveling a steady blue gaze at her. "I'll go with you and Sharon."

"No, I—"

"We'll drive to the airport in Asheville, you and I, during the next two weeks, several times if we have to. We'll sit and watch the planes take off and land. I read about this in a book about phobias." He had driven all the way to Asheville to buy that book, and he'd been debating whether or not he should recommend to Cassie that she read it.

"There was a chapter about people who are afraid to fly," he went on. "Did you know there's a course that helps people confront their phobias?"

"No," said Cassie. "I didn't. Anyway, I'm sure there's no such course here in Scot's Cove."

"Cassie, I'm convinced that you've already done most of the groundwork for getting over this aviophobia of yours. You're much more self-confident now, more relaxed. Now it's time to confront your fears. There's no point in any more suffering, Cassie."

"But—"

"Don't give me that business about Rory and Kevin. You don't have to go on paying and paying for their deaths!" He spoke bluntly, but not unkindly.

Cassie blinked and looked down at the ground. She couldn't deny the logic of what John said.

"What would I have to do?" she said quietly.

"The people who take the course I told you about get used to being around airplanes, talk out their fears, use a lot of positive thinking, and eventually they overcome their phobias and take a flight. We could do what they do. We could go to the Asheville airport, every day if necessary, and work intensively, the two of us."

"Don't make it sound so simple," snapped Cassie. "What happened to me to make me afraid of flying hasn't happened to most people."

"Ah," he said softly. "Don't you think I know that?"

Silence engulfed them, punctuated only by the buzz of a grasshopper's wings. Cassie saw the grasshopper winging through the daisies somewhere on the periphery of her vision, but that was before her eyes blurred with tears.

"Cassie, I'd be there, right by your side to help you. I'd be holding your hand. You made it through dinner at the Juniper Inn, didn't you? And you thought you'd never go away from Flat Top Mountain for anything even remotely resembling social reasons. Trust me, Cassandra."

Tears glittered on the edges of her eyelashes until she blinked. She didn't dare look at him, didn't dare let herself see the beseeching in his blue eyes, the patience and understanding in his expression.

I'm so afraid, she thought. *He doesn't know how afraid I am. I can't get into an airplane again. I can't.*

"I'll make it easy for you, Cassie. Just go along with what I'm trying to do for you, give me that much, and if at the end of two weeks you don't want to climb on that airplane with Sharon and me, Sharon goes alone."

Her cheeks damp with tears, she lifted her eyes to his. She was no longer thinking of herself. She was thinking of her friend. "Sharon can't go alone. She's scared silly about how to act, about where she'll live when she gets there, about all kinds of things."

"She needs you. We both know that."

Too late Cassie realized that she had backed herself into a corner. Sharon had no support group, no loyal family back home pulling for her, no close adviser except Cassie. John couldn't fill Cassie's role for Sharon, nor could Kajurian, as good-hearted as he was. John was entirely right; Sharon needed her.

She bowed her head before wiping the skin beneath her eyes with the edge of her hand. "All right, John," she said, her voice no more than a whisper. "I'll try. I want to help Sharon, and I want you to know I'm trying. You've given me so very much, I can never give you enough, never! But oh, John, if I can't get on that airplane when it's time to go, please understand!"

John's eyes flickered with a spark of hope. He gathered Cassie into the circle of his arms, cradled her against his bare chest, and smoothed her damp cheek reflectively with one finger.

"I'll understand," he said quietly. "You're a courageous woman, Cassie."

She closed her eyes, fighting the panic that so insidiously grappled with the sense of well-being that John had carefully instilled. This time, the well-being won.

"I'll make the plane reservations tonight," he told her. She nodded in silent assent.

John held her close for a long time, listening to their hearts beating. He loved her, and she was trying. When they finally drew apart, his expression was bright and his eyes were sparkling with approval. As a mark of that approval and in an attempt at lightening their mood, he carefully placed the daisy wreath on Cassie's head and kissed her on the mouth.

Cassie drew John's head into her lap and lingeringly traced the fullness of his lips with one fingertip. He was so dear, so loving, so considerate. But he wanted to move the center of herself, to shift her world on its axis.

"I love you, John," she said. "I really do love you."

In answer, he smiled up at her. His smile was confident and sure. "I know," he said.

She smiled back and then stroked his hair absently. She fingered the scar that bisected his eyebrow, drifted the palm of her hand across the pale stubble on his cheek. Still smiling, he closed his eyes, and she bent to kiss him, feeling playful now that her decision had been made and the tension between them released. The daisy crown that John had placed so carefully on her head tipped crazily over one eye, and although she grabbed for it, it fell to John's chest.

Releasing his lips, Cassie plucked two daisies from the wreath and placed them ever so carefully on John's closed eyelids.

"Hey, what are you doing?" he demanded.

"Giving you day's eyes," she said, a smile in her voice.

John could not see her face, and she could not read his mind, a fact for which he was mightily thankful.

He could not help thinking that this was the second set of eyes she had given him, and the thought that Cassie did not yet know the extent of her giving or the effect of her generosity on his life made John's heart ache with sadness.

It also stiffened his determination to bring her to the point where he could tell her the truth.

THE UNPAVED ROAD down Flat Top Mountain twisted and turned, jolting Cassie from side to side of the wide front seat of John's Chevrolet. The motion made her feel sick.

Stop it, Cassie, she warned herself. She turned her eyes toward the car window, hoping that the scenery would take her mind off herself. Shades of green flashed by, green walls closing in on the sides and the top of the road. Bowed branches clutched damply and the wet tentacles of a willow tree slapped against the car as they swept around a curve close to the creek. In a hollow, deep green kudzu vines snaked over the trees, covering them completely, choking out the sun and transforming the trees into tall hunchbacked figures that loomed threateningly. *Stop it,* Cassie told herself again. *This is bad enough without letting your wild imaginings make it worse.*

"Are you all right?" asked John, removing his eyes from the road long enough to shoot Cassie a keen look.

"I think so," she said, clutching at the edge of the seat and turning a delicate shade of pea green.

At the next widening of the narrow mountain road, John steered the car over to the side and yanked on the emergency brake. He turned to Cassie and pulled her into his arms.

"It'll be all right," he soothed, and Cassie wished she could believe him. She stared fixedly at the damp chiseled face of rock outside the car window. It was feathered gently with ferns. John had instructed her to distract herself from her panic by thinking about other things when the panic struck, and they had even practiced this technique. But today, concentrating on the scenery didn't help. Just the thought of seeing an airport again made her stomach do rollovers.

"Let's go," she said shakily, drawing away from him. His eyes held hers for a long moment.

"You're sure?" he asked.

"I'm sure."

He kissed her forehead before he started the car. And he wondered if taking her to the Asheville airport and making her watch the planes take off and land was the only way to help Cassie, or if he was merely being cruel.

But he didn't mean to be cruel, and he didn't know anything else to do, so he threw the car into gear and edged carefully back onto the road again. If the truth were to be told, he was as scared right now as she was, because Cassie, with her unpredictable emotions, might react violently to this sort of do-it-yourself therapy. He wouldn't recommend this sort of thing for everyone. But with Cassie, who had already tried professional help, this was a last-ditch attempt. She was brave and he was determined. He could only hope that their combined bravery and determination were enough to see her through.

THE ASHEVILLE AIRPORT WAS NOT a large airport by anyone's standards. It had a control tower and a small terminal where workmen were repouring the cement sidewalks on that day. Brightly colored buses from area summer camps idled in the parking area, waiting for the loads of campers who hiked off their flights toting tennis rackets and knapsacks and shouting to one another in loud voices.

At first all the noise and activity distracted Cassie, made her want to look in all directions at once. She was still not used to being around groups of people. She held fast to John's hand as they detoured around two workmen wielding trowels on the front walk. When they reached the door, John slid an arm around her slim shoulders, bracing her.

Inside, nonthreatening Muzak piped soft violin music through the terminal. Doors swished open and closed, people noisily trundled suitcases out of their way. Slowly John and Cassie approached the wide plate-glass windows overlooking the runway.

Airplanes looking as bendable as aluminum hunkered on the apron outside the terminal. Bright sunlight glinted off the wings.

Wings of death, Cassie thought to herself before she could help it, and a chill stabbed through her. She shivered.

"All right?" John's eyes, full of concern, searched her face.

The glare of the sun on the airplanes shattered and fragmented into a kaleidoscope of light. She tried to inhale a deep yogic breath to steady herself, but instead she was breathing too fast, so fast she became dizzy. A sick feeling churned up from her stomach, clogging her throat. Oh, she knew it, she should never have come here. A thousand hammers pounded inside her head, and the reverberations turned her stomach to stone and her knees to jelly. John's face whirled and everything in her line of vision tilted sideways.

"Cassie!" John said, and she heard his voice as though he were far, far away as she slumped toward the floor.

But John caught her, clasping her against his broad chest as she sagged, gripping her in an embrace so fierce that she was steadied by his strength.

The world righted itself. The rhythmic *thrum-thrum* of John's heartbeat beneath her ear intruded upon her consciousness. Slowly the numbness in her arms and legs receded; slowly her knees tightened so that her legs would bear her weight. She heard herself breathing, and to her surprise, she was breathing normally.

"Okay?" said John anxiously, leaning back so that he could look down at her face resting against his shoulder. Her eyelashes curled against the fabric of his jacket; she looked like a young child. Finally she opened her eyes, and in their silvery depths he saw a glint of resolve.

"Yes, I'm all right," she said carefully, scarcely believing that she was actually able to speak so normally after almost fainting dead away.

He kept a tight hold on her in case she started to go under again. That had scared him, he had to admit that. But he didn't admit it to her. For her, he managed a facade of buoyant confidence.

"Let's sit down over here," he said, leading her to a couple of chairs facing the window.

She let him guide her. Sitting next to him, she maintained a tight grip on his hand. A voice barked out a flight number over the public address system. Cassie concentrated on silently reciting numbers from one to a hundred backward. She tried to remember the lyrics to all the songs she had ever written, in chronological order. She repeated the Gettysburg Address to herself. Anything, anything, to get her mind off where she was and what she was doing.

Cassie forced herself to watch as a jet angled up to the nearby gate and disgorged a group of passengers. Soon, in spite of herself, she was caught up in watching the many minidramas surrounding her, so much so that she forgot about the plane hulking right outside the window. She stopped reciting numbers, she forgot about the Gettysburg Address. She watched hugs, kisses, cries of happiness as husband met wife, as sweetheart met lover, as parent met child.

"I never noticed," Cassie said soberly, "how happy people are in airports."

John smiled. Cassie could have noticed the couple standing at the end of the terminal, drying each other's tears because one was about to leave and the other was going to stay. But instead, Cassie had zeroed in on the happiness and gaiety of the scene surrounding them, and John knew that this was a good sign.

He squeezed her hand. "Let's go," he said gently. "I think you've had enough for one day. We'll come back again tomorrow. I'm proud of you, Cassandra."

She ventured a weak smile, because sitting in an airport watching planes take off and land had been an ordeal the like of which she could never have imagined, the like of which she never would have attempted a few months ago, before John.

"I'm proud of myself, too," she admitted, slipping her arm about John's waist as they walked together to the door of the terminal. "But John, I still have a long way to go."

"Yes," he said, hugging her close. "All the way to California."

Chapter Thirteen

They fastened their seat belts, or at least two of them did. Sharon, settling into the window seat, had no trouble with hers. Nor did John, sitting on the aisle seat. But Cassie, who was sitting between them, fumbled with hers until John said, "Here, love, let me do that," and he clicked the latch and pulled at the belt until it fit snugly around Cassie's hips.

"Oh, John, I'm so frightened," she whispered, and her fingers gripped his so tightly that it caused him pain.

They'd decided to fly coach instead of first class, because in coach they could sit three abreast. And Cassie was convinced that she needed both Sharon and John beside her if she was to live through this flight.

"Take deep breaths," advised John, and Cassie concentrated on her breathing. She'd been practicing relaxation through yoga in preparation for this flight, and as long as she was on the ground, it had helped calm her fears whenever she thought about leaving the ground. But now, departing from the Asheville airport on the first leg of a journey that would end in Los Angeles, she fought panic with every bit of willpower she possessed.

"They're pulling the service truck away from the plane," Sharon advised with barely contained excitement, craning her neck to look out and down from the little window. In a moment, the door at the front of the airplane slammed shut. The metallic clang filled Cassie with terror. The sides of the plane closed in on her, choking off her breath.

Now I'm in here and there's no getting out, she thought to herself. John squeezed her right hand reassuringly. On her other side, Sharon smiled an understanding smile and reached for Cassie's left hand.

"I feel like such an idiot," Cassie murmured helplessly.

"Don't," said Sharon. "I'm pretty scared, too. I've never flown before."

Cassie heard the piercing whine of the powerful jet engines and listened to the metallic rattle of the pilot's voice over the intercom. These things barely scratched the surface of her consciousness, because unbearable tension was beating against the inside of her skull, scraping on bone, throbbing with edges so jagged that she fought back a scream. She was in an airplane, locked tight inside, and they would soon leave the ground, only she couldn't, she couldn't!

"Cassandra," said John, and his dear, familiar voice penetrated the wall of her fear. He said, "Breathe, love, just as you practiced. You see, we're taxiing down the runway now, nice and easy, picking up speed, more speed now, everything is fine, Cassie..." And he went on in this vein, his voice smooth and calming, just as they'd talked about her fears, talking her through this anguish, taking her up and up. The plane lifted off, and they were flying, *she* was flying, and when she realized that they were actually airborne she turned her head and began to sob softly against John's shoulder, her tears washing away her pain and her fear and ushering in a sensation of wonderful relief.

John handed her his handkerchief. "I came prepared," he said tenderly.

A flight attendant bent over their seats. "Is everything all right?"

"Yes," said John, his adoring eyes never leaving Cassie's face. "Yes, everything is fine."

MORGANA'S LEGS STRUCK OUT in their own unabridged fashion, pacing the floor of her apartment. She alternately sipped Scotch-on-the-rocks and consulted her wristwatch.

Where were they? Where the hell were they? Their plane was already an hour late; Morgana had called the airline God knew how many times. She should have met them at the airport, but John had insisted over the phone last night that they could take a cab, and Cassie hadn't been there to talk to because she had been doing some last-minute drudging about in that garden of hers.

Cassie. How had John ever talked her into getting into an airplane? No mean feat, that. Morgana had talked to Cassie about her fear of flying a few times after the accident, but every time Cassie had turned white, and once she'd nearly keeled over, whereupon Morgana had promptly stopped providing little pep talks and had just as promptly sent Cassie to her own shrink, which had done no good at all.

Morgana felt sorry for Cassie, because the sense of guilt and the terror that had descended on Cassie had ruined her life. No one had worked at a career any harder than she, and she'd given it all up. Not just the performing, but the songwriting, too. A shame. But then, who was to say that she, Morgana, wouldn't have felt the same way if she'd felt responsible for killing her husband and her kid?

Not that Morgana had ever understood the rationale behind Cassie's guilt. *She* knew that Cassie hadn't killed anybody. It had been an accident, pure and simple. Unfortunate. But those things happen. The thing to do afterward is to get on with life the best you can. Well, Morgana had sent John out there to Flat Top Mountain, and he'd worked wonders, apparently. Wonders enough to get Cassie on a flight to L.A., all because of this Rose o' Sharon person, John had said.

Cassie had written Morgana a long letter begging her to let Rose o' Sharon stay with her at her apartment. And since she would do anything to help Cassie, because Cassie had offered her a home in those days long ago when Morgana had been down and out, Morgana had agreed to let Rose o' Sharon stay with her until she found her own place. Now Morgana hoped she hadn't signed on to play shepherdess to a poor little lamb lost in the woods. The woods out here were full of poor little lost lambs. Hell, she knew that better than anyone. She'd been one of them once.

The doorbell chimed. Morgana parked her glass on a convenient table and ran to answer it.

"Morgana!"

It was Cassie at last, thank goodness, and Morgana embraced her. Behind her stood John and a redheaded girl who looked puppyish but had definite possibilities. Not only that, the set of the girl's chin hinted at a large-sized proportion of grit and a whopping amount of determination.

Rose o' Sharon is no lost lamb, Morgana thought with relief. *Not that one.*

Sharon's awestruck inspection of Morgana's luxurious apartment amused Morgana immensely. But Sharon could wait. Morgana centered her attention on her friend.

"Cassie, darling, what have you done to yourself?" No sooner were the three of them inside her apartment than Morgana, thunderstruck at Cassie's appearance, twirled Cassie around for inspection. Cassie wore a knee-length short-sleeved Kamali dress with a loose cowl neck, and the sweat-shirt gray brought out the silver in her eyes. Gray ostrich-pattern pumps, swinging silver earrings and a pocketbook on a glittering silver chain finished the ensemble. No shapeless sack dress, no bare feet, and Cassie's fractious hair was subdued into a neat bun at the nape of her neck.

"Dug in the back of my closet," admitted Cassie sheepishly, swinging the purse off her shoulder. She glanced ruefully down at her legs, bare no more. "Sharon bought me a pair of panty hose in Scot's Cove, I might add."

"Cassie looks marvelous, doesn't she?" John surveyed Cassie's new look with pleasure. "And we're going shopping tomorrow. We're buying a basic wardrobe for Sharon, and a bright red dress for Cassie."

"Red? Why red?" Morgana warmed to the interaction between Cassie and John. If you went by the look of them, the love between them had grown in the past weeks since Morgana had visited Flat Top Mountain. Cassie had filled out, seemed more self-assured. Not since before the accident had Morgana seen Cassie looking so happy and at peace with herself.

"I'm buying her a red dress because," said John, grinning down at Cassie, pulling her close, "I want to see Cassie in a red knit dress from Giorgio's. I want to watch her slip her feet into a pair of classy sandals from Charles Jourdan. I want—"

"I want a glass of water," interrupted Cassie with an impish gleam in her eyes, the way Cassie used to look. Morgana was so glad to see it that she stood in the middle of the room, uncharacteristically speechless. Her eyes filled with tears, also uncharacteristic, but it happened sometimes when she was overcome with emotion.

"Morgana? Are you all right?" Cassie, all concern, crossed the room in a flash, limping still but unselfconscious. She raised a tentative hand, fingernails gleaming with pale pink polish, to Morgana's arm.

"No," said Morgana dryly, blinking rapidly. "But oh, Cassie, you are all right. And that's what counts." Blindly she drew Cassie into a heartfelt hug.

The two old friends embraced for a long time before John said, after clearing his throat, "Hey, I'd like a glass of water, too, Morgana." Then Cassie and Morgana separated, dried their eyes and walked arm in arm to Morgana's spacious gourmet kitchen, John and Sharon following, where they all sat down amid the copper-bottomed pans and the gleaming Cuisinart and the woven grass baskets from Mexico. At Cassie's insistence, they toasted the future with glasses of plain water drawn from Morgana's shiny spigot.

"Next time," said Cassie thoughtfully to John as she rolled the glass of water between her hands, "remind me to bring along a bottle of my famous scuppernong wine."

"Spare me, darling," groaned Morgana.

IT WASN'T SCUPPERNONG WINE that flowed at the cocktail party Morgana gave in Sharon's honor that weekend, but there was no scarcity of other more potent libations.

Cassie had always believed with certainty that the scriptwriter responsible for the bar scene in the movie *Star Wars* had been inspired by one of Morgana's parties. John, after one look around the room, agreed with her.

Morgana, striking in a long, glistening sheath of purple sequins, her platinum-palomino hair flowing, introduced her latest male friend, a stalwart and bearded Viking type named—naturally—Thor. While Morgana acted as hostess, Thor stood impassively in the corner, glaring out from under bushy blond eyebrows, his arms folded across his massive chest.

"Let's get away from him," whispered John to Cassie during a lull. "I have a feeling he's waiting to slice off our heads and offer them to Odin on his shield."

"I see Kajurian," said Cassie, threading through the crowd with John in tow. "We can say hello to him."

Morgana took Sharon, looking bright and angelic in white piqué, under her own capacious wing and introduced her to an army of young studs. Cassie, peering around Kajurian, who looked chipper in his new suit, made a mental note to have a serious talk with Sharon about the danger of too hastily entered man-woman involvements.

"Nice party, eh?" said Kajurian, rocking back on his heels and looking pleased.

"Not really," said Cassie.

"Cassie, you've been away too long. Soon you will be used to these parties again, I promise. The word's out that you're back in town. I can get you a spot on the Carson show. Barbara Walters called me today and she wants an interview. Let me tell them yes, eh?"

"I have plane reservations to go back to Flat Top Mountain next Saturday," rejoined Cassie. "I only came out to get Sharon settled with Morgana."

"Sharon is doing all right. The committee for the AAFA Awards is very interested in Sharon singing at the Awards Spectacular, especially when I told them she could play the mountain dulcimer just like you. And I already introduced her tonight to Jay Heitman, head honcho at WorldWide Records. He wants to talk to you, too, Cassie."

"Kajurian," said Cassie patiently. "When will you believe that I will never perform again?"

"Never. But listen, Cassie. I've sold the songs you wrote. All of them. Snapped up by the same company that published 'Where the Heart Is.' They're talking with a very popular entertainer—no names, you understand—but this guy wants to sing your songs on his new album. You would be astounded at who it is, Cassie."

"I'm glad that somebody is interested in performing my songs. But I don't want to talk about it."

"But Cassie," interjected John, "I think that's wonderful."

"I guess it is," said Cassie diffidently.

"You'll write more songs, won't you?" Kajurian looked worried.

"Of course she will," said John warmly, but Cassie was saved from having to answer because at that moment Kajurian was accosted by a has-been male crooner who was trying to drum up business, and this provided an opportunity for Cassie to drift quietly into the crowd, followed by John.

After fielding the prying questions of an aging actress who, in a predatory fashion, pounced upon them and loudly declared the missing Cassandra Dare found at last, Cassie and John sneaked away to stand beside a lighted easel displaying a painting, which on further inspection proved to be of a magenta cow's udder on an electric-blue background.

"Morgana has interesting taste in art," said John, squinting at the udder.

"And people," said Cassie with a shudder. "Look around this room. Do you see anyone who looks normal?"

John looked. So far he'd met an orange-haired starlet named Duckie, a cigar-chomping motion-picture producer who looked as though he'd been sent over from central casting to play the part of a cigar-chomping motion-picture producer, and a psychic, who, compared to everyone else, seemed surprisingly ordinary.

"No," he said, finally. "There's a full moon tonight, though. They say that brings out the crazies." John gestured at the nearby window, on the other side of which a moon hung so low that Cassie thought she could reach out and touch it. And, from their vantage point on the fortieth floor, it looked as if she almost could.

"You're stunningly beautiful tonight, Cassandra," John told her. He gazed down at her approvingly, and she was glad that he liked what he saw. She wore the red dress he had bought her, and her hair, subdued by Morgana's hairdresser, flowed in shiny ripples down her back. She felt poised and confident. She smiled up at John, proud to be with him. He was easily the most attractive man in the room, even allowing for the Hollywood pretty boys who always turned up for Morgana's parties.

Avoiding people as much as possible, they strolled around the edges of the room, observing instead of mingling. John seemed perfectly at ease in this Gucci-Pucci-Porsche group.

"Maybe we should be meeting more people," he suggested.

"Not unless you want to," said Cassie. "This room is full of people who leave behind perfectly ordinary lives in Kalamazoo or Altoona, arrive in California, and invent themselves. I don't know how I could have survived being a part of this scene for so long."

The scene was a familiar one to John. As an eligible bachelor he was invited to many such parties.

At that moment John was mobbed by three nubile young women, and Cassie decided after a worried glance at the wolf pack closing in on Sharon that, instead of waiting until after the party, she needed to rescue Sharon and talk with her now.

With a look that said "Help!" John watched her go, but Cassie simply smiled and lifted her eyebrows, leaving him to muddle through as best he could.

Cassie fought off the wolves and dragged Sharon down a hall to one of the four bedrooms, opened the door and then closed it again rapidly when she realized from the flash of bare rippling skin that coats weren't the only things lying on the bed.

"Here," she said, shoving Sharon into the room the two of them had shared since arriving. She collapsed gratefully into a moire-upholstered chair. It was quiet here, blissfully quiet. The smoke, the loud music, the noise and the crowd seemed far away from this ruffled, pastel-decorated haven, with its canopied twin beds and its pristine pale carpet.

"What's wrong, Cassie?" asked Sharon in concern. "Are you not feeling well?"

Total innocence, thought Cassie, thinking of Sharon surrounded by overeager men, and she wondered how to initiate the conversation. She drew a deep breath.

"Those men in there," she said finally. "They may come on a bit strong, Sharon. Don't let any of them turn your head."

"Or get me in bed?"

Sharon's bluntness surprised her. "I'm sure that's what a few of them have in mind," Cassie replied.

Sharon was silent, but she turned thoughtfully to the window and drew back the sheer curtain with one graceful hand. The sky beyond was hazy with moonglow, and stars twinkled here and there. Below this concrete-and-glass tower in Century City, the L.A. metropolis sprawled in front of them, lit in all its neon glory.

"See that?" mused Sharon softly in the gentle flowing accent of her native North Carolina. "I never dreamed I'd be here in this fabulous place, at a party given in my honor by Morgana Friday. Or that you would be my friend, my *best* friend, Cassie."

Cassie started to remonstrate, but Sharon dropped the curtain and knelt quickly at Cassie's side.

"You've given me an opportunity so rare for somebody from Flat Top Mountain. Oh, Cassie, I wouldn't give it up for anybody. Not for any *man*. The only person I would give it up for is me, my own self." The stars in Sharon's eyes burned as bright as the stars in the sky outside, and she was luminous with a light glowing brighter than all the neon below.

"You won't let your head be turned by all the attention? The flattery?"

"No, no, never. I came out here to succeed as a singer. I won't let myself be sidetracked. I'm going to give it all I've got. That's a promise, Cassie." Sharon's face shone with sincerity.

At that moment, after a quick rap on the door, Morgana burst into the room. "Say, what's going on in here? Something private? No? Well, come on out here, then. Mrs. Applebrenner is going to give readings. Sharon, you're first." Morgana propelled both Sharon and Cassie into the hall.

"Who's Mrs. Applebrenner?"asked Cassie, turning to Morgana with a degree of bewilderment.

"The psychic. *The* psychic. Oh, she's the latest craze in town. I was lucky to get her. She works parties so seldom, you know. She's sitting at a card table in my bedroom giving readings. Cassie, she can read you next."

"No," said Cassie, backing away even as Sharon disappeared behind the indicated bedroom door after an encouraging shove from Morgana.

"Well, she claims to be eighty percent accurate with her predictions, Cassie. She's going to tell me what she thinks about the success of my latest documentary."

"I certainly wish you well with your documentary," replied Cassie, edging out of Morgana's reach. "But I have no desire to know about my future."

"You don't? Why?" Morgana wrinkled her forehead in puzzlement.

"Sometimes the future holds things we'd be better off not knowing," said Cassie quietly. If she had known about the airlane crash five years ago, if she had known she was going to give up her career—but what was the use of speculating? It was over and done with.

"I see," said Morgana finally in a flash of understanding.

"So if you don't mind, I'll avoid Mrs. Applebrenner. Besides, I want to find John." She smiled briefly at Morgana, then slipped away in the wake of a man wearing a turban, who leered at her suggestively once they reached the living room.

"My name's Sinbad," he said, twirling the ends of his mustache with a wicked laugh. "It's easy to remember. Sin, and bad, that's me!" He roared in laughter, rearing his head back so far that his turban slipped. Cassie fled.

"Where *have* you been?" John murmured in her ear, surprising her as he walked up behind her.

She explained as briefly as she could.

"Look, can we leave now? I can hardly wait to get you out of here."

"I promised Morgana we'd stay until the end, John. The party *is* in Sharon's honor, you know." He nuzzled at her ear, and her physical response was lightning quick. She would have liked to leave, too, and the sooner the better. But she felt a responsibility to stay.

"I've been looking forward so much to your seeing my place," he told her, curving an arm around her waist. "I was hoping there'd be time for a walk on the beach tonight."

For the past week, Cassie had been staying with Morgana, but this was the night she was going to leave. John had used the week to open up his house in Malibu. Cassie had been surprised that John lived in such an exclusive area; he had said nothing previously to lead her to believe that he made enough money with his photography to support a Malibu life-style. But when she'd commented, John had mumbled something about family money, and she'd thought no more about it.

She was looking forward to the beach, however. It had been a long time since she'd strolled in the sand, delighted in little wavelets tickling her toes, or watched in hushed reverence as the sun slipped below the horizon. She and Kevin and Rory had done those things often enough. Now that she had John, the beach and the ocean and sunsets would mean something again, something special. As everything did, now that she had John.

After an energetic tap-dancing demonstration by a starlet who had imbibed too much, and after a woman with hair sprayed and quivering like a chocolate mousse had spilled a whole pitcher of martinis on Morgana's white flokati rug, the crowd began to thin out.

While Morgana was bidding her guests good-bye at the door, Cassie hugged Sharon and quietly gathered her possessions from the room they had shared.

"Now, Sharon, follow Kajurian's advice. He'll take good care of you," Cassie said as her eyes swept the room one last time, searching for belongings she might have missed. "And if you need to reach me, don't hesitate to call me at John's house."

"Cassie, don't worry," Sharon said with an impatient grin. "I'm ready to be on my own now. Really. And Morgana is wonderful. I'll be fine."

At the door, Morgana leaned over and pecked John on the cheek. At Cassie she leveled a long, penetrating look.

"Be happy, Cassie," was all Morgana said after they embraced in farewell.

Be happy? Cassie reflected as she and John sped away in John's BMW, headed for Malibu. How could she not be happy when she was with John, when being with him meant loving him and learning more about him every minute?

Chapter Fourteen

The waves rolled one by one to the shore, each one closer to John's and Cassie's toes. The tide was coming in; soon they would have to move their blanket farther up the beach if they didn't want to be inundated. But the baking heat of the afternoon sun had made them sleepy and lazy, and they didn't want to move.

They'd been at John's house in Malibu for five days now. Cassie loved the house and had been amazed at the luxury of it. It was an unabashedly modern house, its exterior a gleaming white, architecturally designed to look as though it were swooping like a great sea gull to light at the edge of the Pacific Ocean. Inside, it was tastefully decorated, casual and comfortable, with a great gleaming kitchen, baths with Jacuzzis, and a number of bedrooms, all angled for an ever-changing view of the ocean.

This had been a halcyon time, the two of them together and for the first time free of any responsibilities. Their days had been full of love and laughter and sharing and fun.

"Augh," cried John suddenly when a wave outreached its companions and washed over one leg as far up as his knee.

Laughing at his disconcerted expression, Cassie scrambled to her feet. She helped John gather up their soggy blanket and grabbed the bottle of suntan lotion and her sandals before they were carried away on the next wave.

"It must be time to go inside," she said. "The waves are chasing us away."

"I should go in anyway," John said, draping an arm around her shoulders. "I'm expecting a phone call."

"Another one?"

"Yes, another one," he said, thinking that maybe she would ask him about all the phone calls, and there had been a lot of them in the past five days. But Cassie didn't ask. She wasn't the prying kind; she herself was such a private person that she seldom inquired into anyone else's business. Still, he wished she were more inquisitive. A question from her would have given him the lead-in he needed to initiate the discussion he had to have with her. She was ready now. All he needed was an opening.

They climbed the spiral staircase to the long, low terrace overlooking the beach.

"Shall I cook for us tonight?" asked Cassie. She'd been entranced with his kitchen, and after he'd shown her how the pasta maker worked, she'd begun making pasta with a vengeance. The pasta—spaghetti, linguine, fettucini—was delicious, too. She was quite a good cook, was Cassie.

"We could go out," he suggested. After having lived in seclusion so long on Flat Top Mountain,he enjoyed seeing Cassie dressed up, watching other men's heads swing after her when she walked into a restaurant like L'Orangerie.

"Let's think about it. Oh, you know we have that marinated steak in the refrigerator. I'd forgotten about it."

"Right. We were going to grill shish kebabs."

He held the door open for her, and at that moment the phone rang.

She slid under his arm to go inside. "Your phone call," she said, smiling up at him. "That means I get first dibs on the shower."

Cassie disappeared into the bathroom while John scooped up the receiver on his bedside telephone. It was Gordon, one of his managers at AirBridges. An Air-Bridges plane in Hawaii was grounded because of engine problems, and Gordon wanted John to okay the use of another plane that had recently undergone an overhaul.

"Yeah, okay," said John. "Keep me posted, Gordon."

He hung up, pondering the situation with Cassie. How was he going to break it to her that he wasn't who he said he was? And all the rest of it—the cornea transplants, his search for her, everything. It was a lot to heap on one fragile woman at one time. Then his lips curved into a smile. Fragile? Cassie had certainly been fragile when he met her, but, he corrected himself, she was fragile no longer. She might look soft on the outside, but she had proved herself to have a core of steel.

Cassie came out of the bathroom, a towel wrapped around her and tucked neatly at the cleft of her breasts, her hair damp and hanging. With her hair wet and molded to her head like that, her eyes took on a new importance in her face. Round and radiant, they smiled at him even before her lips did. His expression softened, and he bent his head to kiss her gently, lingeringly.

"Your turn at the shower," she said, her breath sweet against his lips. She sat down on the edge of the bed and began to towel her hair with a large bath towel.

As he was about to disappear into the bathroom, she called out, "John? Shouldn't you call about rescheduling our airline reservations for Wednesday? I'll do it, if you'd like."

He'd talked Cassie into postponing their trip a few days, until the following Wednesday, because they were having such a good time at Malibu. No amount of sweet-talking had persuaded her to put their return to North Carolina off for another whole week, however. Her garden on Flat Top Mountain would be ruined from neglect if they did that, she claimed, despite Bonnie Ott's promise to look after it in Cassie's absence.

"Sure, go ahead and call. No point in waiting until there are no seats available," he told her, heading for the bathroom. "My travel agent's number is on a card in my wallet."

Quickly he stepped inside the shower stall, which was still steamy from Cassie's shower. He had the quixotic thought that he'd never heard Cassie's voice over the telephone. Tomorrow he'd make a special point of running an errand and calling up from a pay phone. He wanted to know how she'd sound over the phone, her high little-girl voice with its underlying whisper conveyed by cables and wires. Her voice was one of the things about her that he loved most. Talking with her in bed after the lights were out, the way she laughed, the way she gasped his name when they made love, her voice that had thrilled millions, only for him in those moments...it excited him just to think about her voice.

He washed the sand off quickly, wanting to spend as little time as possible away from Cassie. He slammed the shower door, toweled himself nominally dry, and walked naked into the bedroom.

Cassie sat on the bed, her face expressionless, her gray eyes stony. He sensed immediately that something had gone wrong. Something had gone totally, terribly wrong.

"You!" she said in a choked voice. His wallet slid from her lap to the ground, and with a whopping jolt like a swift foot connecting with his solar plexus, he understood. He saw his driver's license lying on the carpet, with its incriminating photo and information. And other identification, too. But no, it was all wrong! He hadn't meant for her to find out this way!

Cassie's chest heaved so hard that the towel, so carefully tucked between her breasts, untucked itself. The towel loosened to reveal the white swimsuit line and more, but John was immune to the sight of what would have stimulated him tremendously only a moment ago.

He strode across the room, and Cassie's eyes lifted to his, and now her eyes were not silver-bright but gray and flat, the color of lead. He wanted to reach out and touch her, to smooth away the pain and doubt on her face, to kiss away the horrid accusing expression that seemed so foreign on the beautifully asymmetric face of Cassie, his love.

But he dared not touch her.

She spat out the words.

"Your name isn't John Howard! Your name is John Bridges! Isn't it? Isn't it?"

Slowly, numbly, he nodded. He had wanted her to know for so long. But he hadn't wanted her to find out like this. Not like this.

"Cassie—"

"I don't even know you! Keep away from me!" In a fury she rolled out of his reach, the white towel unwinding and falling to the carpet. John's king-sized bed lay between them, and they faced each other over its expanse, each of them naked, neither of them able to hide behind a facade of any kind.

Cassie had never hidden anything from this man. Everything about her had been true and real and honest. Her soul had been naked before him from the night when she had made her body naked before him, and she had thought she knew him, knew all of him. Because she had trusted him, dammit, had placed all her love and her trust in John Howard, only to find out by happenchance that there wasn't any such person as John Howard.

And in a flash it hit her: What else did she know about him? In their dreamlike existence on the mountain, their lives and their love had taken on a surreal feeling, had seemed magical somehow. In that atmosphere of magic she had told him everything about herself, leaving nothing out, and she had trusted him to do the same. But now she saw what a fool she had been.

If he wasn't *who* he said he was, then perhaps he wasn't *what* she thought he was. A photographer? What did she know of that? Where were his pictures? Certainly there were none in this house, this magnificent house with its ocean and its fabulous kitchen and its fashionable Jacuzzis. And now she stood naked before him as she had always stood naked before him, and he stood naked before her, and she didn't know who he was!

"Who are you?"

John had not known that Cassie's gentle soprano could grate so harshly on his ears. He winced, but she did not give him time to reply.

"Who are you?" she repeated. "Some hustler who wants me to come back to L.A.? Who do you work for? Kajurian? A record company? Who sent you to Flat Top Mountain?" For suddenly, she realized what she had been too stupid or too wrapped up in herself to realize before—that John, the quintessential Californian, the sophisticated and worldly John who was so at home in L.A. and here at this house in Malibu, would not have come to so remote and bucolic a place as Scot's Cove without a purpose. God, what a fool she had been to have been taken in by him!

"Morgana gave me your address," he said as calmly as he could. "But Cassie, don't—"

"So Morgana was in on it! *Morgana?* My friend, who just happens to need publicity for 'All the Way Home'.And who else was in on it? Kajurian?"

It horrified him that she would think he'd use her, but in the world she'd left behind, that sort of using was commonplace. He drew a deep breath. He'd make her understand.

"No, Kajurian had nothing to do with it. It's not what you think at all. I've wanted to tell you all about it for so long, but I didn't think you were ready to hear it. Whatever I've done, Cassie, I've done out of love for you. And out of gratitude. Please, Cassie, you must believe it." His eyes pleaded with her for understanding, but no understanding was forthcoming.

"I've been hustled and hassled," Cassie said, her anger subsiding suddenly, leaving her feeling deflated. "By people who want to use me for their own purposes. I had Kevin to protect me...once." She spoke brokenly, and the fire went out of her. She stood before him exposed in all her vulnerability, and he loved her with all his heart. But she was a stranger.

Like a person sleepwalking, she went to the closet and pulled a big white cotton shirt on over her damp hair. Wearily she tugged on a pair of baggy green drawstring beach pants and tied the string around her waist, not bothering with underwear.

"Where are you going?" he asked, dreading the answer.

"Back to Flat Top Mountain," she said. "I never should have left." She slipped her feet into a pair of sandals and moved heavily to the phone, where she looked up a number in the Yellow Pages of the phone book. She stabbed out a number and asked that a cab be sent immediately.

Swearing, John went to his own closet and began to throw on clothes.

"I'm going to get Morgana over here," he said forcefully. "She can help me explain this mess."

"Morgana? I don't want to see her," said Cassie coldly. She began to toss clothes into a suitcase. In those baggy clothes she looked small and defenseless, but there was something tough about her, too, something that hadn't been there when he'd first seen her sitting under that tree on top of the mountain.

John picked up the telephone and punched out Morgana's number. After several interminable rings, he reached Morgana's answering machine. A lot of help that was.

"Cassie, listen to me," he said, slamming the phone down in exasperation and following her as she gathered her few cosmetics from the bathroom and collected her terry-cloth robe, which she had carelessly draped over a chair only that morning. She was calm, eerily calm. He couldn't tell if she heard him or not.

"My name is John Howard Bridges, Cassie. I'm not a photographer. I wish I'd never started that business; it gave me nothing but trouble. But the fiction that I was a nature photographer made it seem logical that I'd be living on Flat Top Mountain, and I had to see you, to tell you—"

"Don't talk to me," said Cassie, whipping her head around so that he'd be out of her line of vision. Water droplets flung from her hair stung his cheek. "Just don't talk." He spoke with the sincerity that had earned her trust in the first place, the sincerity that she had thought was inviolable. In the face of his deceit, her trust in him was laughable.

"I'm the one who wrote you all those letters a couple of years ago," he said in desperation. "You returned some of them; you refused to see me. Remember? I signed my name John H. Bridges on all of them. I was afraid if I told you my real name when I got to Flat Top Mountain, you'd turn me away."

"You're right," she said. She looked him straight in the eye. "You have to be careful when you're in the public eye. You meet a lot of nuts." She slammed her suitcase closed.

"Wait! You can't just walk out of here like this!"

"Oh, can't I? You just watch me!"

"Cassandra, I—"

"Don't call me that! You said you'd call me by that name when what you said was important and real and true and meant only for me! Is anything you said real and true, John? Is it?" She lifted her suitcase off the bed and stood glaring at him, her chest heaving.

"That's too heavy for you," he objected, but she only tightened her lips as well as her grip on the suitcase handle and marched limping down the hall, where she unlocked the front door. The cab drove up in front with perfect timing. John cursed the cabdriver, the cab company and taxicabs in general.

"Need some help?" called the driver from his open window, but Cassie was there before he could get out of his cab, heaving the suitcase into the back seat and climbing in after it. She didn't look back as the cab drove away.

John stood staring at the cab's exhaust before turning to go back in the house. He couldn't believe it; it had happened so fast. It was as though she had turned into a completely different person as soon as she had found out that he wasn't John Howard. She had become a different person as soon as she had perceived *him* to be a different person.

Oh, God, what had he done? Cassie was the best thing that had ever happened to him in his life, and because he had handled the situation so sloppily, he'd blown it. He couldn't believe that a mission he'd begun only out of gratitude and with highly honorable intentions had turned so sour.

The front door slammed behind him with a definite and final thud, and he stood for a moment on the tiled floor of the foyer, not knowing what to do next.

Give her time, said a voice inside him. Bleakly John saw that he could not reason with Cassie in her present state of mind. Nothing he could say would soften what, in her mind, had been the ultimate deception.

And so he would give her time, but what was he to do in the meantime? He who hated to be away from Cassie long enough to take a shower, who delighted in her gentle presence and her tinkling laughter, who found the way she moved and the way she looked unbelievably titillating—how was he to live without her? In his chest began a dull ache, and the weight of the world settled on his shoulders. *Oh, Cassie,* he thought in despair. *Why wouldn't you listen?*

He walked aimlessly into the living room, decorated in white on white, its curtains drawn back to reveal the azure blue of the ocean. On the horizon, the sun slipped slowly down, washing the waves with gold. He and Cassie had watched several such sunsets, hand in hand at that very window. Sunset here at Malibu had always been one of their closest times. He never forgot, not for one minute, that he wouldn't be seeing sunsets if it hadn't been for the new corneas he had acquired from Kevin, because Cassie had signed the waiver that had made it possible for K. J. Muldoon to become a donor.

Why wasn't I honest with her from the beginning?

Blindly he sank down on the couch, buried his face in his hands, and let the first hot tears of grief trickle slowly through his fingers.

"WHERE TO, LADY?"

The cabdriver's voice cut through the fog that had eclipsed Cassie's consciousness.

"What?"

"I said, where do you want to go?"

"The airport," she said, but suddenly she knew she didn't want to go to the airport after all. Not because she was afraid. She had left her phobia behind forever, she hoped. But she needed time to regroup, to think; she wanted to return to the place where she had known so much love and happiness and the security of a warm family life. She wanted to be where she could feel, if only for a few days, close to Kevin and Rory.

"Would you drive me to my house near Occidental? Do you know where that is?"

The cabdriver slowed the cab and shot her an incredulous glance in the rearview mirror. He saw a small woman with beautiful eyes and damp brown hair, and her chin was set in an expression he knew enough not to question. This was clearly a woman who knew her own mind, and she wasn't one of those crazy ones, spaced out on drugs or booze.

"Sure, it's north of San Francisco, in Sonoma County. That's hundreds of miles from here. It'd be an expensive ride," he said, dubiously.

"I can pay." She named a more than adequate sum, one that made his eyes pop. With that amount of money he could take the rest of the week off. He could take the rest of the *month* off.

"Sure," he said, as though this sort of thing happened every day.

Cassie settled back in the seat for the long drive. She watched the houses of Malibu whipping by in a blur, wondering dully how she could have been tricked and for what purpose.

Who was John Howard? Some out-of-work third-rate actor who could have been bought to bring her back to L.A., to talk her into performing again, to get the Cassandra Dare money-making machine going? Before the accident she and Kevin had employed a cadre of people—secretaries, hairdressers, makeup artists, a public relations man, an agent. Any one of them or all of them could be responsible, along with Morgana or Kajurian, for trying to bring her back on track.

Kevin, Kevin, she thought, *I wish you were here to take care of me.*

She hated John Howard, hated him!

For the man she had known as John Howard had changed her past, and he had failed her in the present. Cassie could see no hope at all for her future.

IT WAS RAINING and cold when she arrived at Wildflower, the walled retreat that she and Kevin and Rory had once called home. The cabdriver carried her single suitcase in through the wide double front doors and stood dripping on the marble floor while she counted hundred-dollar bills into his hand. The man was clearly impressed by the Waterford crystal chandelier, the majestic spiral staircase and the obvious trappings of wealth. He narrowed his eyes at Cassie as he closed his fingers on the money.

"You look like somebody," he said.

Cassie managed a smile. He had been kind to her. "I'm Cassandra Dare," she said.

"You? You're Cassandra Dare?"

"Yes."

"I should have guessed. Cassandra Dare!" A shadow passed over his face. Cassie knew that he was thinking of her tragedy.

"Well, I'll be going." He nodded uncertainly, as though he were reluctant to leave her in this isolated house, so gloomy and dark and lonely.

"Thank you," she said.

He ran through the rain to his cab, and Cassie watched his headlights swing across the heavy gray curtain of rain before the gates automatically swung closed behind his cab.

She closed the door and locked it. The house had the musty odor of a house too long closed up. But it was too late to do anything about it at that hour. She went to the wall thermostat and flipped it on. The place needed some heat. It was so cold and damp.

She walked quickly through the house, switching on lights until the whole first floor was lit up as though there were a party going on. The rooms seemed so much bigger than she remembered them, probably because she was used to living in Gran's little house now.

She must still be numb from her discovery about John, because she did not feel as she had expected to feel upon her return here.

The house was special to her, named after "Wildflower," her very first hit single, a song she'd written herself. She and Kevin had been newlyweds then, and this house had been the embodiment of their hopes for the future.

There was the old walking stick, made from a section of gnarled tree root, that Kevin had often carried when they strolled in the woods. It was standing at its usual place beside one of the French doors. At Cassie's orders, nothing in the house had been changed since the day of the accident. She picked the walking stick up and turned it over and over in her hands as though mesmerized by it. She remembered the walking stick so well, but she couldn't picture Kevin carrying it. She couldn't even picture Kevin.

Cassie went slowly up the stairs to her bedroom, hers and Kevin's, and lifted a small framed picture of him from a round skirted table on her side of the bed. Yes, he had looked just this way in their first year of marriage when she had snapped that photo. Absently she set the picture back on the table and looked around at the pretty French furniture, the antique Chinese screen that hung above the bed, the windows with their plantation shutters shut tight against the night.

She wandered into Rory's room, decorated in bold blue and white, with its mural of sailboats on one wall. His clothes hung in the closet, and she touched the sleeve of his parka with the fur-lined hood, momentarily burying her face in the fur, wanting to smell the sweet little-boy smell of him again. But no, people's fragrances must fade along with their memories, because she couldn't smell Rory there. She closed the closet door and made a furrow with her finger in the coating of dust on Rory's dresser.

She was wet from running through the rain, and she should change her clothes. Her leg ached from the cold and the damp. But she was overcome with a deadening lassitude. She didn't have the energy to do anything about her wet clothes.

Back in her bedroom, she sat down on the edge of the big bed she had shared with Kevin. It seemed like such a long time ago. Yet they had loved each other so much, it seemed as though she ought to be able to recapture Kevin in some small way, here at Wildflower, sitting on the bed they had shared.

When she had fallen in love with John, Cassie had learned that you never love the same way twice. Everything with John had been fresh and new and different, and she had grown to depend on him, had learned John's face, had learned John's quirks, had learned how to respond to John and how to live with John until John was all she knew.

Or thought she knew.

She crumpled into a heap on the big bed and let the sobs rack her body, echoing through the big empty house. She cried until her throat ached from the effort. Finally the tears ran silently from her eyes, the sad seepage of her broken heart.

Chapter Fifteen

From the cockpit John watched the toylike shadow of his plane scudding swiftly across the landscape below. He'd already passed the San Francisco Bay area and was descending now, looking for landmarks.

Trees. There were lots of tall redwood trees, and hills. Cassie's estate, Wildflower, lay in the valley between two hills, and Morgana had told him to look for the distinctive swimming pool in the shape of a diamond. And there it was, glimmering aqua blue behind the L-shaped house. Wildflower, where Cassie almost certainly must be.

He'd been frantic, trying to find her after she left him. He wanted to make sure she was all right. She'd looked so broken, so hurt. He needed to know that she wasn't planning on doing anything rash.

"Sure, John, I can check up on Flat Top," Ned Church had assured him when John had phoned the day after Cassie left Malibu. "But I ain't heard she came back. I hear just about all the local news, what with owning the only gas station in town and the store, too. Yeah, I'll drive up there right now. You say Bonnie Ott is looking after the garden? And the cat? Well, I'll talk with Bonnie, then. She'd know."

John had waited interminably by the telephone for Ned Church's call, and when it came, Ned was less than encouraging.

"Nah, she ain't there. She ain't *been* there, either. It's deader'n a doornail up at Cassie's place. Bonnie Ott says she ain't heard nothing."

"Call me right away if Cassie shows up, will you, Ned? Or if Bonnie hears anything?"

"Sure John. I'll bird-dog it."

But Ned Church hadn't called.

When John had finally reached her by phone, Morgana had been alarmed, to say the least.

"You mean she's gone? Just like that?"

"I'm afraid so," John said tersely.

"Oh, my God." There was a heavy silence on Morgana's end of the line. "And just when she was doing so well, too."

"The worst of it is that she thinks that I'm somehow part of a plot to get her to resume her career. She thinks that you and Kajurian were in on it. No matter what I said, I couldn't convince her otherwise."

"You've got to," said Morgana. "You're the best thing that has happened to Cassie since the accident. Listen, John, you've got to find her."

"I know," John said, but his heart ached. "If only I hadn't—"

"Don't blame yourself," interjected Morgana. "You did what you had to do, and it worked. You got her down off that mountaintop and made her feel good about herself. Just find her and tell her the whole truth."

"I will," said John heavily. "If only she'll listen."

In the next few days, neither a worried Morgana nor Sharon heard from Cassie. Nor did Kajurian.

It was Kajurian who suggested Wildflower.

"Cassie loved that place before the accident," Kajurian said. "She used to say that going there recharged her batteries. My bet is that she's gone up there, maybe just to check on the property, maybe to stay awhile. Who knows? But I bet that's where she is."

John called Wildflower, but the phone had been disconnected long ago and it wasn't working now. That left only one thing to do and that was to go up there.

But first, making use of his connections as the owner of AirBridges and as a pilot, he called on a friend of his who was an air safety investigator for the National Transportation Safety Board.

What he learned there was something he was sure that Cassie did not know.

And that truth, along with everything else, was what John was going to tell her when he reached Wildflower.

SHE WOULD SELL WILDFLOWER.

There was no point in keeping it. Why pay for maintenance on a place she wouldn't use? She'd never come back here. Once she got back to Flat Top Mountain, once she left on Wednesday, it would be good-bye to Wildflower forever.

Living so close to nature on the mountaintop had made Cassie aware of the natural rhythms of life. She saw that she would have to slough off the old season's skin before getting on with the new. Anyway, it was time. Time to sort through Kevin's clothes. Time to give Rory's things to someone who could use them.

So she spent her days engaged in the tasks that no one else could do for her, tossing out the remnants of her past life.

Kevin's walking stick was put aside. She'd take it to Flat Top Mountain, maybe use it when she walked through the rugged part of the woods to Gran's gin-seng patch, when her leg often hurt her. Rory's parka with the fur-lined hood went into a big green plastic bag to donate to the Salvation Army. It was joined by Kev-in's wading boots, by Rory's toy Micronauts, by her own evening dresses.

Every day was good-bye. She fell into bed at night exhausted, both physically and emotionally. She'd asked the gardener to arrange for the nearest grocery store to deliver a box of food, food that she picked at but didn't really eat. Trying not to think about John didn't work.

Why, *why?* Cassie asked herself this question over and over.

She had never questioned his sincerity or his hon-esty. It had seemed so very real, so much a part of his character. She'd detected the goodness in him as soon as she'd laid eyes on him, and she had never been one to misjudge character. So what had gone wrong? Why had he lied about who he was? Sadly she admitted to herself that she would probably never know the whole story. At this point she wasn't even sure she wanted to.

On Monday she heard the heavy drone of a plane's engine as she dug through the kitchen cabinets, sorting out the pots and pans. There were some really good-sized pots that she wanted to ship to Flat Top Moun-tain. They'd be good for making jam; Gran's pots were old and dented.

The plane circled the house. Years of having been married to a pilot had made her more aware of planes than most women would be. Cassie stopped what she was doing to listen. It sounded as though the plane were about to land on her runway!

Was it an emergency of some sort? Once a pilot whose Cessna had ruptured a fuel line had landed at Wildflower. The pilot had been grateful to find an honest-to-goodness runway where she needed it in the emergency.

Cassie wiped her hands on the housekeeper's smock she wore over her shirt and slacks and ran through the breakfast room and out the French doors. She wasn't over her aviophobia well enough to take possible flying emergencies as a matter of course. She never would be. Her heart pounded in her ears, her mouth went dry and her tongue cleaved to the roof of her mouth.

The plane banked, then spiraled downward. It began a slow, descending glide.

The swimming pool and its cabana occupied a neatly landscaped plateau directly behind the house, and beyond that the manicured lawn sloped gently to another plateau where there was an asphalt landing strip. On the other side of the landing strip lay the woods.

Running...she was running toward the runway. She kept her eyes glued on the plane, hoping that with her uneven gait she wouldn't trip. The plane was a small one, and it didn't seem to be in trouble. But she would never for the rest of her life be able to see a small plane landing without all the pain and tragedy of her own horrible experience hitting her hard.

It was the moments before the plane's wheels touched ground that were the hardest for her. In her heart she was begging, *Please, please, let it land, let it be all right,* because imprinted on her brain was the picture of the runway rushing toward her, speeding by, and then the hell of knowing that something had gone wrong, that she wasn't going to land, and then the awful sensation of spinning, rolling...

JOHN FLICKED HIS EYES ACROSS the instrument panel before lowering the flaps and maneuvering the Mooney into a glide. The runway sped toward him, still in good condition, even though it hadn't been used in years. The wheels touched, smooth as butter, he thought with satisfaction. He'd always exulted in the sensation of takeoff, but he also liked the feeling of competence that a good landing gave him. He taxied the plane to the apron in front of the hangar and cut the engine.

And then he saw her, running as though something were chasing her, running frantically with that funny little hitch because of her leg. Her hair was a pale-brown tangle, burnished with golden highlights by the sun, and he couldn't wait to bury his fingers in it, to smell the fresh scent of her skin, to feel her delicate bones melt in his embrace.

"I love you, Cassie Muldoon," he said out loud, and then he got out of the plane.

THE PLANE WAS A SINGLE-ENGINE Mooney, the Cadillac of small planes. It could carry four passengers and flew at over 200 horsepower. It was a beauty of an airplane with a custom paint job—bright white, with a distinctively intertwined blue-and-green swoosh.

And it landed safely.

Cassie slowed to a walk, her pulse pounding in her throat, only now realizing how much her leg hurt. Her heart stopped hammering, and she drew a deep breath in relief. Whoever it was, he was safe. She needn't have worried so. But then she wrinkled her forehead in consternation, wondering who this was and why he had landed on her runway. She was close enough to read the logo on the side of the plane. It said *AirBridges*. Something about the name sounded vaguely familiar, but she didn't know why.

She was only sixty feet away or so by this time, but the plane was situated on the hangar apron so that her view of the pilot inside was blocked. And then the door opened, the pilot stepped out and down, and he turned toward her.

John Howard Bridges.

Cassie stood as though rooted to the spot. As much as she had thought about him, as much as she had cried over him, she had never thought to see him here at Wildflower. Not in her wildest imaginings would she have dreamed that he would swoop down upon her from the sky. She hadn't even known he knew how to pilot a plane.

If she had thought she could outrun him, she would have run. If she had thought she could force him to get back into that plane and leave, she would have forced him. But she knew that she could do neither of those things. And besides, he stood there, his blue eyes warm on her face, wearing a white shirt and white pants that only served to show off his tan and his trim physique to good advantage, and he was smiling at her in a way that she'd never been able to resist.

"Cassandra," he said. His voice brought back memories of another time and another place when he had said that he would call her by that name when what he was going to say was important and real and true and meant only for her.

But then he had lied.

"Get out of here," she said.

"No, Cassie, we have to talk. Finally, we have to talk."

She turned her back on him and began walking up the slope away from him. "I told you I don't want to talk."

"No."

"There's an old mountain saying that I heard from Gran. It goes, 'You fooled me once, shame on you. You fooled me twice, shame on *me*.' I'm not going to be fooled twice, John Bridges." Her eyes flashed at him like quicksilver.

"I told you why I didn't tell you my whole name. And I want to explain to you why I didn't tell you that I'm not a photographer. Does the plane give you any clue?"

"No. Should it?"

They had reached the diamond-shaped swimming pool by this time. Cassie kept walking.

"If you think about it, it might. Think, Cassie."

She went inside through the French doors. John followed right behind her. She turned to face him.

He flung a file folder on the breakfast-room table. "If you won't talk, at least read that."

Her anger flared suddenly. "I don't want to read anything, I don't want to talk about anything. Don't you understand?"

"I only understand that what's in that folder is important. It's a file I got from the National Transportation Safety Board. Read it, Cassie." His voice was firm, his eyes steady.

The National Transportation Safety Board was no stranger to Cassie. They were the people who investigated airplane crashes. She'd talked with their investigators at length after the accident. Then she'd put them and their investigation out of her mind as much as possible. But now John Howard Bridges was asking—no, *demanding*—that she read this file. And she couldn't. It would bring back such painful memories.

"I'm in no mood for this," she said, feeling suddenly exhausted. She couldn't take any more of this conversation.

She turned her back on John and his folder and walked from the breakfast room through the hall to the living room. A wide grouping of sectional sofas covered in soft chamois took up one side of the room. Kevin had picked out this particular furniture grouping. In addition, he had chosen the round revolving cocktail table topped by a small basalt sculpture entitled *Mother and Child.* He'd fallen in love with the sculpture, he'd said, because it reminded him of Cassie with Rory. This room had been the center of their family life. There was no place at Wildflower that reminded Cassie more of her husband and son.

John was silent, but she felt his presence behind her and she knew he had followed her.

"You don't have to read the file," he said softly. "I'll tell you what it says."

A chill swept through her. "What—what does the file say?" She couldn't stop herself from asking, even though she was sure she didn't really want to know.

"Cassie, it's about Kevin, but I think it will ease your mind. I wouldn't tell you about it if I didn't think so."

She turned to him and saw his gaze, so caring and so sympathetic, and once again she felt trust. She didn't want to trust him. In fact, she couldn't understand why she trusted him. How could she, after what had happened? And yet, in spite of everything, she did.

"Tell me," she said unevenly, sinking down on one section of the sofa. John sat beside her and set the file folder on the table. He took both her hands in his, and his touch unnerved her momentarily. But he was talking to her urgently in that sweet voice of his, and she tried to focus her attention on what he was saying.

"Cassie, Kevin wouldn't have survived the accident, even if you hadn't lost control of the plane."

She gasped, went cold and tried to snatch her hands away. He held fast to her hands, and his voice inexorably pursued her through the twisted channels through which her mind raced.

"The required autopsy report shows that Kevin died of a myocardial infarction, Cassie. He was dead of a massive heart attack before the plane hit the ground."

Her thoughts were transformed into pictures clicking through her memory one by one like a slide show. Kevin slumped over the yoke, his face pasty in the blue light from the instrument panel. She couldn't tell if he was breathing or not, she was too scared. She had touched him, his skin was clammy, and he was not responding to her touch. Wondering if he was dead—but no, he couldn't be. Kevin was only thirty-three.

"The heart attack killed him. Not the crash. Do you understand what I'm saying, Cassie? There is no way that you can consider yourself responsible for Kevin's death. No way at all."

"I—I—" But she couldn't talk. She couldn't speak. John released her hands, and she buried her face in them.

"There's always a pilot autopsy in a crash like yours. The autopsy report was released a couple of months after the accident. You could have had a copy of it if you had requested it."

She lifted her head. "I didn't know. I wasn't thinking clearly afterward. I never thought to ask. It was the kind of detail Kevin would have seen to. You see, before the accident, I never had to do things for myself."

"I know. I thought to check on it because I was curious and because I've heard of similar cases. You know how it is with pilots, don't you? We sit around airports and swap flying stories with our buddies."

"You're a pilot," she said. "I didn't know."

"Cassie, I didn't want you to know I'm a pilot, not after I saw the way you reacted at the very idea of Morgana's getting on a plane. How could I tell you that flying is a part of my life, that it's how I make my living?"

"You make your living by flying?" She stared at him.

"I'm the owner of AirBridges Cargo Transport. We're one of the prime air cargo movers on the West Coast and in Hawaii. I not only fly my own cargo planes from time to time, but I fly for business and pleasure in any one of a half-dozen other company planes like that Mooney out there."

"I had no idea," she said, still staring. "You said you had family money."

"I do. SeaBridges Shipping made my grandfather and father millionaires. With my interest in aviation, AirBridges was the natural extension of an existing business. But I couldn't tell you I was John Bridges of AirBridges, not when you were in the state you were in about flying. How could I watch you fall apart because you feared for me? I knew how much you loved me. I had to get you over your fear before I could tell you the truth. You do understand, don't you?" He studied her face anxiously.

Her eyes never left his. She nodded, once, twice. "I do understand," she whispered. She blinked. "But then that means I was wrong about Morgana! And Kajurian! You weren't...they weren't trying to get me to perform again!"

"No, Cassie," he said gently. "Morgana and Kajurian want only for you to be happy, whatever happiness means to you. If it means performing, all well and good. If it means never stepping onto a stage again, then that's fine, too. We all want the best for you."

"But I thought—oh, John. How could I ever have thought—. I was so shocked to find out there was no such person as John Howard that I was ready to accuse everyone of anything. How will I ever make it up to them?" She looked distraught.

"It's time to stop thinking of your life in terms of making things up to people," he reminded her. "Morgana and Kajurian are none the worse for this misunderstanding. What's important is that now you know the truth."

"The truth," she said slowly. Her eyes glazed in a look of ineffable sadness. "Thank you for telling me about Kevin, John. It does help. But Rory..." She bit her lip to stop the tears.

"I'm sorry about Rory, Cassie. Really so, so sorry." His expression was one of shared grief and pain. "It's one of those things that there's no understanding, love. I wish it hadn't happened to you. But oh, Cassie, you've tried to escape the harsher realities of life by shutting your heart up tight. You can't go on that way, you know. You have to stop looking backward and go forward now."

Cassie's eyes filled with tears, but John was right. There was no understanding such senseless grief and misfortune, but she had to go on. All her guilt had accomplished nothing. It had held her down and held her back. Perhaps now she was ready to put the past behind her for good.

He watched the successive expressions flit across her face. Each side of her face was so different, each side so lovely. Tears like tiny diamonds quivered on the tips of her eyelashes. His heart went out to her in her grief. Because he loved her, he wanted to share that burden.

He was a toucher, and never had he wanted to touch Cassie more than he did at that moment. Yet he hesitated, not knowing whether she would slap him or welcome him. Finally, unsure of himself, he reached out and rested his fingers tentatively along the soft inside part of her wrist, and then before he knew it, she was in his arms, sobbing against his shoulder, and he was murmuring to her and kissing her and comforting her. He inhaled the sweet familiar scent of her; as usual, she wore no cosmetic fragrance to conceal the fresh natural scent of her skin.

"I love you, my Cassie," he said tenderly, when her sobs had faded to hiccups. He hoped that she would say she loved him, too, but she didn't.

Cassie's mind was overwhelmed with thoughts of the past. Here in this room, where Kevin and Rory were so much a presence, it was hard to detach herself. But they were gone, Kevin and Rory were gone, those two people whose lives had revolved around hers. The specter of the coming years loomed before her. There was no one to revolve around her now, and nothing to evolve, either. She couldn't face the prospect of a life spaced through with emptiness.

"Will you stay?" she said quietly to John. "It's late to be flying back to L.A."

His arms tightened around her. Would he stay? It was what he had hoped for. "Yes," he said gently. "I'll stay, Cassie. As long as you want me."

"YOU HAVEN'T BEEN EATING PROPERLY," John said, peering into the refrigerator.

Cassie shrugged. "I suppose not."

"Do you feel up to eating an omelet? I'll whip one up." She was pale, and in the few days since he had seen her, her cheeks had lost some of their fullness, so that shadows hid in their hollows.

"Sure," she said, busying herself by stacking up the pots she had left on the kitchen floor when she had so precipitously run out to meet his plane.

She watched him as he cooked, and they sat down to eat John's omelet supper together in the breakfast room overlooking the pool.

"You're going to have to do better than that," he cajoled as she picked at her omelet.

"It's very good," she said. "I'm just not hungry. I keep thinking about..."

"Thinking about what?"

"Kevin. Rory."

"What about them?" Maybe it would be good for her to talk it over, talk it out.

"Oh." Her face softened. "Rory had such a good sense of humor. He used to say funny things. Once I was baking something, a soufflé, I think. And I had to watch it through the glass oven door to make sure it didn't burn like the last one I'd made. I sat down in front of the door with my arms clasped around my knees, and while I was watching the soufflé, Rory marched through the kitchen and said, "Enjoying the show, Mom?" She laughed a bit in remembrance.

John smiled at her. "I think it's good for you to remember the happy things. It's good for you to be able to laugh. You don't laugh enough."

Her expression became somber. "I suppose not. And there are a lot of happy things that I could remember."

"I could help you remember. It doesn't bother me to hear you talk about Kevin and Rory. And I love to hear you laugh. Laughing is the easiest form of breathing, did you know that?"

She smiled across the table at him. It was so good to see him there. There was a warm feeling of friendship between them. He watched in approval as she finished her omelet and drank a whole glass of milk.

Later, when the sun had gone down, he suggested a swim in the pool. "Unless the water is too cold," he said. The air temperature fell swiftly after sundown here.

"It's heated," she said. "I turned the pool heater on to make sure it still works. I'm going to sell the house, John."

"Are you sure that's what you want?"

"Yes," she said, wanting to add that she planned to go back to Flat Top Mountain and stay there permanently. But something held her back—a wish, a hope, a longing that the two to them could have a future together, that her life could somehow be made bright by his presence in it. She still didn't know how such a future would be possible. John's business was in L.A. She was sure he couldn't move to Flat Top Mountain to be with her. She was equally sure that she couldn't be happy in L.A.

They swam in the lighted pool, self-consciously staying at arm's length from each other. John swam lap after lap, while Cassie merely paddled. In the back of their minds was the question: What happens when it's time to go to bed?

"I think I've had enough," said John finally, hoisting himself to the edge of the pool. Water glistened on his face, and it ran down his chest, diverted into many rivulets by the curly hair there. Cassie averted her eyes from the revealing swimsuit he wore; she dared not look. Reflected light from the swimming pool glimmered in his eyes, giving them depths of turquoise, of azure, of cobalt blue. His eyes stirred a hungering passion in her, and she found that she could no longer bear the caress of the water on her skin.

Cassie climbed up the pool ladder and tossed him a towel from a nearby lounge chair. She wiped the water from her face, blotted her hair and wrapped her own towel around her waist. Her casual movements belied the heat rising within her.

Silently, each of them occupied with their own thoughts, they went in through the French doors. Cassie closed and locked the doors behind them.

He thought, *We've slept together so many times. Will we sleep together tonight? Is this a reconciliation or just her way of saying good-bye?*

She thought, *I want to feel his arms around me. I want to feel the muscles of his back sleek and resilient beneath my fingers. I want to feel the hot pressure of his thighs against mine, his breath heavy in my ear, his lips caressing my lips, my breasts, everywhere.*

He followed her through the swaying shadows of the unfamiliar house until they reached the huge foyer where the magnificent spiral staircase led to the upper floor. One light burned, a dim light meant to be used as a night-light. Cassie reached for the wall switch to flick it off, and then, without warning, her left leg collapsed beneath her.

John saw her tremble and instinctively reached for her before her leg actually gave way, and then he was sweeping her into his arms as he would a child. The cold marble was no longer against her bare feet, and she was dizzy with the heady sensation of his lips upon hers.

"My leg," she said against his lips.

"Does it hurt?"

"A little. It just gives way like that sometimes." She tried to hide her pain. "Maybe it was the running today, or the swimming. It's not a very reliable leg."

And then he was carrying her up the wide spiral staircase, and she was looking dazedly down, down, through the stairwell, his heartbeat strong against her cheek, her wet hair splayed against his taut biceps.

The upper story offered a profusion of doors. "Which door?" he asked her.

She pointed to the master bedroom. And then he was carrying her there, kicking back the bedspread with one foot and depositing her tenderly and with infinite care on her bed.

Exploratory fingers touched the scar below her left knee. Her calf muscle was tense and hard. John massaged it slowly, carefully, taking his time.

"Better?"

She nodded. When he stopped massaging, she struggled to sit up.

"No, love. You'd better rest." His eyes were intent upon her, and there was no hiding the desire in their rich blue depths. He seemed mesmerized by her face, his gaze taking in every detail. Cassie stopped breathing.

Slowly, slowly, he lowered his mouth to hers, and she was waiting. Only his mouth touched her, but all of her yearned toward him. Yet he only kissed her, deepening it by degrees, making her hunger for him.

And then his fingertips were on her cheeks, drifting to her chin, feathering across her throat, delicately outlining her ear, winding in her wet hair.

"Cassie," he said unsteadily into the hollow of her throat. "Cassie, I've missed you so much." He lifted his head, and she saw the anguish in his eyes.

"I've missed you, too," she breathed.

"I was afraid I'd never see you again," he said brokenly.

"I didn't intend for you to," she replied, wondering how in the world she could ever have left Malibu without giving John a chance to explain.

She moved over on the bed to give him room, and he lay down beside her, cradling her in his arms. She stroked his hair, kissed his shoulder.

He pulled away from her slightly so that they were both lying on their sides, their heads sharing the same pillow, looking into each other's eyes.

"It helps, you know," she said. "Knowing about Kevin's heart attack helps. It's so hard to deal with what happened to them. Wondering why...wondering why something so awful happened, something out of which nothing good could come."

A sudden stillness captured John's heart.

"But Cassie," he said, gently, tenderly, smoothing an unruly strand of pale brown hair back from her face and looking deep into her marvelous silver-gray eyes. "Something good did come of it. Something very good."

She was puzzled, as he had known she would be. "No," she breathed, and her sadness made his heart ache. "Nothing good."

"Darling Cassie, if it weren't for your generosity, I would not be able to see your lovely face. Not your beautiful eyes—" and he kissed them one by one—or your charming nose—" and he kissed it too "—or your sweet, soft, lips—" and he touched his lips gently to hers.

"What do you mean?" she said, confused. His eyes, their pupils dark with love, gazed steadily into hers.

"Because you gave me the precious gift of sight, my love. Because you signed the papers that made it possible for Kevin to be a cornea donor. I was the one who received Kevin's corneas, Cassie. And I thank you from the bottom of my heart."

"You?" Startled, she stared at John. It was not possible. It couldn't be true! She dimly recalled signing the paper, one of many papers that had been shoved at her after the accident. She had thought at the time that it was what Kevin would have wanted. And then she had completely forgotten that she had given permission for Kevin's corneas to be transplanted to someone else's eyes.

"I was in a freeway accident. A truck demolished my car and my corneas. The scars on my corneas were so deep and so widespread that I could only see things in a blur, as if through frosted glass. I was afraid I'd never see again, and it meant that I couldn't fly, I couldn't drive. I thought my life was over, until the doctors advised a cornea transplant. I waited over a year for a donor, Cassie."

"Kevin was the donor?" Her thoughts spun, dizzying her with their force.

"Yes. Afterward I was like a new person, filled with optimism for the first time since my accident. I had plunged to the depths of despair, thinking that I would be blind for the rest of my life. I wanted to die. Afterward, I had to find Mrs. K. J. Muldoon and thank her, no matter what the cost. It became a matter of honor to thank you in person. But you wouldn't see me, and I knew that if it took moving heaven and earth to find you, that's what I would do."

She'd been wrong about him all along. Wrong, all wrong. For John Bridges had fought his way out of the deep, dark caverns of the spirit just as she had. He knew where she'd been, understood as perhaps no one else could understand, how hard it had been to pull herself out of the depths to which her soul had fallen.

Mutely she lifted a hesitant fingertip and trailed it along the scar bisecting John's eyebrow.

"The scar?"

"A result of my accident," he affirmed.

"But when you found me, you didn't tell me who you were," she breathed, still unable to believe it.

"How could I? You were in pieces, afraid of me, afraid of the world, afraid to fly. You were enslaved by your fear, Cassie. And because your gift—yours and Kevin's—had given me back my life, I wanted to give you back yours. Can I help it if I fell in love with you in the process?" He smiled at her, and the eyes she loved so much crinkled at the edges.

She didn't know tears were streaming down her face until John gently wiped them away with the edge of the sheet.

"Crying? Why are you crying? It's a story with a happy ending."

"Because I was the one who was blind," she managed to say.

"It's all over now," he comforted, stroking her damp hair. "We've both been through hell, and the worst part is that we've each been through it separately. We don't have to be alone anymore, Cassie. We can be together, sharing the good things and the bad. Can we put the past behind us and go on from here?"

She swallowed. "I love you," she said. "I love you. But how can we fit our lives together? I don't like L.A. I want to go back to Flat Top Mountain. You have a business to run. The practicalities make it impossible."

John enjoyed nothing more than a challenge. He was the kind who perceived a problem, defined the solution, and hung on until the solution was reached. He wasn't through fighting for her, not by a long shot.

"Sweet Cassandra," he said, loving her with all his heart. "We will find a way."

And then slowly and deliberately, he took her for his own, knowing that this time he would never let her go.

Chapter Sixteen

Flat Top Mountain
September 1985

John Kevin Bridges lay in the woven willow basket that had once served his mother and his grandmother as a bassinet, and he yawned. Then he laughed.

"Cassie, your son just laughed out loud for the first time," said John, reaching into the basket and lifting little Kevin out of the nest of blankets he had managed to kick into a heap.

"It's gas," said Cassie, who was gathering the last of the marigolds for drying.

"No, look, it's more than a smile. He's actually laughing," insisted John.

Cassie dropped the marigolds into a burlap bag and hurried to where John sat in the shade of the maple tree, holding Kevin in his lap.

Kevin chortled again, subsided with a great drooling grin and energetically bicycled his legs.

"You see? He's laughing for you."

"So he is," said Cassie, entranced with her small son. She reached for him, but suddenly he wrinkled his nose and let out a wail.

"It's the scent of marigolds on your hands," said John, jiggling Kevin to make him stop yowling. "I don't think he likes it."

Cassie sniffed at her fingers. "You're right. Marigolds aren't the most fragrant flower in the world, are they? Shh, Kevin, it's all right. I'll leave you to your daddy." She backed away. "I'll be finished gathering these marigolds in a few minutes. Then I'll feed the baby." She smiled reassuringly at Kevin.

"Anyway, there's the mailman," said John, flipping Kevin expertly over his shoulder. "Let's go for a ride, fella, okay? Say, the way you're growing, you'll be big enough for piggyback rides before long." John set off toward the road where Joe Clutter in his U.S. Mail jeep was stuffing an assortment of envelopes into the mailbox.

"Hi, Joe," greeted John. "Anything special today?"

"Nope, just the usual. How's the baby?"

"Fine, just fine," John told him. Kevin blinked at Joe, fascinated by the jeep.

"Say, John, you and Cassie will be leaving soon, won't you?"

"Yes, we'll be going back to California next week. We'll drop our forwarding address off at the post office for you."

"Just put it in the mailbox and I'll take care of it," said Joe with a grin. John nodded in agreement, took the mail and headed toward the house, where Cassie was waiting on the front porch.

"Come on, Kevin, that's the boy," crooned Cassie, holding out her arms. John caught the fragrance of

Cassie's homemade rose-scented soap on her hands, a scent that brought back fond, beautiful memories.

Cassie sat on Gran's old cane-bottomed hickory rocking chair and unbuttoned her blouse. Kevin took Cassie's nipple eagerly, making contented noises deep in his throat. Cassie rocked contentedly, feeling peaceful and happy as she always did when her baby suckled at her breast. She smoothed his silky blond hair and gazed at his dear face. He looked so much like John.

"Here's a letter from Sharon," said John, tearing the envelope open. He scanned it quickly. "She says her new apartment is perfect, and that she can't wait to see us when we get back to the Coast. Her latest record release is already number twenty-one on the charts and climbing."

"Mmm," said Cassie. "How wonderful for her." Rose o' Sharon's singing career had taken off like a rocket after she had sung Cassie's song "Where the Heart Is" at the AAFA Awards Spectacular a year and half ago. The national exposure had made her an instant sensation, and Cassie's joy at her friend's success had eclipsed her own delight at winning the Best Songwriter of the Year award and the fact that "Where the Heart Is" had been named best theme song by a female vocalist. In a clean sweep, Morgana's *All the Way Home* had also won in its category.

"Sharon volunteers to baby-sit," continued John. He let Sharon's letter drop to his lap, and his eyes resting on Cassie went soft. He could never watch Cassie nursing their son without feeling moved by the beauty of mother and son together, and with it the perfect harmony of their lives as husband and wife. "I'd like to take Sharon up on that baby-sitting offer," he said softly. "I want us to have some time together, alone."

Cassie's shimmering silver eyes met her husband's. "We will," she said, reaching toward him with her free hand, gripping his. "We will."

They sat like that, hand in hand in the deepening dusk, until their son fell asleep at Cassie's breast. John lifted him from Cassie's arms and carried him to the spare bedroom, which now housed neither raccoon nor skunk but which served admirably as a nursery.

Cassie was just stepping inside from the porch, closing the screen door softly behind her when her husband emerged from Kevin's room.

"Hush," he said, holding a cautionary finger to his lips. "He's sleeping soundly." He walked quietly across the wooden plank floor, no mean feat in that old house where the hand-hewn boards creaked so readily. He drew her into his arms, his eyes gleaming like black water in the room's rising shadows.

Cassie wrapped her arms around the strong, straight bulk of him, feeling his arousal almost immediately.

"Ah, love," she said against his chest. Then she raised her lips to his.

Their kiss was long and infinitely gentle, a kiss that bespoke more than passion and headlong pursuit. It was a kiss of commitment, a kiss of caring, a kiss that reflected their deep and continuing love for each other.

He lifted her into his arms and carried her to Gran's big brass bed. Slowly, knowing the way now, they undressed each other. There was no fumbling, no insecurity. As always, Cassie was aroused by his desire and by the love in his eyes.

If two could truly be one, then Cassie and John were. Cassie bloomed beneath his touch, flowering open. When they made love, she never failed to be dazed by the delight she felt in his caresses, by the way she was able to let her cares spin away so that the essence of her self melded with his body, merged with his mind and mingled with his soul. John's lovemaking took her to the place that had too often eluded her in the past. His total love and commitment had freed her so that she could lose herself completely to the passion of their union.

She pressed against him, absorbing him into every pore, breathing him into every cell of her body, letting herself soar, letting herself fly, up and up and up in space until she saw the sun, and the sun was hot and it burst inside her in waves, gilding her world again.

Afterward, as they lay with their bodies intertwined, John spoke.

"Will you want to leave next week as we planned, love?"

"Mmm-hmm," she replied, stroking his chest. "The garden will be harvested by then, and Bonnie Ott is looking forward to taking over the dispensing of medicine to my seekers." Bonnie had proved a willing pupil, as talented with herbs as her sister Sharon was with the mountain dulcimer.

Tigger jumped from nowhere onto the bed, meowing to be let out.

"And how about you, old boy? Ready to return to the sands of Malibu?" A year and a half ago, when they had first transplanted Tigger, they had worried about his adjustment. But the tomcat had weathered the change from mountain to beach with great aplomb, although he had been initially mystified as to why anyone would want to live on the edge of one big sandbox.

As for Cassie, the adjustment had been more of a struggle. But she and John had agreed that the important thing was for them to be together, and in the spirit of compromise, she had offered to try living at Malibu for eight or nine months of every year. The beach at Malibu, after all, was not the hard, bright city of Los Angeles. Living at Malibu turned out to be nothing like living in L.A.

Cassie loved the beach. The changeable sea satisfied her yearning for nature, and it nurtured the stillness of her spirit. Best of all, she and John had made good friends there, both from within and outside the entertainment community.

Cassie, her imagination fueled by the ocean and her spirit renewed by her marriage to John, had entered an especially creative period where she could scarcely write her songs down on paper as fast as they came to her. Kajurian was delighted, and Cassie quietly blossomed in this new phase of her career.

She and John eschewed the hectic pace of Hollywood and Beverly Hills. In line with Cassie's wish for it to remain uncomplicated, their life was quiet and centered on their home. Because they knew that if their marriage was to survive they'd have to tailor it expressly to their needs, they'd built a structure, through trial and error, with which they both felt comfortable.

John had found it easy, because he employed such reliable managers at AirBridges, to leave the Coast and spend the summers on Flat Top Mountain as he had before. This year they had left soon after Kevin was born, and they planned to continue the pattern of living at Malibu during the winter months, on the mountaintop in the summer.

"And if, after a while, it's not working," John had said, "we'll try something different. The important thing is that we'll always be together."

Always. A beautiful word.

"What are you thinking of, love?" He asked her this often, and she never hesitated to tell him.

"About us," she said dreamily. "About how much we would have missed if we hadn't found each other."

"I found *you*," he said. "Remember?" His voice lowered an octave. "And then I almost lost you."

"Almost," she agreed. Her fingertips caressed the scar above his eye. "If you hadn't seen me through eyes of love—"

"Through eyes of love. What a lovely way to say it."

"If you hadn't seen me through eyes of love, you might have let me go. I was so irrational, I wouldn't have blamed you if you had."

"Let you go? Never. Never, my Cassandra." And John's eyes told Cassie that his love was for always and always, as once more, with joy and exquisite tenderness, two became one.

Readers rave about Harlequin American Romance!

"...the best series of modern romances I have read...great, exciting, stupendous, wonderful."

–S.E.*, Coweta, Oklahoma

"...they are absolutely fantastic...going to be a smash hit and hard to keep on the bookshelves."

–P.D., Easton, Pennsylvania

"The American line is great. I've enjoyed every one I've read so far."

–W.M.K., Lansing, Illinois

"...the best stories I have read in a long time."

–R.H., Northport, New York

*Names available on request.